Lee Harvey Oswald on Trial:
A Novel

Keith Pruitt
Rebekka Pruitt

2015
Words of Wisdom Educational Consulting
Old Hickory, TN

Dedicated to Erik and Jason
I pray truth will always be
important

Dedicated to Mawmaw

A Note of Thanks

I owe a special note of thanks to many people who have fired up my love and passion for studying history. And particularly in the writing of this book, I have endeavored together with my daughter Rebekka, whose determination to learn truth has passionately equaled mine. I will forever treasure our trip to Dallas to commemorate the 50th anniversary of that horrible day in November.

Of immense importance has been the work of a very special lady...Joyce Click. Joyce has encouraged and edited with a sense of professionalism and dedication that has kept us on track. Thank you seems inadequate. Joyce has read every word in this manuscript at least twice. While she has been an immense help editorially, do not lay to her charge any failings in the writing. Those go only to me. Thank you, Joyce for your time and talents. Your hard work has made this book far better than it would have been without you.

Preface

Tom Cavendish was sitting in his office in the downtown area of Dallas. While most everyone else on his staff was excited over the Presidential visit, Tom, who was always slaving away in the coal mine, decided to catch the action on local television. He just had too much to do to take the time to walk the couple of blocks over to the motorcade route and brave the large throngs of people who were showing up on the sidewalks of Main Street.

And here it is, Airforce One is landing at Love Field after the short flight from Ft. Worth, the news reporter for WFAA-TV announced.

Scott, can you bring me the Smith file? Tom called into this box sitting on his desk. *Scott? Scott? Are you there? Everyone must have gone.*

I'm here, Tom, Scott finally responded. *Sorry. I was tied up with files and couldn't get to the desk. I'll bring the file in just a few moments.*

That's fine. I need it for the hearing tomorrow.

OK. I've got a couple more things to copy for Sylvester and then I will bring it up.

Excellent. And could you stop by the shop downstairs and bring us up some lunch? My treat. Just take it out of petty cash.

Will do. Your usual?

Yep.

And there she is now, Jackie Kennedy. This crowd is large and cheering for the First Lady. She looks radiant in this pink suit with the pill box hat to match. And now there is President Kennedy. He is waving to the crowd.

Well, I'm glad this trip to Texas is going well. The Democratic Party is so divided right now. That Yarborough has just about divided it between the liberals and conservatives, Tom was now speaking to the television set. It was a newer

General Electric model that had a clock and radio built in to the large console box. On the top were pictures of his family. *The President will stay with LBJ at the ranch tonight. Bless his heart, Lyndon will talk him to death if anything. He won't get a moments rest out there.*

The President has now broken from his security detail and is walking over toward the fence where adoring Texans are gleaming with pride and will now get to greet their President personally. Jackie is following her husband carrying a bouquet of red roses. It looks like Dallas is excited that the President is here, the reporter added.

Tom picked up the Dallas Morning News on his desk and began to look through some of the articles. When he saw the ad that had taken an entire page welcoming the President to Dallas, paid for by the American Fact Finding Committee, Tom knew that not everyone was thrilled JFK was in Dallas. If he had only known that the President showed that ad to Jackie that very morning. It would be the very last paper the President would read.

The motorcade has now begun. It will wind its way down Mockingbird Lane to Lemmon through the Turtle Creek Blvd. area and then into downtown via Cedar Springs Road to Harwood and then to Main Street. It will go all the way through downtown to Dealey Plaza where from Elm Street it will get on the Stemmons Freeway to the Trade Mart where President Kennedy will address a luncheon gathering.

I wonder how much those tickets cost? Tom asked to no one.

I suspect a bundle, Scott responded as he walked in with the file. *I'm going down to get our food. Be back in just a moment. Has the motorcade started yet?*

Yep, just got underway.

The motorcade is coming within just a couple of blocks, you sure you don't want to go? Chance to see the President and Jackie?

Nope, wouldn't venture through those crowds for nothing.

Could be your only chance. I doubt he will come back to Dallas during the campaign.

I'll pass.

You a secret Republican or something? I bet you voted for Nixon.

No sir, I actually voted for Kennedy and I'm a loyal Johnson Democrat. But I'll still pass. I detest crowds.

OK, be back in two shakes of a hen's feather.

Tom chuckled and returned to his perusal of the newspaper.

The President's motorcade·has now stopped and the President has gotten out of the car and has gone over to greet some Nuns who were holding up a sign.

Scott soon returned with the disappointing news that the deli downstairs was closed for the Presidential motorcade and would not be opening until 1.

Hum, well I guess we will figure out something.

The motorcade is now turning slowly around this awkward left turn from Houston Street on to Elm Street. And this is the end of the motorcade. We will...wait something has happened in the motorcade. We are getting reports that shots have been fired at the Kennedy motorcade and that the car sped away. Some folks on the scene are saying that the President has been hit. We are getting...

Oh dear God. Did you hear that Scott? Tom was standing at his desk now glued to the television set. The local news station was attempting to get information as the hosting commentator was puffing away on a cigarette. *This can't be happening.*

Scott stood in the middle of the room near the desk, his mouth open in shock at what the reporter was saying.

We understand that the President's car has gone to Parkland Hospital. Reports are coming in that someone in the President's car was hit when shots were fired at the motorcade. Repeat, there has been an assassination attempt in downtown Dallas, Texas.

I can't believe this, Scott, how could something like this happen? With all that security and all, you would think this couldn't happen. I hope the President is OK.

My heart is about to pound out of my chest, Tom. I have a really bad feeling about this.

For the first time Tom looked at the clock on the television. It read 12:33.

The President's car has arrived at Parkland Hospital. We are being told, and this is not confirmed, that the President has been hit as well as Governor Connally and Vice President Johnson.

Oh dear God, no, no, no! Tom pounded his desk repeatedly.

Sylvester Donelson Tom's law partner and close friend rushed through the door breathless.

What?

Oh dear, oh my dear Jesus, did you, oh I can't believe this, Sylvester was near collapse and sat down on the sofa and buried his face in his hands and wept.

We have spoken to a reporter who was in the Presidential motorcade media pool car just behind the Vice President's car who has confirmed that shots were fired. He is saying three or four shots. He is now at the hospital, at Parkland and says that he has been told that the President was hit in the head. He believes that Governor Connally has also been hit. He had no word on the condition of Vice President Johnson.

I was down there in the crowd just around the corner from Elm. I was about to leave because they had just passed us on Main Street and when they turned into Houston I figured it was over, Sylvester was now explaining. *I heard what sounded like a backfire and I assumed it was one of the motorcycles. There were several of them. Then when I heard a woman scream and commotion, and then I heard two more sounds like the one before and I knew immediately that it was gunfire. I ran down there but they were all gone by that time and there was just people running every which way. Some of the police were looking up at a window and others were running to the railyard. Up that little hill there, you know.*

Do you know, did anyone tell you if anyone was hit?

I talked to this one person, and oh they said, he began sobbing. *I-I- walked down Elm a little bit and saw blood on the pavement. Someone standing by told me they saw the whole thing. They seemed to be somewhat in shock. There was a motorcycle leaned on its side. I don't know where the officer went, but it was covered in blood and...oh I just can't believe it.*

What?

What appeared to be brain tissue.

We have just received word, and this has been confirmed, that the President has been hit by at least one maybe two or more shots during an apparent assassination attempt that has taken place today in downtown Dallas, Texas. We have been told that the President's condition is grave. Also injured was Texas Governor John Connally. We are told that Governor Connally's condition is serious. We are now getting word, it is now about 12:45, and we are getting word that a call has gone out for a priest to come to Parkland Hospital.

The office had now filled with numerous secretaries and interns who had returned from Main Street. Some didn't know of the shooting when they returned, but with the latest bulletin, most all were in tears.

This is a dark day for our country, Tom said.

It is even a darker day for Dallas. The nation will never forgive Dallas for what has happened, an intern insisted.

Tom looked at the clock for only the second time that afternoon. He had never become so cognizant of time in his life, not since he was in grade school wishing to rush along each hour of the day. He waited with the others holding their collective breaths, praying for a miracle. But it seemed that miracles were in short supply that day.

Walter Cronkite, the voice of CBS news, delivered the news to the country. *From Dallas, Texas, this flash, apparently official. President Kennedy died at 1 pm Central Standard Time...*

Chapter 1- The First Appearance

All rise, the court is now in session, the honorable Joe B. Brown presiding, announced the clerk. The packed audience made plenty of noise sitting back onto the old wooden pews, but when the noise had subsided the judge began.

Clerk will announce the next case the judge requested his drawl accentuating each and every syllable.

State of Texas vs. Lee Harvey Oswald, the clerk projected saying his last name as though it were two different words *Oz-wald.*

Is the defendant represented by counsel? the judge asked.

He is your honor, a man stood at the front table on the left. He was handsomely dressed in a dark suit, white kerchief in the pocket, wearing dark rimmed glasses. His hair was in a crew cut and appeared to be freshly cropped. His black narrow tie was secured by a bar across about midway down the shirt. It had an emblem on the bar, perhaps a masonic pin. *Tom Cavendish for the defense, your honor. I'm representing Mr. Oswald in this matter.*

Does the defendant understand the seriousness of the charges that have been brought against him? He is accused of the murder of police officer J. D. Tippit and of the assassination of President John Fitzgerald Kennedy.

Yes, sir, your honor, Mr. Oswald is acutely aware of the charges and of their seriousness.

They ought to just hang the bastard, a man stood in the back and screamed. He was wearing a dark pinstripe suit and had what appeared a name tag of some sort hanging over the breast pocket. The judge hammered the gavel full power.

There will be order in this court, the judge demanded hammering the now startled crowd back to silence. *Bailiff, remove this man from my court. Ladies and gentlemen, I will not permit this court and its proceedings to become a circus. I will exercise the tightest of controls on these proceedings and any outbursts of this nature will not be tolerated. Now where were we?*

I was introducing myself and attesting that my client realizes the seriousness of these charges.

Very well, counselor. Mr. Wade, is the State ready to proceed with this preliminary hearing?

Wade stood. The seasoned attorney was crowned with large waves of gray hair. His white starched shirt and creased pants were perfectly matched. His chiseled face and square jaw were set as though he could bulldoze through any obstacle. He was undaunted by the magnitude of the prosecutorial obligation he now faced.

Your honor, prosecution is ready to move forward with this proceeding. He quickly sat down but not before taking a glance around the courtroom. In all his years even Wade had not seen such a large group of people packed into Judge Brown's courtroom. There appeared to be more reporters present than citizenry, he thought, which suited him. Election time would be coming next year.

Will the defendant please rise? the judge requested. Oswald slowly and timidly got to his feet his coat jacket a size or two too large for his small frame had been borrowed from his brother Robert. His eyes darted about the front of the room fear etched on his face, the apparent brazenness that had evidenced itself on television the day of the assassination and following now seemingly gone.

The judge turned his attention to Oswald, his eyes blazing right into the accused killer's forehead. *Mr. Oz-wald, you have freely selected Mr. Cavendish to represent you in these matters?*

Oswald started to open his mouth, turned to his lawyer for direction, the lawyer whispered something to Oswald and the defendant turned back to the bench. *Yes, sir.*

And he has apprised you of the charges leveled against you by the state of Texas?

Yes, sir, he has. His accent sounded less eastern European than it had on television especially when he was asking for counsel to come forward to assist him.

And what plea will you enter to the first charge the killing of Officer J.D. Tippit, guilty or not guilty?

I have not killed anyone, your Honor. I do not know any such man named Triplet, Tippit. I am completely innocent.

Mr. Cavendish, would you instruct your client to answer the questions directly? We do not need anything but guilty or not guilty at this point. This is not a trial and he does not need to testify.

Cavendish moved closer to Oswald and spoke to him softly. Oswald's face turned red and he took a step back and then looked at the judge. His demeanor quickly changed and he looked down at the table. After a moment or two of silence, he looked at the judge. *Not Guilty!* Oswald screamed.

Mr. Cavendish, you will need to control your client. Do I make myself clear? I will not hesitate to find both of you in contempt of court for his actions. A simple guilty or not guilty will suffice, Mr. Oz-wald, and you need to lower the tenor of your voice by several decibels. Do I make myself clear, Mr. Oz-wald?

Yes sir.

Mr. Cavendish?

Yes sir, your honor. I am most apologetic of this disrespect.

Very well, counselor, let's see that it does not become a pattern of behavior.

The guards standing behind Oswald shielding him from the direct sight of the audience looked at one another with disgust. The older of the two leaned forward and whispered something in Oswald's ear. Cavendish put up his hand motioning for the guard to stand back from his client.

Your honor, it is very obvious, Mr. Cavendish continuing his face contorted with anger, *it is very obvious that my client is being constantly harassed by the authorities in the*

Sheriff's department including these two guards who have done nothing but taunt Mr. Oswald all morning.

Mr. Cavendish, those guards are there to protect your client from a mob of folks that would like to hang him from the nearest tree. We aren't going to have none of that in my court room, but I'm also mindful that this is no ordinary defendant. He is accused of two very heinous crimes. There is a great deal of emotion involved in this case. Now can we just pro-ceed with the pleas? The judge finished his remarks with more of a demand than question and returned his attention to Oswald.

Now Mr. Oz-wald, your plea in the charge of the murder of Officer Tippit is guilty or not guilty?

Not guilty, your honor, Oswald responded his voice steady and firm with a hint of the New Orleans accent cultivated from years of living in the Crescent City.

And on the second count of the murder of John Fitzgerald Kennedy, how do you plea, guilty or not guilty?

He turned to his lawyer and then back to the judge. Absolutely not guilty.

A buzz lit up the chamber as the crowd registered their thoughts.

Whack! The gavel cracked against the wood of the judge's large desk. Order! he barked.

Mr. Wade, Mr. Cavendish, seeing that this is such a high profile case, I'm going to allow a bit of leeway in regards to time. Let's see, today is November 25th, let's say we begin this trial on January 18th. I'm going to...

Your honor, Cavendish exploded. Defense can't possibly be ready by then. There are hundreds of depositions that will have to be taken; discovery alone may take three months. Mr. Oswald deserves, as does any American, a fair trial. We would ask that the trial be scheduled no earlier than March 15.

Mr. Wade?

Well, your honor, Mr. Wade rose slowly from his wooden club chair, Mr. Cavendish is correct in regards to discovery. We have begun the slow process, or rather the fine

Dallas police department has begun the process of interviewing eyewitnesses, but even they admit that there are hundreds of witnesses to be interviewed and deposed. It has also come to our attention that there are numerous video recordings of the assassination of the President as well as pictures that must be expertly reviewed and television coverage that we will wish to comb through for evidence. So prosecution would ask that no docket date be set at this hearing. However, your honor, according to my paperwork, there are two more charges that have been filed against Mr. Oswald that should be addressed at this time.

The judged turned to the court clerk his eyebrows raised in points on either end of his face. *Mr. Smith, are you aware of any additional charges.*

Yes, your honor, they are in the additional folder I placed on your desk. He rose to move to the side of the judge, locating the folder, handed it to the judge.

The clerk will read the other charges.

Lee Harvey Oswald is also charged with the attempted murder of Governor John Connally, and the attempted murder of James Tague.

Mr. Oz-wald, how do you wish to plea on these two charges?

Not guilty.

Be seated, Mr. Oz-wald, Mr. Cavendish. I'm going to delay setting a trial date. Mr. Wade is it your intention to try all charges at once?

Yes, your honor.

Very well. Bail, Mr. Wade?

Your honor, these are very serious charges. While little is known at present about Mr. Oswald, we have been informed by the Secret Service that he at one time denounced his United States citizenship and fled to Russia and that as early as just this past summer was in Mexico attempting to get to Cuba. We believe that he is a substantial flight risk and would ask that he be remanded to the custody of the state prison in Huntsville.

Your honor, if I may, interjected Cavendish.

Counselor.

My client has a wife and two small children, his mother and a brother who all live in the area. Moving Mr. Oswald to Huntsville would be a major inconvenience on his family...

Say what? the judge blasted. He looked over his glasses and snarled at Cavendish. *It isn't my desire to make anyone comfortable or to make things convenient for this defendant or his family. Do I make myself clear?*

But your honor...

There will be no bail! The judge picked up the gavel and smashed it into the bench so hard that the head broke off the handle. *Are there any other issues to be brought before this court?*

Your honor, Mr. Cavendish rose, *we shall be filing a motion for change of venue.*

You can file the motion if you like. I'll read it. But I'm not so inclined. Anything else?

Before anyone could respond, he banged the head of the gavel, rose quickly from his chair and was down the stairs and out the back door before the bailiff could command the courtroom to rise.

Lee Harvey Oswald

Chapter 2- The Interview

Cavendish asked to meet with his client after the preliminary hearing ended. The deputies handcuffed Oswald and placed shackles on his ankles and led him out a side door. Five deputies surrounded Oswald as they led him from the courtroom protecting him from potential harm. The narrow hallway led toward the judge's chambers and to numerous deliberation and conference rooms as well as bathroom facilities.

After Oswald was allowed to go to the restroom, he was led into a small conference room where Cavendish was already seated at a large oval oak table.

Well, that really went well, Mr. Cavendish, Oswald offered sarcastically. *A few more minutes of that and they would have hung me in the damn courtroom! I thought you said you could help me.*

I did. I am. Lee, sit down and listen to me. I have not seen the evidence they have against you yet. I'm hearing a lot of stuff in the news. The Police Chief thinks they have an open and shut case against you. You have to tell me exactly what happened Friday. This is privileged. Lawyer/client relationship, you know. The only person that will hear what you have to say is me.

Yeah, I've heard that before. Police done tried to get me to talk. Said they could protect me. They don't know what they are talking about. They can't protect me. I didn't shoot nobody, Mr. Cavendish. I'm just a patsy.

For whom, Lee? A patsy for whom? OK, let's not do this again. I want you to start with that morning, November 22. I want you to tell me every detail.

I woke up that morning not feeling so good. I'd spent the night at Ruth Paine's place. Marina and I argued. I played with the babies. Oh my girls, Lee seemed to almost tear up as he smiled in thought about his children. *I got up Friday morning and went to work.*

Did you carry anything to work with you?

Yes. I carry my lunch with me.

Why did you hitch a ride with Frazier out to Irving on Thursday evening?

I wanted to see my wife and daughters.

It wasn't to pick up a rifle?

No. Why would I take a rifle to work with me? Everyone would see that, yes? Oswald was beginning to slip into his Eastern European accent he sometimes was known to do.

So what did you do at work that morning?

I fill orders. That is what I do every day. I pack up books in boxes and get them ready to ship to schools.

When did you learn that President Kennedy was going to be coming through Dallas?

I had heard about it a couple of days before, I think. I think everyone in the Book Depository knew that Kennedy was coming through there. Most went out to see him

But you did not.

I went outside the front door for just a couple of minutes, but I needed to use the telephone and came back inside. Plus it was my lunch time. I was getting pretty hungry by then.

Oswald moved about his chair the way a nervous man does. He was fidgeting with his fingers and biting his nails. His eyes shifted from his lawyer to the corners of the room.

Who did you call?

Call?

On the telephone at the Depository?

Oh, I call Marina.

I don't think so, Lee. I have already talked to Marina. She told me and the police that she hadn't spoken to you since Thursday night. So don't lie to me! Cavendish slammed his hand flat against the table. Lee flinched when the thudding sound pierced the air.

Alright. I talked to my friend George.

What is his name? I will need to talk with him.

No, you cannot. You leave George out of this! Lee was becoming agitated, his face flaming with red blotches around his neck and veins showing on his cheeks. The swelling of his eye from where he was struck by an officer during his arrest was subsiding but a purplish bruising was prominently taking its place.

Cavendish was already tiring of Lee's antics. It was obvious even to a relative novice lawyer like Cavendish that Oswald was hiding something. *Lee, I am here to help you, man. If you are found guilty they will fry you in the electric chair. If you didn't do this, if you didn't shoot that officer or the President and Governor Connally, then you have to let me help you. Now what is George's last name?*

Mr. Tom, I did not kill anyone. I didn't shoot anyone. But let me make something plain to you. Because this is just us, right? They cannot hear this. Am I right?

You are correct, Lee. They cannot hear this and what you say to me is privileged.

President Kennedy was a good man, Mr. Cavendish. I liked President Kennedy. I didn't kill him. There are bad guys out there. They will try to kill me, don't you know? I'm the patsy. The patsy! The patsy has to die, Mr. Cavendish.

No Lee, we aren't going to let you die.

YOU CAN'T STOP IT! Lee tried to stand up from the metal chair, but the restraints caused him to stumble and he fell to the ground. A guard immediately opened the door.

Is everything OK in here? the young officer asked. His hair was cropped close and his cap seemed larger than his head. *What the...* he moved over to Oswald in two steps and had him back up in the chair. He gave him a shove that nearly knocked Oswald from the chair again. Oswald leered up at the young officer.

You just try something you sob, and I'll blow your head off just like you did the President's. The young man, who couldn't have been much more than Oswald's age of 24, rested his hand on his holster.

Cavendish stood and faced the officer. *You may leave now.* The officer looked at him and smiled a half-cocked smile and then turned back to Oswald. He stormed out the door and closed it hard.

For the first time Cavendish realized his prisoner, and perhaps himself, were not safe. The Dallas police and the County Sheriff's office could not be entrusted with the safety of one of the most despised men in the world. Oswald had within twenty-four hours been convicted by the press of the assassination of the President and the other crimes he was now charged with. A friend from Chicago had phoned just this morning to tell him the lead in the Chicago Tribune. Made it sound as though the case had already been proven, and that was that. Tom Cavendish may only have been a few years older than Oswald, but he had been around Dallas politics long enough to smell a rat.

Lee, I don't think you did this. But you have to help me prove it.

Mohrenschildt, Lee said softly as though protecting a secret.

What's that, Lee?

George de Mohrenschildt. That's who I was talking to on the phone.

Tom smiled a bit nervously. At least now he had another name to pursue. He had heard of this guy, some big shot in the Dallas Russian community. He wrote down the name and looked at Oswald who was starring over at the side wall. A picture of Kennedy hung on the wall.

Oswald looked up at Cavendish. A trail of moisture was edging down his swollen cheek. Tom just nodded his head.

Chapter 3- Discovery

The office phones rang constantly in the law office of Cavendish and Donelson. Their small suite of offices was located in an upstairs floor of a building on Jackson Street in downtown Dallas a block over from the famous Adolphus Hotel on Commerce Street. A couple dozen interns had been hired to assist with discovery. The police in the weeks following the assassination of JFK had conducted at least 200 interviews with witnesses or others thinking they might know something about Oswald.

The request for Oswald's military records had been turned down by the Department of Defense. The response said the records were classified.

Why on earth would his military records be classified? Cavendish said to Scott as they looked over the response. Cavendish grew exhausted as long hours seemed to lead in so many different directions that soon he felt as though he were chasing his own tail. He would have gladly bitten such if he could have just caught one break in the case. Oswald had given him the name of George de Mohrenschildt, but the Russian immigrant was being less than forthcoming. He alleged that he hardly knew Oswald although he readily admitted to knowing Marina, the young Russian woman Oswald had married while in the Soviet Union, as well as many prominent people in Texas including Congressman George Bush.

Tom had gathered relatively good, credible information regarding Oswald's whereabouts over the last five years. But there, as there always seemed to be in this case, was conflicting information. Robert Oswald, the defendant's brother, had given Cavendish some information about his client. He was a loner who seemed eternally unhappy about most everything. Their father had died years ago. They had grown up with relatives in New Orleans. Dad had mob connections.

Cavendish had also interviewed Marguerite Oswald his client's mother. There was an odd bird. He found her to be very flighty, nervous and filled with fantasy stories of what her young son had been up to in the last few years. She told Tom that Lee was a good boy and that she had arranged for him to be used by the government when he was just a teenager. They had trained him in intelligence operations in Japan, she insisted, and sent him to Russia where he had acted as a double agent. Cavendish couldn't help but chuckle when she told him that the government had used him for misinformation and brought him, his bride and child back to the United States without a hitch.

In an effort to check out the story, Cavendish again asked for the military file. His partner Sylvester Donelson contacted the State Department to determine the scenario around Lee's defection and reentry into the United States. The State Department likewise refused the request on the grounds of National Security. Cavendish was getting more information from the newspapers than from his own government. The story in the paper he had read confirmed that Lee had been in the military and had denounced his citizenship and traveled to Russia. He had returned with a Soviet wife and child with seemingly little difficulty and few questions being asked. Even Cavendish now was beginning to believe Lee was telling the truth when he said he was *just a patsy*.

Discovery was extremely slow in coming. A handful of pictures had been placed in an envelope, clearly marked and given to his staff. There was a photo taken just about the time of the shot that had hit President Kennedy in the head taken by a Mary Moorman. She was contacted and explained that after the assassination she and her friend Jean Hill had gone up the grassy knoll to find the gunman because they were certain the final shot had come from there. There, she and Jean were detained by Secret Service officers and taken to a building for questioning. In the conversation, Mary revealed that she had a number of other pictures she had taken, but these were taken from her. Notation was made of this and a staffer, Billy Andreous was sent down to inquire as to the location of the other Moorman pictures. Moorman and Hill had been practically beside the President when he was hit. If Mary had taken pictures earlier than this, it stood to reason that earlier pictures moved the car back toward Houston and would give a greater view of the scene.

Boss, Billy began while walking in through the open door to Cavendish's office.

Yes Billy, Tom responded looking up from a stack of papers.

I went over to the police department and talked with a couple of the detectives working the Oswald case. They had no idea of any other Moorman pictures existing. I walked over to the FBI office and talked to a Mr. James Hosty. Seems he had been investigating Oswald or something. Hosty went over and talked to Marina Oswald just a few weeks before the assassination. Was trying to meet with Lee, but never did.

What? I don't understand what the FBI would want with Lee. That makes no sense. According to the paper, the government is saying that Lee is just a loner, nut case who was seeking fame? Does that sound right to you? You were with me the last time we spoke to Lee.

Boss, you saying something isn't right?

I'm saying I'm really getting confused. If Lee is seeking fame for killing the President, then why is he denying that he did it? What interest would the FBI have had in this guy if he is just some lone nut? And why won't the government tell us anything about his military stay, defection and return?

Mr. Cavendish seems to me that someone knows a whole bunch more than they telling.

Well, and I was just reading a report from the FBI ballistics. Ballistics on the gun Oswald was carrying at the Texas Theater doesn't match the bullets taken from Officer Tippit. He was killed with an automatic. Oswald was carrying a regular pistol. Same caliber but different guns. And get this. Says in the police report I get on the crime scene that cartridges were found thrown in some bushes nearby of both types.

Oh and boss, concerning the Moorman pictures, didn't Mary tell you that her and that Hill lady were questioned by Secret Service?

Yes. That is what they said. Questioned for hours, they said.

Couldn't have been.

Why not?

All the Secret Service folks were at the hospital with the President. Never left him or Johnson.

Tom Cavendish looked up at Billy as though he had heard something that left him gasping for breath. He shook his head and rubbed his temples with his thumb and index finger. He felt a mighty powerful headache coming on.

Hey Billy, I need a drink.

****

The man came into the bar and sat down at the table beside Billy and Tom. He handed Cavendish an 8 ½ by 11 envelope with a clasp at the top. The lawyer opened the envelope and took out a picture. It looked like a number of people standing in the doorway of an office building.

Taken literally a second or two into the assassination, the man commenced his explanation. *That is the Texas School Book Depository at the corner of Elm and Houston Streets. Dallas police believe the shots were fired from the sixth floor window of that building. That is where they found the three spent cartridges and the Carcano rifle belonging to your client. Pretty damning evidence until this picture comes along.*

What's the significance of the picture? Billy asked.

Look in the doorway. Recognize anyone?

That's Oswald in the doorway, exclaimed Tom. *He couldn't have been on the sixth floor firing the shots if he was on the first floor in the doorway!*

Tom looked closely at the picture.

Where did you get this?

Guy name of Ike Altgens photojournalist for AP. Picture been in a couple of papers. I happen to see it. Thought it appeared to be Oswald. Several people got either videos or pictures including the front of the depository. There were a lot of folks up there, but I'm not sure of the clarity of any of the pictures.

It's obvious that the Secret Service guys are looking directly at the building. You can see the President has his hands over his throat and Connally is turned sideways in front of the President. The first shot has been fired. Now if that is Oswald in the doorway...

Then he didn't fire the first shot.

Or any shot, Cavendish insisted.

But why would Oswald not tell you that he was on the front stoop of the building when the President was shot? Billy asked.

Perhaps he did, Cavendish responded, when I talked to him at the preliminary hearing. He said he was on the first floor and had gone outside for just a moment but went back in to call Mohrenschildt. He had no way of knowing this picture had been taken—he probably thought no one would believe he was out there. Maybe we need to talk to Lee some more. Let's go over to the jail. I need to talk to Oswald.

He still over at county?

Yes sir, Mr. Jackson, he is still at county. David Jackson didn't work PI work for many folks these days. He had been on the Dallas police force until booze had gotten him out of line one too many times. Spent a lot of time at the Carousel Club back in 62. Guy named of Jack Ruby owned the joint, or so he told all the cops in town. They covered him. He was a weasel of a guy. Mob connected for sure out of Chicago. They've kept him over there instead of sending him to Huntsville for safety reasons. Lots of death threats. If Oswald gets to trial, he might be lucky.

I'd say. I was over on Houston the other day and runs into that Jack Ruby guy.

Who? Billy asked.

Ruby, you know the guy that owns the Carousel Club. I'd met him a time or two over there at the club. He recognizes me just walking down the sidewalk. He starts chatting me up and then all of a sudden he starts talking about the Kennedy thing. Got himself all worked up.

That's odd. Why would someone you hardly know just start talking about the assassination on a sidewalk?

Maybe cause we was standing in front of the Dal-Tex building right across from the Depository. I dun no. But he sure was torn up about it. Said it was the worst thing ever happened to Dallas.

Did he see it? Was he down there?

Said he wasn't. Seems odd him being so close to the parade route and all. He's a strange one though.

So how are we going to know, Tom continued, if indeed the police are turning over to the state all the pictures, videos and stuff connected with the case?

Dallas police are going to turn over just what they think you need to see. And with the ties and glasses breathing down their throats...

Ties and glasses? Billy interjected.

FBI, CIA, Military Intelligence, and no telling who else. Why that J. Edgar himself has already released enough statements about Oswald to put him away for life. Because you know all these here people think Hoover is a god.

Did you follow up that lead I gave you the other day? Tom asked David.

Which one?

What I heard about that doctor over at Parkland?

Oh, Crenshaw, was it?

Something like that. Said what he is being told doesn't mesh with what the doctors saw in the ER. Said he was very certain the President was hit at least twice and both times from the front.

I'm on it, he said getting up to leave and grabbing his white Stetson. I'll let you know what I find out. And hey boss, David added as he walked toward the door.

Yes, Mr. Jackson.

You might want to be careful like. I got a friend over in lockup at the city jail said he heard a cop say the other day that *someone was trying mighty hard to cover their tracks. Lot of strange things been going on down there.*

Like what else?

You know, they brought in a bunch of people that day for questioning, people that were loitering in the train yard, on the trains, hobos and all that. Let them all go, no records, names, or anything. Yard worker over there told me himself that he saw some guys in uniform behind the picket fence during the assassination. He told me...ah, let me look at my notes here, David said while fishing a small writing pad out of his shirt pocket. *Name of Lee Bowers. He said that as best he knew there were only four people in the yard during the parade. Two of them were parking attendants that he knew and the other two men were standing behind the picket fence near the overpass.*

But then you got Jean Hill and that police officer, what's his name, Billy tried to remember,...

Hargis, Cavendish supplied the name.

Yeah, Hargis, Bobby Hargis who said that as soon as they got up that hill there were police and Secret Service agents all over the place.

And you know, David that Hargis guy was riding to the left and behind the limo and got splattered with blood and brain. How could that happen if the shot came from behind?

Some suggest it was the wind blowing, Billy injected.

Did you see the pictures of the assassination from that Zapruder film that was in the magazine?

Yes, David responded. *It was obvious to me that there were at least three shots. Kennedy grabs his throat. Connally turns around to see what has happened. Jackie is looking right at Connally when the Governor is hit and falls back into Mrs. Connally's lap. Then the head shot.*

In your opinion, David, Tom asked, *what direction did that head shot come from?*

Very difficult to say. Hargis told the paper that Kennedy was hit in the side of the head. The White House spokesperson speaking at Parkland when he announced the

President had been killed pointed to the side of his head, like the temple.

I'm going to subpoena all the doctors at the hospital.

Smart move.

They were the first medical professionals to see the President. And even though no autopsy was done here, I believe their testimony will be extremely insightful.

I would think it could be critical.

I'm betting the farm on this one fact. If any of the shots that hit the President came from any other direction or place other than that Depository, then one thing about the Dallas chiefs continuous statements are found wanting. Oswald may be a nut, but he wasn't alone.

Chapter 4- Discovering a Dark Path

Discovery wasn't going well, and the Cavendish team was working overtime trying to get the government to give them information. Each time they insisted on receiving a file or asked the wrong question, they would get stonewalled by the officials. Dallas police, sheriff, Governor's office, FBI, White House, CIA, military...no one seemed to be cooperating in this case. It was not a federal offense to assassinate the President; it was just like any other murder. But the authorities weren't treating it with the same level of transparency. Nothing seemed normal about this case. The body was taken back to Washington before an autopsy could be done, violating state laws. Now the chain of custody having to do with evidentiary value, if there were any, pertaining to the President's body was questionable.

The President's body had not been properly examined by a forensics team and what possible evidence it contained was probably contaminated by the Secret Service agents taking him from the limo. While Parkland doctors maintained that JFK had a pulse when he entered the emergency room, one can hardly imagine life not almost immediately being gone the moment that bullet hit his head. But then the body had been handled by nurses and doctors at Parkland, then again by the doctors and Secret Service who placed his corpse in the coffin. They take him back to Air Force One to Bethesda Naval where later even more doctors perform an autopsy. Not once was a forensic team asked to gather evidence from the car or the body of JFK. Not one picture was taken of the body as it presented at Parkland. And now President Johnson wants us to believe the report of the FBI and Secret Service that they are convinced that my client murdered the President all by his little ole lonesome, Tom Cavendish shook his head back to reality. He had sat transfixed at his desk looking out the office window trying to determine his next course of action.

Even the Tippit shooting Oswald was accused of committing was shrouded in mystery, he continued in thought unable to shake his own mind. *Some of the "witnesses" could not identify Oswald as the shooter of Tippit. Others said there were two shooters who killed the officer.* Cavendish attempted to determine why Tippit was even in the Oak Cliff neighborhood. This wasn't his patrol area.

Oswald wasn't being very helpful. When his lawyer would inquire about specific information, Oswald would become sullen and clam up. On one such occasion, Oswald asked if his family was safe.

What do you mean, Lee? Do you mean if they are OK?

Sure. Nobody has tried to hurt my family, right?

No, they are fine. Why do you ask that? Do you think someone would hurt them?

Mr. Cavendish you have to understand something. If I tell you everything I know, none of us would live very long.

Oswald clammed up and would not explain what he meant. When Cavendish tried, Oswald would ask the guard to take him back to lockup.

Cavendish determined that one of the first things he must do is establish a time line for Oswald's whereabouts. He brought his team together including Sylvester Donelson his partner who would now act as second chair.

Billy, you determined that the exact time of the shooting in Dealey Plaza was 12:30. So at 12.30 we have President Kennedy in a motorcade taking fire. The shooting lasted approximately 6-10 seconds according to what I'm being told by Dallas police. Is that about right?

Yes sir, Billy responded.

Now during that time Kennedy is hit at least twice, correct?

Well, now there is something to hang your hat on, boss, David replied, *because according to the doctors that I talked with at Parkland, including Crenshaw, and don't none of them want to talk. Did you know they were all told by the chief of the hospital that they were to keep their mouths closed about what they saw?*

Say what? Donelson expressed alarm that the chief of the hospital would tell doctors not to cooperate with the investigation.

But Crenshaw was willing to talk and says he will testify in court.

Well, Tom Cavendish added, *we can compel the others to testify. So what did Dr. Crenshaw tell you?*

Dr. Crenshaw said that everyone saw the wounds in the President. The wound in the throat was obvious to them an entrance wound...

Say what?! Billy jumped up from the table. *An entrance wound? Well that proves the case right there, but that isn't what the autopsy is reporting. Had a copy of an official report sent to me last week. It says the President was hit in the back and that it exited the President's throat. And here is the picture they say proves it,* he continued handing over a picture taken of the President's back showing what is obviously an entrance wound.

And that was the official autopsy report?

No it was a report summarizing the autopsy issued by the Navy.

But this wound seems too low to have exited his throat. You got to remember that they say the shots are fired from the sixth floor window. And by the way, I'm not sure this is a real picture or a drawing.

Thing is that in the report they are referring to the entrance wound as being in the neck and not in the back. But clearly from the picture this is parallel to about the 3rd or 4th thoracic vertebra. I could see, Billy continued, *there being a possibility of the bullet exiting the throat if the trajectory wasn't at such a high angle. But this would just almost be impossible.*

Then it also begs the question of what happened to the bullet? David followed up. *I mean if it exited the President at throat level, you would think it was continuing downward in the trajectory.*

Unless the bullet hit something in the President that caused the angle to change.

True.

But it would still have to go somewhere.

Gentleman, Tom interjected; *let's not forget that we have a trained medical doctor, one of the first to see the President after he entered Parkland Hospital saying the President's throat wound to be an entrance wound. And if so, then that means there was more than one person firing at the President that day. And we could put the prosecution in the position of having to prove that the bullet that killed the President was absolutely fired from Oswald's gun, even if they can prove that Oswald was firing the gun.*

And something even more critical, boss, David added.

What's that David? Cavendish asked.

One bullet enters the throat, another hits the back, another hits him in the head and at least one shot hit Governor Connally. That's at least four shots and the government is only willing to say that three shots were fired from the Depository window. Four shots equal two gunmen. And let's not forget that the government is speculating that the first shot may have missed entirely in order to explain the wound to Tague.

A secretary entered the conference room disrupting the meeting.

Mr. Cavendish, the secretary politely begins, *a report just came over from the DA office marked to you and the currier said he was told it was of great importance. It is part of discovery.*

Cavendish took the envelope and opened it. He reached in and took out a handful of pages and began to read them. His face grew tense for a moment and then softened.

What is it? Billy asked.

Cavendish held up his palm facing Billy. About half a moment later, he looked up and began to tell the assembled investigators how the case may have just turned.

I have here some of the ballistics reports. As we had already been told, the pistol Oswald was carrying when he was arrested at the Texas Theater does not exactly match the bullets taken from Tippit. They have confirmed that the Carcano rifle found in the Depository is Oswald's. But oddly enough, they say it has almost no fingerprints on it. They found one partial print and what they believe to be Oswald's palm print.

But Tom, Donelson chimed in for the first time, *if the gun is Oswald's and he has handled it at all, wouldn't one expect his finger prints and palm prints to be all over it?*

Precisely. Proving ownership, however, begs the questions of why the gun was found in the Depository where Oswald just happened to work.

Perhaps it was planted, Billy interjected. *If Oswald is right about being a patsy, then someone has got to make him look guilty, correct?*

But even if it is the murder weapon, and I say if, Donelson continued, *that doesn't prove that Oswald fired the gun at the President. I recall that just shortly after the assassination when a gun was reported to have been found at the Depository it was said by one of the police detectives to be a Mauser.*

Not only that, Cavendish added, *but a reporter was allowed to go up to the "sniper's nest,"* using his fingers to draw quote marks, *a Tom Alyea, and he says that the pictures that were released showing the three spent shells were not at all what he saw. And it was the first time the police showed them. He said the three casings were lying together in an area, and I quote, that could be covered by a bushel basket. Now look at this picture. Does that look as though they are that close together?*

That's a mighty large bushel basket, Billy joked.

Cavendish also explained how the reporter said that Captain Fritz picked up the three casings with his hands so that he, Alyea, could film them. He wasn't sure what Fritz did with the casings once they had finished. *He has seen the picture that was released and is willing to testify that the placement, as seen in the picture, is not where they were when he saw them.*

Did the reporter, Donelson asked, *say anything about seeing a paper bag, you know the one they are saying he used to bring the gun to work?*

No sir, not anywhere in sight, and there are no pictures of it at the crime scene, only the photo of them taking it out of the depository.

Sounds to me, David sighed heavily, *that the Dallas police de-part-ment done botched this one up real good like.*

It would sure appear so, Cavendish confirmed. *This report also says that Oswald's palm print was found on one of the boxes in the snipper's nest.*

A moment of quiet seemed eerie at first until David broke the silence. *Boss, he worked in the place. I suspect his palm and finger prints might be all over many of those boxes as would be a number of other people for that matter.*

True enough, Cavendish replied. *Let's take half an hour for lunch. When we come back, we have to get cracking on that time line.*

The group took a break to check messages and to grab a quick bite to eat. David and Tom held up in Tom's office with the door closed for most of the half hour. About halfway through the conversation, Tom opened the door and said to his secretary, *I would like for you to get a detective Seymour Weitzman, Deputy Sheriff Eugene Boone, Lieutenant J.C.Day and Deputy Sheriff Roger Craig on the line please one at a time. I'll need to arrange to have a chat with them. When we arrange that, there will need to be an official stenographer present and a recording device. Got it?*

Yes sir, she smiled.

Cavendish closed the door.

******

When the group reconvened, Cavendish began the discussion. *We know that any number of things happened in the hour between 12:30 when the assassination happened and approximately say 2:00 when police have Oswald and have taken him to the station. We have got to put together as tight a timeline as is possible for every minute of that time. I believe that when we do, we will have Oswald's case. Because something isn't going to match up and immediately we establish doubt.*

12:30- What do we know for sure?

Carolyn Arnold, David began, *has given an affidavit to the FBI that at 12:25 she was standing just outside the Book Depository and that Oswald was standing just inside the doorway on the first floor.*

Seems to stack up with the picture of him in the doorway stoop taken by Altgens, Billy asserted.

Yes it does, Tom agreed.

This is confirmed by two other employees James Jarman and Harold Norman who say they both saw Oswald on the 1st floor between 12:20-12:25. Then we have the Altgens photo, if that indeed is Oswald in the picture standing in the doorway, the picture was taken at exactly 12:30 the moment the bullets started to fly.

The room was quiet for a moment as they all took in the impact of what was just said.

And I, Tom stated with energy, *with just that information could gain an acquittal. But something tells me that if things are not as they seem and Oswald is indeed a patsy, that whoever is behind the President's assassination...well, all bets are off, fellows.*

*Simultaneous to this, we have a witness...*Donelson looked down to his legal pad to check the name, *Arnold Rowland that has attested to his seeing a man on the sixth floor holding a rifle at 12:15 or thereabouts.*

And we also have the testimony of Carolyn Arnold that she saw him in the 2nd floor lunch room at 12:15 as they started to leave. Eddie Piper, who also works there, reported to police that he saw Oswald on the first floor at 12 and he said he was going up to eat his lunch. We know he went back downstairs after that where he appeared at the doorway and was seen by several witnesses and photographed. Then he would have gone back to the second floor where he got a soft drink and is seen at 12:31 by Officer Marion Baker and building supervisor Roy Truly leisurely drinking the pop.

OK, so we have all these folks that said they saw him at the time just before the shooting and immediately after. We have the photo assuming that is indeed Oswald, puts him on the stoop as the shooting was happening. Sylvester Donelson was trying hard to bring a point around. The atoms were working doubly hard realizing that he was near a critical part. *But do we have anyone who can testify that he wasn't on the sixth floor at any time critical to the assassination?*

There is the testimony of Bonnie Ray Williams who said, Billy continued to add, *that he had returned to the 6th floor at about 12:00 and there was no one there.*

Well, boss, David spoke up, *there is that Givens fellow.*

Oh, Tom interrupted, *do you really believe that anyone is going to believe that guy. He first has the police looking for him because he takes off from the Depository; and you know he has a police record. Then he gives two statements to the police neither of which mentioned anything about seeing Oswald. Says he left to visit a friend who worked out in the train yard. Now all these weeks later, he is inventing this story about returning to the sixth floor to retrieve his cigarettes he has left and sees Oswald. Trouble is there are a number of other people who have already located Oswald downstairs. Smacks of collusion and perjury not to mention he had previously told the FBI he saw Oswald on the first floor reading a newspaper.*

So we have a relatively good idea of Oswald's whereabouts through 12:31 for sure when Officer Baker sees him in the second floor lunchroom drinking a soda pop, correct? asked Cavendish.

Everyone agreed.

So what's next?

Billy went first with his information stating that Oswald had left the School Book Depository at 12:33 heading east on Elm Street where he catches a west bound bus on Elm just past Griffin having walked five blocks. *The bus is heading back toward Dealey Plaza and runs into traffic, of course, within two blocks.* Billy stands from the table, walks over to a map of Dallas that is hanging on the wall. With a wooden pointer he begins to show the locations he is addressing. *Oswald gets off the bus and walks two blocks south on Lamar to the Greyhound Bus Station. Here he catches a cab to Oak Cliff the neighborhood just across the Trinity River from downtown where he is renting a room. But instead of getting out at the boarding house at 1026 N. Beckley Avenue where he lives, he gets out at the corner of Neely and North Beckley some 4 blocks away and walks back to the rooming house.*

That's mighty odd, David interrupts.

Thought so as well, Billy agreed.

And what time did Oswald arrive at the rooming house? Donelson asked.

Approximately 12:58.

Wait, he did all this moving around and got back to his boarding room in 25 minutes? That seems mighty quick given all the walking he is doing. What else?

It seems that all he got at the boarding house was his pistol and a jacket. But while he was in the house, according to Earline Roberts, the housekeeper, a Dallas police car pulled up in front of the house, blew the horn and drove off. She has reported to police that she saw Oswald standing outside the house awaiting a north bound bus at no earlier than 1:03 pm. Tippit's shooting was approximately one mile south of that location at about East 10th Street at Patton. Boss, even walking briskly, it would have taken Oswald nearly 15 minutes to walk that far. That would put him at the murder scene no earlier than 1:18.

When was Tippit murdered? Donelson asked.

That's what I looked into, David took over. *According to three eyewitnesses Tippit was gunned down no later than 1:10. There are some who are trying to say that it was later than that, honestly because I think they know Oswald could not have gotten to that location that quickly.*

No way could he walk that in less than seven minutes, Donelson insisted, *unless he was running full sprint. Or someone had picked him up. But best report we can get is that Tippit's gunman was on foot.*

I checked with Dallas police, David continued, *and they report that a call came in from a civilian from Tippit's car at approximately 1:15-1:16. And the bus in front of Oswald's boarding house, by the way, goes by the Texas Theater.*

Do we know what time Oswald was seen at the Texas Theater?

It is reported, David answered, *that he arrived there around 1:30, but some of the other businesses in the area report him in there as well. It is only about 7 blocks from where officer Tippit was killed to the Theater.*

Tom Cavendish had a look of concern on his face. *Is there anyone that can place him on that bus in front of the boardinghouse?*

Silence.

Then we have a problem, gentleman.

Cavendish commended the work they had done in putting together the timeline. It gave them rough areas that needed further investigation and raised a number of questions. Cavendish told them he had only at lunch discovered something he believes will blow the lid off the case.

I discovered at lunch in another envelope that had come over from the DA's office that four officers have signed affidavits testifying that the rifle found in the TSBD was a Mauser and not a Carcano.

That would mean it wasn't Oswald's rifle, Billy blurted.

That's correct. I believe Dallas PD know they have a problem with this case. Even their circumstantial evidence is starting to fall apart.

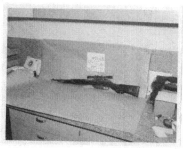

Chapter 5- Hiding the Truth

A bitter wind blew straight off the Rockies that January morning as Tom Cavendish made his way down the sidewalk of Commerce Street in downtown Dallas. He had on his wool top coat over a gray, pinstripe suit. The only hint of color in his clothing came from a narrow red and blue paisley tie. The lead attorney in the most important trial of 1964 was on his way to see his client in lockup at the county jail. Lee had been successfully moved in early December but not before some nut tried to break the police barricade and go into the basement of the Dallas Police station. Jack Ruby was a nightclub owner with reputed ties to the mob. He had a loaded pistol in his pocket. Police took him into custody but later released him. Those in the know were certain that Ruby's bosses, whoever they were, had the police on the take. Tom wondered if there were more to the story.

Cavendish had some news for Lee, but it wasn't good. The judge had refused to recuse himself or grant the change of venue. He had moved the trial date to May 25th giving the defense a bit more time to prepare. All the witnesses were lining up well. At this point, Cavendish and Donelson had prepared a preliminary witness list of about 42 witnesses. It was sure to grow he thought. In an effort to bolster his chances, Cavendish had granted a couple of exclusive interviews with CBS correspondent Dan Rather and Bob Schieffer of the Star-Telegram. Both interviews tanked when both men, who had been way too close to the reporting took issue with Cavendish on a number of accounts. Rather was hostile refusing to accept any version of the assassination that discounted the official version offered by J. Edgar Hoover. He had been one of a handful of reporters allowed to see the Zapruder film the night of the assassination just moments after the copies had been made. He was sticking by his story that there were only three shots and all came from behind. Rather even said that on the film it showed the President violently pitching forward when the shot hit him from behind.

Sylvester Donelson had attempted to speak with Mr. Zapruder regarding what he saw in his view finder, but he kept declining each invitation. *Speak to my lawyer, Mr. Donelson. I have nothing more to say. I've said everything I'm going to say to the Dallas police. Just go away and leave me alone.* He would be subpoenaed. What good it would do only time would tell. He had already given a full statement to police and his lawyer was refusing to cooperate in regards to a deposition. Judge Brown didn't seem all that interested in compelling Zapruder to testify but had signed the subpoena. Donelson had also asked the Judge to allow the Zapruder film to be entered as evidence. He was taking that under advisement and Time, who now owned the rights to the film, weren't playing nice.

Cavendish entered the county jail on the Main Street side and went through the security procedures. He always felt strange realizing this building was the last JFK passed by before the assassin took aim. In fact, from a small window in Oswald's cell, he could look out onto Dealey Plaza and even the TSBD where he once worked, although Cavendish doubted that Oswald did either.

The conference room was smaller than the one at the city lockup, but it had a small table, two metal chairs that were bolted to the floor and a mirror. Cavendish was reasonably sure that each time he had met with his client someone had been watching. And while everything Oswald would say in here was privileged, he was reasonably certain that their words were being listened to by others if not actually recorded. Today they might well get an ear full because Tom intended to ask Mr. Oswald some very pointed questions.

Cavendish had been waiting about five minutes when the guard brought Oswald into the room. He wore an orange jumpsuit and was shackled both ankles and wrists bound with large chains.

Good morning Lee, Tom Cavendish began. *How are you doing?*

Fine, Mr. Cavendish. Have you seen my wife and babies? My mother? Robert? Are they all ok?

Oswald seemed unusually panicked, more so than normal.

Lee I saw them all within the last few days and besides being worried, they are all doing OK. Robert has taken a leave from his job for a few weeks to let things die down some. He was getting some flack at work. Has Marina been to see you, or Robert?

Yes, Robert was here yesterday I think. I have not seen Marina in several weeks. Robert thinks I did it.

Did he tell you that?

He keeps saying that he doesn't know me. He thinks I am hiding something because I do not talk about it. What do I have to talk about? I did not kill anyone. I did not shoot at the President. I was on the first floor at the door when the President passed by and then I go to lunch. There are witnesses who saw me. I did not shoot that cop, Mr. Cavendish. I was on a bus going to the theater.

Cavendish's heart was racing. This was the first time that Lee had gotten into talking about what happened that day without being prodded. He thought it extremely important to let him continue talking, but he needed to ask him some questions.

They do not let me read the papers much here. But I read the other day. It said my rifle was found in the Depository. How did it get there?

The police believe you took it there that morning from Ruth Paine's house. But we have witnesses who said the rifle found was a Mauser. I intend to press that point. Wesley Frazier told police that you had a package on the backseat of the car. When he asked you what it was, he said you told him "curtain rods." Linnie Mae Randal, Buell's sister is also telling police that you had a package when you arrived at her house. So what was in the package?

I don't know why they say these things, Lee responded his Russian accent kicking in. *I only have a bag with my sandwich and an apple.*

Tom knew that is what Lee had told the police when they questioned him, and that an employee at the TSBD who saw Lee enter the building, Jack Dougherty, confirmed that when Lee entered the building he had nothing in his hands. Tom figured that a gun wrapped, even if it were broken down, would be rather suspicious looking. No one at the building reported seeing Lee with any such package. Marina had also confirmed that Lee was carrying his lunch.

Cavendish thought about this for a moment. If Oswald had indeed murdered the President, as Hoover had phrased it, for notoriety, then why is he denying it so vehemently? He didn't know if Oswald knew this or not, but Frazier had also told police that the bag Oswald had was like one you get in a grocery store and wasn't big enough to have had the gun in it. But Cavendish was testing Oswald to see if his story remained consistent. Of all the pictures that the police photographer had taken that had been turned over in discovery, Cavendish had yet to see a picture of the bag in the depository.

Lee, I need to ask you some questions. I want you to just look me in the eyes and be honest and tell me exactly the truth. This is so important. Your real name is Lee Harvey Oswald, correct?

Yes.

Your father died before you were born, correct?
Yes.

You have lived in New Orleans, Louisiana, correct?
Yes, several different times. I was born there.

When was the last time you were in New Orleans?
Last summer.

Did you hand out pro-Castro leaflets on a street corner there?

Yes, I did do that.

Did you have an altercation with some anti-Castro supporters?

Yes. And I was arrested by the New Orleans police for causing a disturbance.

Afterwards, did you appear on television to have a discussion or debate with an anti-Castro supporter?

Yes, I did that. He was very mean.

Are you a communist?

No sir, Mr. Cavendish, I am an American who believes in Marxism..

Do you know a Guy Banister from New Orleans?

Yes.

How do you know him?

I ran some errands for him several times while I lived in New Orleans.

Isn't it true that the address you listed on the back of the leaflets you were handing out was Guy Banister's office?

I don't think so, Mr. Cavendish. What does this have to do with my defense?

Well, Lee, it's this simple. If you are a patsy, then that tells me that you probably know who the men were that killed the President.

No, I know nothing about that!

Then how do you know you are a patsy?

Lee sat quietly looking at the table and then looked up, his right eye twitched as he looked at Cavendish.

It's ok. Let's continue. Did you go to Mexico last summer?

Mexico?

Yes, the feds are saying that you went to Mexico last summer. They have audio and pictures of you at the Russian, Mexican, and Cuban embassy. They say you were trying to go to Cuba.

I must see these pictures. Obviously someone is pretending to be me if they say I was there. I was not there. How do you think I could afford to go to Mexico? I barely make enough money to rent a room.

But you traveled to New Orleans last summer, yes?

I did.

How did you get there?

Bus.

You had enough money to pay for a bus ticket?

No, it was paid for by someone else.

How did you come to have the job at the Depository?

That Paine lady, she told me about the job. Wesley Frazier's sister is a friend of hers. I went to see about it and Mr. Truly hired me.

When did you start working there?

Sometime about the middle of October.

So what had you done between the time you left New Orleans and when you came back to Dallas? Where had you been?

Here and there, I guess. I was in Houston for a bit.

Like maybe Mexico.

His lips smash together and his face turned a slight red. He wasn't going to answer the question. Perhaps no more questions, at least not today. A guard appeared at the door and suggested that time was up.

One final question before you go, Lee, do you own a rifle.

They say I did; what do you think?

I'll be back in a few days and we will continue. The case is coming along well.

You believe I am telling the truth?

Sometimes. Cavendish grabbed his satchel and hat and walked out of the room.

Chapter 6- The Trial Begins

Mr. Wade, are you ready to begin your case? Judge Brown asked as the day began. It was an unusually warm day for the later part of May in Dallas. It was the foretaste of what would become one of the hottest summers on record. The courtroom was packed with those who were fortunate enough to get into the courtroom. A pool reporter and photographer were to the side of the courtroom. Judge Brown decided having just these two recording the events for the public was sufficient. Fans fluttered throughout the courtroom.

State is ready, your honor, Wade responded. He had his normal gray pinstripe on with a narrow black tie and white long-sleeved shirt. The black Florsheim shoes were polished to a shine that any Marine sergeant would have envied.

Mr. Cavendish, the judge continued, *is the defense ready?* Cavendish sat to the right of Lee Oswald who for the occasion was dressed in a tailored suit bought by Donelson at his favorite place in town. Sylvester sat to Oswald's left. The entire table was facing the jury box so that everyone in the courtroom had a direct line of site on Oswald. The prosecution table sat across the room right next to the rail of the jury box. Oswald looked sheepish as dozens of folks stared at him including all twelve of the jurors.

Selecting jurors had been an extremely difficult task. The state ordered a pool of 1,000 prospective jurors to come to the Dallas Memorial Auditorium. About 750 showed up with warrants issued for the 250 no shows. Forms were filled in, questions were asked in small groups of 20. Before lunch on that first day, which was a week before the trial was to begin, over 200 persons had been dismissed from service. Most of those had confessed belief that Oswald was guilty and were intransigent in that belief regardless of the evidence to be submitted. It was not until late Thursday evening that the twelve jurors, consisting of 12 white men, had been impaneled. Since the day was late and Judge Brown had a prior commitment on Friday, it was decided to delay opening statements till Monday.

   Before Mr. Wade begins his opening statement, the bench would like to reiterate two things to the jury and to the folks who are in the courtroom today. I will not, under any circumstance, tolerate any outbursts, talking, or any semblance of disrespect for this court. This is the only warning I will issue. Secondly, let me remind the jury that opening statements are merely the statements of counsel as to what their intent will be in going about attempting to prove their case on the part of the prosecution, and what defense might be planning in regards to defending Mr. Oswald from the charges that have been brought against him. The opening statements are not proof; they are not evidence. You will form your decision on a balance of the evidence that is presented after the opening statements have been presented.

   Mr. Wade you may begin your opening statement.

   Thank you, your honor, Wade responded bouncing quickly from his seat. His speech, however, was slow, deliberate and with a pronounced Texas drawl.

   Gentlemen of the jury, you hold within your hands the ability of deciding the fate of this man (pointing to Oswald), *whom the state is convinced is guilty of committing one of the most atrocious acts in the annals of American history. Only four times in our nation's illustrious history has someone gunned down a sitting President. In the three prior assassinations, a lone gunman took the life of first Abraham Lincoln nearly 100 years ago, then another shot President Garfield in the back; he would later die from complications of his wounds. Still another madman would pull the trigger at the Pan-American Fair in Buffalo, New York some sixty three years ago taking the life of the much beloved William McKinley. It is the contention of the state of Texas that on November 22, 1963, in Dealey Plaza and from the Texas School Book Depository, that Lee Harvey Oswald fired three shots from a cheap Italian Mannlicher-Carcano rifle taking the life of President John Fitzgerald Kennedy, and seriously wounding Governor John Connally along with a* bystander James Tague. It is further the contention of the state that Lee Harvey Oswald left the Texas School Book Depository, went back to his boarding house where he retrieved a revolver which he then used to kill police officer J. D. Tippit as he planned his escape from the city. A few moments later, Mr. Oswald was found hiding in the Texas Theater not far from this very courtroom. When affronted there by police, he grabbed his pistol and attempted yet again to fire it at the police.

That, in brief, is what the state will prove to you to a moral certainty and beyond a reasonable doubt. It is the contention of...actually let me restate. Lee Harvey Oswald is a troubled man. Some might suggest that he doesn't look like a killer, he doesn't look dangerous. He's a small man at about 5'8" tall, and he doesn't weigh but about 135 pounds. But he is a troubled man, nonetheless. He was troubled as a youngster, nearly taken from his mother by New York authorities who thought he was schizophrenic. He joined the marines to be like his brother Robert, to prove himself. But he was such a convert to Marxism that he denounced his United States citizenship, a citizenship that each of us holds in highest regards, and deserted his country to go live in Russia. While he was there, he married Marina, his Russian bride. He became a father, but he couldn't make a living there; he found out just how horrible communism is and he begged to come back home. And...gentlemen of the jury, this is the part that seems so incredible to me...we, our government, took him back! We may never understand everything having to do with that episode of his life, but that has little to do with what happened in November last year.

And you will need to know that Mr. Oswald's excursion to Russia is not his only adventure. Oh no. Just the summer prior to his evil deed, Mr. Oswald was down in New Orleans campaigning for a pro-Cuban group in support of Castro. And then, were that not enough, he left there, according to the FBI and Secret Service, went to Houston and then on to Mexico where he attempted entrance into Cuba.

I do believe that Mr. Oswald is a confused young man. But in his confusion he has taken from our nation its beloved leader and left a path of destruction. We intend to prove to you, gentlemen of the jury, that Lee Harvey Oswald had opportunity to shoot the President and Officer Tippit and did just that. We believe that he killed the President with malice aforethought because of his belief that the President had wronged Cuba and the Soviet Union. And we intend to prove that this man (again pointing to Oswald) is a cold blooded killer who deserves to pay for his crimes. You will hear testimony from eye witnesses who have identified Lee Oswald as the owner of the gun that killed President Kennedy and as the one who owns the pistol that killed the Dallas police officer. You will hear from witnesses who positively identified Mr. Oswald as the one who shot the officer.

Now I will admit to you that the crux of our case may seem circumstantial. And that is ok. If the pieces of a puzzle seem to fit together, they often do. And we will show that every piece of this puzzle leads but to one person...Lee Harvey Oswald. It is not imperative that we prove without any fear of contradiction as a fact that Oswald did what he has been accused of doing. It is sufficient that we prove to a moral certainty, that it seems very evident, and without a reasonable doubt. Now if we fail to meet that challenge and you have any doubts that we have proven our case, then it will be your obligation to acquit this young man. But when all the evidence is presented, we believe you will render a verdict of guilty. I thank you gentlemen for your service in this trial. I know your service comes at a sacrifice to your personal lives. This trial could go on for a number of days, and the fact that you are being sequestered shows how important we deem your seclusion from outside pressures will be. You know you are not allowed to discuss the case with each other or with anyone else or to listen to or read news reports having to do with this case.

But there is one thing I will expect of you. I will expect of you what is incumbent on any American citizen. I will expect you to listen carefully to all of the evidence presented. I will expect you to weigh that evidence, and if the preponderance of the evidence convinces you of the guilt of Lee Harvey Oswald, I will expect you to return a guilty verdict on all the counts in the indictment.

Let's review those counts, if you please.

First, the defendant, Lee Harvey Oswald is charged with first degree murder of John Fitzgerald Kennedy. We will support this charge with eyewitnesses who saw Oswald in the sixth floor window of the School Book Depository. In addition, it will be shown that three spent cartridges were found in the "snipers' nest" as it has come to be called, the same number of shots as the FBI believe were fired at the President's limousine. Furthermore, the state will show that on the sixth floor of the Depository an Italian made Mannlicher-Carcano rifle was found, with Oswald's prints on the gun, and that this same gun was both bought and owned by Lee Harvey Oswald and was brought just that very morning from the house of Mr. and Mrs. Paine to the School Book Depository. Gentleman, I will concede something very important to you now. There is no witness who actually saw Lee Harvey Oswald pull the trigger of that rifle, but the circumstantial evidence is overwhelming. He had both motive and opportunity.

Second, that the defendant, Lee Harvey Oswald fired the bullet that seriously wounded our Governor John Connally. Governor Connally was riding in the same car with the President. He was riding in a jump seat just in front of the President. One of the bullets wounded the governor in the thigh, chest and wrist. It seems strange that such a bullet could cause such damage, but we will present evidence, via both still photographs that were made and the now famous Zapruder video, that Governor Connally had placed himself in a twisted position in the seat in an attempt to turn to President Kennedy and was struck by one of the shots that was fired from the depository. We believe that we have in evidence the very bullet that caused this damage.

Third, there is the injury, though slight as it might be, that occurred to a bystander, a Mr. James Tague. Mr. Tague was standing near the Triple Underpass on Main Street where his car was part of the traffic jam that occurred because of the motorcade. He got out of his car and stood by the curb. He did not realize at first that he had been wounded by the gunfire, but one of the bullets caused damage to the curb and pieces of the concrete lacerated his right cheek. The state believes that Mr. Oswald bears responsibility for this was equally a crime. We plan to show that he is guilty of criminal assault with a weapon with intent to commit murder. That concrete could have just as well hit him in an eye or the throat; in fact, that bullet could have just as easily hit Mr. Tague as it hit the curb.

Fourth, Mr. Oswald is charged with the murder of Dallas Police Officer J. D. Tippit. The state contends that Mr. Oswald, having assassinated the President and shot Governor Connolly and wounded Mr. Tague, left the School Book Depository, eventually taking a taxi to his residence at 1026 N. Beckley in Oak Cliff, a rooming house where he had been living for just three weeks. Here he retrieved from under his mattress his pistol. At first, Mr. Oswald is going to take a bus, as will be testified by a housekeeper, but instead decides to walk. As he is walking along, Officer Tippit sees him near the corner of 10th Street and Patton. He stops the car and rolls down the window and speaks to Oswald through the passenger window. Tippit becomes suspicious of Oswald who matches the APB that is out and gets out of his car. Oswald then takes out his pistol and fires three shots into Tippit's chest and then at point blank range fires a last shot into the right temple. We will present eyewitness testimony that it was Lee Harvey Oswald who shot and killed Officer Tippit.

Fifth, resisting arrest and attempting flight, as well as assaulting an officer. When Officer M.N. McDonald approached Lee Oswald in the theater having snuck into the theater without buying a ticket, Oswald stood and struck the officer and attempted to use his pistol to shoot McDonald. McDonald managed to strike a blow to Oswald and wrestle the gun from his possession before other officers subdued the defendant.

District Attorney General Wade, that was what he was thinking as he walked over to his table, put down his pad, and picked up a piece of paper. The election was coming later in the year and he intended on winning the highest prosecutorial office in the area. When he put Lee Harvey Oswald on death row, he knew the populace would not be able to resist.

Gentlemen of the jury, let me close my opening remarks by stating you are going to see evidence, lots of it, that hasn't yet been seen by the public. You will hear things about this defendant that others don't know. But there are limits to our ability to share with you everything you might wish to know. Some things we would like to know are sealed, and while we have attempted to break the seals so that we could have what we believed would be a fuller picture, such has not been forthcoming. Now I know that Mr. Cavendish may perhaps attempt to raise doubt based on this. Don't let him deceive you. This is about what we do know and that evidence points clearly and absolutely to one person—Lee Harvey Oswald.

Mr. Oswald killed our President, wounded our Governor, murdered our police officer and brought grief to millions of mourning souls worldwide. You must take the action that guarantees, after you have heard all the evidence and the arguments that will be made, that this defendant, Lee Harvey Oswald, receives justice for his deeds. And I know you will do just that. Thank you.

Mr. Wade walked slowly to his seat, looked over to his second, a young man in his early twenties, and faintly smiled. He was satisfied that he had laid out the case. Now he was anxious to hear what the defendant's lawyers were going to attempt in his defense.

Chapter 7- The Defense Opens

After a fifteen minute recess, Judge Brown asked Mr. Cavendish if he was prepared to present his opening statement.

Before I begin my opening statement, may counsel approach the bench for a private conference?

Does this need to go to chambers?

That might not be a bad idea.

What is this about, Mr. Cavendish? Mr. Wade rose from his seat to inquire. *If counsel is seeking some trick already this early, then..."*

Now, Mr. Wade, pipe down, why don't you. Approach, gentlemen.

Both lawyers approached the bench. Their voices lowered as they moved to the side of the dais on which the judge was sitting.

Your honor, Mr. Cavendish said in a very low voice, *Mr. Wade made it clear that there was information his office had not been able to obtain. Since I have seen no mention of that in his discovery to us, and while we have had our own difficulties in obtaining some information ourselves, I believe that it is proper that a listing be given to the defense of said information.*

I object, your honor, in that we can't provide a listing of that information since we haven't received it. We don't know what the information is that we didn't receive.

But you know what type of information it was that you were after in general. I believe we have the right to know what information you attempted to receive in which you were unsuccessful.

Your honor, this is ludicrous.

I don't agree, the Judge insisted. *Isn't this part of the rules of discovery? If you attempted to find out about something that would greatly change the perspective of the jury or the information they should know about the subject, his culpability, etc., then you have a responsibility to let the defense know. I want this done and on their desk by noon tomorrow. No excuses. I'm very disappointed Mr. Wade that you would not see this as your responsibility. May I ask the nature of any examples you could give me about this?*

My apologies to the court and to Mr. Cavendish. We did not provide the listing because we simply did not know what bearing it had on anything. For example, we were unable to get information regarding Oswald's military service.

Nor were we.

Say what? The Judge seemed surprised.

Evidently, Cavendish added, *the government considers it classified. And I might add that Mr. Oswald has not been too awful forthcoming in regards to his history himself. This has been the darnedest thing I've ever seen.*

Well, for now, gentleman, Judge Brown continued, *I want that list made and I want to see it as well. Let's get back to it.*

Wade and Cavendish moved back to their positions, Cavendish taking his place at the lectern. He nodded to the jury and then looked at Judge Brown for his cue to begin.

Mr. Cavendish, please begin your opening statement.

Gentleman of the jury, I submit to you that the prosecution has correctly spoken on one particular count...their case is based primarily, if not in whole, on circumstantial evidence. In fact, I would go so far as to say that the prosecution will go a long way in suggesting that you believe facts that are not in evidence and could not be in evidence. Why? It is because the prosecution has no evidence. For example, the prosecution will attempt to place my client on the sixth floor of the Texas School Book Depository at the time of the assassination. In order to do this they will use questionable testimony or might even just say it without any proof as much of their case against my client seems to entail. It is almost as though by saying it they believe it becomes true. While asking you to believe that Oswald was there in that sniper's nest, they will also ask you to ignore the testimony of fellow workers that Oswald was elsewhere in the building within just moments of the assassination including one witness who places Oswald at the door of the Depository on the first floor at the exact moment of the assassination. We are going to ask that you listen to their testimony.

So if Lee Oswald was not on the sixth floor of that building, then he did not fire the shots that killed President Kennedy, wounded Governor Connally, or any of the charges having to do with the events on November 22, in Dealey Plaza. But that is given one additional factor. That is given the factor that the prosecution can prove beyond reasonable doubt that, as the government wants us to believe, that all three shots (and only three shots) came from the sixth floor of the Depository. The prosecution will attempt to lead you to believe that Oswald's rifle was used to commit this horrendous crime. But you will hear testimony from no less than four of those investigating the Depository that the rifle discovered there was not a Mannlicher-Carcano but a German-made Mauser. Why is this of any importance? Because the state knows that Mr. Oswald did not own a Mauser, he owned a Carcano. So if indeed it was a Mauser that was found in the Depository as originally noted and sworn to by these officers, how could Oswald have been the shooter? How could this be?

You will hear testimony that less than two minutes after the assassination had taken place, meaning at about 12:32, a Dallas police officer encounters Oswald drinking a soft drink on the second floor of the Depository.

As you have already learned, Lee Oswald, moments after the encounter with the police officer, leaves the TSBD. When a head count is conducted and it is learned that Lee Oswald has left the building, an all-points bulletin is issued for a man somewhat fitting Oswald's description. But as you will learn, there were other employees who left the building as well, and yet, the police did not issue APBs for them. And they did this in less than half an hour after the shooting took place.

And then we come to the killing of Officer Tippit. The prosecution is going to waffle on the time of his shooting because they know if Lee Oswald were waiting for a bus shortly after 2:00 nearly a mile away, he could hardly have been at the scene of Tippit's shooting just a few moments later. We will use the eyewitnesses that the prosecution believes bolsters their case to actually show that Oswald couldn't possibly have been involved. But why was Lee going to the Theater?

At this juncture, gentleman of the jury, I must tell you that I am a bit flustered. I sense that there is much that Mr. Oswald has not been willing to tell me. But one thing is very clear from day one. The nation heard him say it himself...Oswald said, and has repeated to me on several occasions that he is a patsy. That being the case, there should be plenty of evidence that indicates that all is not as has been purported by Hoover's FBI.

First, there is the official account given by Hoover. Three shots fired from the sixth floor window. Two hit the President and one hit Connally. And what of the bullet that hit the curb that ended up wounding James Tague? And what is to be made of all the witnesses who report more shots or from different directions? You will even hear testimony from people in the motorcade itself who believed that at least one of the reports came from the front of the motorcade.

But let me also point out that you will hear from witnesses having to do with the facts of the case that the official story does not equate with what they have seen with their own eyes. We will look at forensic evidence and medical testimony that disputes the official findings.

Was there a conspiracy to assassinate the President? Everybody keeps asking this. Even Bobby Kennedy wants to know that answer. He has authorized at least two investigations into his brother's murder. But that isn't what this trial is about. Oswald is not charged with conspiring to assassinate the President. He is charged with murdering the President. The prosecution will put on the stand some impressive witnesses who will testify to all sorts of things. We will press hard against their testimony.

Keep in mind, gentlemen, we will also be presenting a very strong defense. My client is not guilty of the crimes he has been charged with and we will actively pursue this defense. I believe that the evidence will not only vindicate my client but will in fact show that he is being set up to take the fall for this heinous crime.   And that, my fellow citizens defines a conspiracy, doesn't it? Thank you.

Chapter 8- The First Witness

The crowd was frenzied with excitement with the court came back into session following the lunch break. They knew the trial was ready to begin. The opening statements set the stage, but now the real drama would unfold. The court was crowded mostly with men in suits and a few women with spring fashion in evidence. The trial had become a social event for those fortunate enough to have won the lottery seats. Judge Brown gaveled the session to order.

Mr. Wade, you may call your first witness.

General Wade stood and said slowly *the state calls Chief Jesse Curry.*

The rear doors opened and the guard ushered in Chief Curry. Curry removed a brown fedora as he entered the courtroom and walked toward the witness chair, another clerk opening a swinging door at the rail separating the spectators from the bench. The jurors' eyes focused sharply on the aging chief of police.

Mr. Smith was stationed beside the witness stand to swear in the witness. Holding a bible he indicated the chief should place his hand on the bible and raise his right hand which he did.

Do you swear to tell the truth and nothing but the truth, so help you God?

I do.

Be seated in the chair, Chief Curry, the judge directed.

Would you state your name for the record, Mr. Curry? Wade requested.

My name is Jesse Edward Curry.

And what is your occupation, Mr. Curry?

I am the current Chief of Police for the city of Dallas, Texas, the chief responded. His typical north Texas twang was evident in his perfect articulation. He was dressed in a gray wool suit, white shirt and narrow black tie. Curry had been involved with every aspect of the assassination investigation and had acted as a conduit for the press with the police department choosing to do so instead of funneling information through a media contact. His voice sounded eerily similar to President Johnson's. The receding hair was short and still dark on the sides of the fifty-year old man.

On the day of November 22, 1963, were you involved in the Presidential motorcade?

Yes sir, I was.

Please tell us about it from the time you left Love Field.

The President's plane touched down at Love Field at approximately 11:40 A.M. When the President and Mrs. Kennedy got off the plane, they were greeted by then Vice President and Mrs. Johnson and Governor and Mrs. Connally. As they were making their way to the cars, the President decided to go over to the fence and shake some hands. He did that for just a few moments which put us a bit behind schedule. The Secret Service had removed the bubble top from the Presidential car because the rain had stopped and the sun had come out. I was told by Secret Service agent Forrest Sorrels that President Kennedy always wanted the top off the car when he was in a parade so he felt closer to the people.

Objection, your honor, Tom Cavendish offered. *Hearsay.*

The objection is overruled, counselor. He is only testifying to what he had been told not to the veracity of the statement made by Mr. Sorrels. The witness may continue.

Oh, yes. Well, we got into the cars. There were three pilot or lead cars in the motorcade. I was driving the third car.

What kind of car was it, Chief Curry?

It was a white Ford Mercury four door sedan.

Were there others riding in the car with you that day?

Yes, sir, there were.

Would you name them for the record, please?

Sitting in the front with me was Secret Service Agent Win Lawson. In the back directly behind me was Sheriff Bill Decker. On the right side was Dallas Secret Service Chief Forrest Sorrels.

You stated that you were driving, is that correct?

Yes, sir. I was driving this lead car.

And this car was directly in front of the Presidential limousine, correct?

That is correct.

Was the President's car in such a position as to allow you to see the car clearly in your mirrors?

Most of the time we were close enough to have a very good view of the President's car and the occupants.

Were you in radio communication with the President's car?

A system of communication had been established on the Charlie frequency, but we were having difficulty hearing the Secret Service agents who were in the front of the Presidential car.

Who were those agents, Chief?

Secret Service Agent Greer was driving the President's car and in the passenger seat was Agent Kellerman.

Who was in charge of the President's protective service?

I believe that was Roy Kellerman as I understand it. Forrest Sorrels was in charge of the local contingent of agents who were also servicing the event.

Who else was in the President's car, for the record, of course?

Of course. Jackie Kennedy was riding in the back on the left side of the car. There were jump seats just in front of the President and Mrs. Kennedy. Governor Connally and Mrs. Connally were in those. Greer and Kellerman in the front.

Now these jump seats as you've called them, tell me about them.

Oh these were small little seats that popped up from the floor and allowed four people to ride in the back of the car instead of two.

Were they full sized seats?

Oh no, they were a lot smaller especially the backs. The back would fold down and the President and Mrs. Kennedy could enter the side and just step right into the back. Then the seat backs would be lifted up so the Governor could be seated.

We have heard different things regarding these seats. It has been stated that these seats were slightly in from the door. From your first-hand experience of that day, would you say that the seats were parallel with those of the back or were they slightly set in?

Well, sir, I would say it is hard to compare. The back seat was a bench going all the way across the car. These were just small jump seats. But they were set in from the door just a few inches. The seats were very small and weren't built for comfort, I'd say.

Thank you, Chief. Now were there other cars in the motorcade?

Oh yes. Right behind the President was the Secret Service car. It maintained a very close proximity to the rear bumper of the President's car.

Who was in that car?

Well, I don't know all their names. I know that Clint Hill was in that car, or actually riding the outside riding board of that car. He kept going back and forth to the President's car and riding the back foot platform. I believe there was also a couple of the President's staff in the car. Ken O'Donnell and Dave Powers I believe were riding back there. We had some communication with them in preparation for the trip. I'm sorry. I don't know that I have the names of the other Secret Service Agents in the car.

That's fine. We will get those. Were there other cars?

Yes, right behind the Secret Service car was the car carrying the Vice President and...well, then Vice President and Mrs. Johnson as well as Senator Yarborough. This car was followed by another Secret Service car; Mayor Cabell was in a car right behind that, and oh Congressman Roberts was in that car as well. Let's see. Oh I believe, Mr. Wade there were about three or four press cars behind that with some more White House staff and then a Congressional Car or two and then the

Press Bus. Of course, we had some Dallas Police officers on motorcycles interspersed.

Of course. In fact, weren't there like four of them right behind the President's car?

Yes, we had two riding on his left and two on his right flanks.

And I suppose it was just another added layer of security, correct?

Yes.

Chief Curry, was there any point before you reached Dealey Plaza at which you became concerned about security?

Objection, relevance, Cavendish appealed to Judge Brown.

Your honor, we are merely attempting to place the whole episode in a great context and to point out how the President was placed in harm's way during this motorcade. It is very relevant to the very murder of the President.

Overruled. Continue Mr. Wade. I will allow it, but let's get to the point sooner than later.

Yes sir, (turning to Chief Curry), *do I need to repeat the question?*

No sir. There were several times I grew concerned for the President's safety. He was in a sea of people sometimes pressing right up to the car. At one point on Main Street, the crowds grew so large we didn't think we could get the motorcade through them without possibly hurting someone. They had swelled out into the street itself.

Was there any point at which the President's car came to a stop?

Yes, once on Main Street the car halted and the President got out and spoke with some Catholic nuns, I believe. And oh, actually we had stopped back before that around Lemon Street and Lomo Alto. There were some kids holding a sign asking him to stop. And he did.

Were there any other stops?

Well, it came to a pretty substantial crawl on Main Street. We tried to maintain about 10 miles per hour at least. It was very difficult. And of course when we made the turn onto Houston, and then again that turn onto Elm. The car about stopped there. In fact, I ended up a considerable distance from the car because Greer seemed to have a great deal of difficulty navigating that turn.

Where was the car you were driving approximately on this map (pointing to map of Dealey Plaza that is on an easel in front of the courtroom) when you heard the first shot?

Do you want me to...?

Please come down to the map and show us the approximate location of your car.

Chief Curry stepped out of the witness box and took the woodened pointer, walked to the map and indicated a position close to the stairs going up the grassy knoll to the Bryan Pergola just shy of the picket fence.

Please let the record indicate that Chief Curry has indicated a position just shy of the beginnings of the picket fence. Is this correct, Chief Curry?

That would be approximately where the car I was driving was at when I heard the first shot.

When it was determined that there was danger and the motorcade sped up, what action did you take?

Sorrels instructed us to head to Parkland Hospital which was the closest hospital to us. He had turned around and saw what was going on. Greer had hit the gas and so I did as well.

So you did not oversee the immediate investigation at the scene, is that correct?

I did not. I went to the hospital.

After you got to the hospital, what were your activities?

I assisted in the protection of Lyndon Johnson.

When did you learn that someone had been arrested in the shooting of the President?

I was informed while I was at the hospital that a suspect had been apprehended in the shooting of Officer Tippet.

I was told that he could possibly have been responsible for the President's murder.

While you were at the hospital, is that your testimony sir? Wade asked puzzled at what the Chief was saying.

Yes. I distinctly remember receiving information there that Oswald had been apprehended.

How long were you at the hospital?

We left the hospital at about 1:15. I was requested by the Secret Service to have two cars ready to take the President, President Johnson, to Air Force One. We left at about that time.

And so you received information...let's think about this. Are you sure you received information of Oswald's arrest at the hospital? Could it be possible that you are mistaken about that? Mr. Oswald wasn't arrested until sometime around 2:00. In fact, about the time that you say you left the hospital is when Officer Tippit was killed.

Objection, your honor, Mr. Wade is now testifying.

Sustained. Mr. Wade, let Chief Curry answer the questions. You ask them. Is there a question in there somewhere General?

Your honor, I believe that Chief Curry is a bit confused about these details, and this is important.

So ask questions, counselor. You know better.

Yes, sir. I'm sorry, your honor. Chief Curry, when did you get the news that an officer had been killed?

Well, that I'm very sure of. It was just about the time that we were leaving the hospital. An officer came over and told me that there had been a shooting and that an officer was down.

Did you have any reason to believe that there was any connection between that shooting and the events in Dealey Plaza?

Objection, leading the witness.

Overruled. The witness may answer the question.

No sir, Chief Curry answered. Since the police shooting was in Oak Cliff that is a little distance from downtown. It never occurred to me that there was any connection.

When the defendant...well let me ask it this way. When was the first time you saw the defendant?

That was at the city jail.

Did you question Mr. Oswald in connection with either the Tippit shooting or the shooting of the President?

No sir. Captain Will Fritz did most of the questioning. I saw Oswald a couple of times in the office and of course I was present numerous times when we moved him from place to place in the police station. That was about it.

How has Mr. Oswald been treated while in custody?

I suppose he has been treated like any other prisoner. While he was in our custody, he was treated fairly.

In whose custody does he now reside?

He is at the county lockup.

Is that usual for a prisoner charged with these types of crimes to be held in county lockup and not at the state prison?

It isn't unusual.

Was Lee Oswald assaulted by police?

I do not believe he was. I have been told that he resisted arrest at...

Objection your honor, Tom Cavendish was now standing, his face turning red. *Chief Curry was not present at the arrest of Mr. Oswald at Texas Theater. He cannot testify as to what happened at that location. Anything he would say would be hearsay.*

Sustained. Move on Mr. Wade.

The audience was beginning to be restless with the questioning as Wade droned on regarding just factual information about what Curry was doing. The shuffling was enough to catch Judge Brown's attention. He inquired of Mr. Wade how much longer his questioning would continue and when he determined that Wade was about to wrap up, he moved for a break. Half hour was ordered and both counselors were asked to join the Judge in chambers.

******

During the break, Cavendish and Donelson met with their client. Oswald was not in a very good mood having sat through the last bit of questioning and knowing that the police had banged him up pretty good at the theater. They also had been very reluctant to provide counsel to him even though he asked numerous times including one now well viewed televised plea for someone to come forward to represent him. Telephone records showed that Oswald had attempted to call a lawyer in New York City, but the connection with that lawyer was very unclear. There were efforts being made in New Orleans by powerful men to get a lawyer for Oswald. Cavendish had stepped forward to represent Oswald after he viewed the appeal on television and was contacted by Judge Brown personally. He knew it could spell doom or catapult him to legal stardom depending on the outcome. Nothing was guaranteed.

Lee, the prosecution may have just hung themselves on the Tippit charge, Donelson began.

How do you figure that, Mr. Donelson? Oswald asked obviously flustered from the lack of truth in that last exchange.

I know that last exchange bothered you, Cavendish remarked. *But remember, I still get to cross examine this witness. And when I do, the fireworks will begin in earnest.*

I sure hope so. It seems like they are just going to cover up how they treated me.

We'll get them. Don't you worry.

Back to what I was saying, Tom and Lee, I think they just backed themselves into a corner. The Chief said under oath that he learned of Tippit's shooting while he was at the hospital but that they left at around 1:15. We have an eyewitness placing you at a bus stop in front of your boarding house at a bit after 1:00, around 1:02. The shooting was almost a mile away. That only gives you 13 minutes to walk nearly a mile—actually less than that. The shooting would have happened earlier than 1:15 if the chief heard about it around 1:15. So we have that.

Lee sat silent as he often did when he didn't wish to talk about something.

Lee, Cavendish reached over and placed his hand right in front of Lee's on the table, *I know there are many things you aren't telling me. I hope that as we go through this, you will* trust me enough to tell me more. We have an excellent case. We are going to get you off most of these charges, but it would help us so much more if you would tell me more.

Lee Oswald looked up from the table, square into the lawyers' eyes and with moisture building and a quirky twisted smile uttered words that chilled Cavendish and Donelson.

If I do, we are all dead.

Chapter 9- Curry Cross Examined

After the break, General Wade continued his questioning of Chief Curry. Most of the questions had to do with procedure of the arrest and booking. Few substantive questions were asked or answered that in any way did more that tell why it was that Oswald was now on trial. It was obvious that Chief Curry had left to Captain Will Fritz the heavy lifting in this case. Fritz and his team had interrogated Oswald, along with FBI and Secret Service Agents, for hours during his confinement in their facilities. But it suddenly became apparent that at some point that investigation somewhat stopped.

It is our understanding that Lee Oswald was questioned for numerous hours by the Dallas Police, but always in the presence of either FBI or Secret Service agents, is that correct?

Yes sir. They were always present. I wanted Fritz to question Oswald alone. I felt he could get a great deal more out of him, but the FBI and Secret Service always insisted they be present during questioning.

Do you know why they made such a request?

No sir, I do not.

Chief Curry, about how long was Oswald confined in the Dallas City Jail?

We carried out his transfer on January 13th of this year.

Were there any difficulties in so doing?

Curry paused and thought about the question for a moment.

Chief Curry, did you understand the question? Judge Brown asked.

The Chief continued to stare at Oswald. His face contorted like he had eaten green crab apples.

Chief Curry, General Wade yelled, *are you OK?*

Wade moved toward the Chief who was mumbling something under his breath.

I'm sorry, General Wade. I got lost in my thought. I just need a little water, please.

Mr. Smith handed Chief Curry a glass of water which he slowly drank. When he had finished the water, he smiled.

I'm good now, Judge.   Could you repeat the last question, sir?

Certainly. When the transfer of Lee Oswald took place on January 13th to the County facility in Dealey Plaza, were there any difficulties.

Yes, sir. Actually there was. We had a fellow name of Jack Ruby who attempted to break our parameter line and enter the basement where the transfer was taking place. One of our police officers took him into custody.

And why do you think...what was his name?

Jack Ruby, he is a small time club owner here in Dallas. He runs the Carousel Club here in downtown.

Oh that place? In fact...

Mr. Wade turned toward the crowd just in time to see a short man with a dark suit exiting the courtroom. He was fairly certain that Jack Ruby had been in the courtroom earlier in the day. *Perhaps that was him leaving,* Wade thought to himself.   He was himself somewhat familiar with Mr. Rubenstein, as was his real name, having run into him at a couple of events and, perhaps even having seen him inside his club.   But he wouldn't talk about that, not today, probably never.

So what was Mr. Ruby attempting to do?

He was trying to get into the basement in order to see the transfer he said. But we thought it best to take him into custody for the time being. He had a loaded 38 pistol in his pocket.

Objection, your honor, relevance. What does this Jack Ruby have to do with anything?

Counselor, I tend to agree, the Judge said. *Mr. Wade, is there some kind of connection or something that you are trying to establish? You seem to be fishing for something.*

No sir, your honor. I'm merely asking about the treatment of the prisoner while under the jurisdiction of the

Dallas Police Department. I want to establish that Lee Oswald was treated as he should have been in accord with his rights.

I think that point was established early on, counselor, the Judge scolded. *Time to move on.*

We have no further questions for this witness.

Cross, Mr. Cavendish.

Yes, your honor. We have plenty of questions for this witness your honor.

Chief Curry, when did you become the Police Chief in Dallas?

1960.

And during that time, have you had additional training in murder investigations?

Well, before that time I was trained at the FBI school, and I have had additional continuing educational courses to stay current.

And have you investigated or led in the investigation of numerous murders?

Yes.

And have you ever seen a case with a higher profile than this case?

No sir, I have not.

And sir, would you agree that it is important to be certain of the facts even in circumstantial cases?

Absolutely.

On November 22, 1963 you were driving the car directly in front of the Lincoln Continental the President was in, is that correct?

Yes, sir, that is correct.

And you have testified that when the first shot was fired that you heard, the car you were driving was approaching the triple underpass just about the beginning of the picket fence, is that correct?

Yes sir. We were just approaching it.

How far would you estimate that the President's car was behind you at that point?

Oh, I don't know for sure, but I'd say at least 20 yards perhaps.

And in your estimation, where did you think that shot had originated?

Objection, calls for speculation. Wade was on his feet and clearly agitated that the defense had gone to this line of questioning so early.

Your honor, how could it be speculation when this gentleman is an eyewitness, was present, and surely had a thought in regards to the origin of the shots?

But your honor, nothing having to do with that subject was introduced in the questioning. He isn't cross examining as much as he is breaking open new lines of questioning that should be reserved for his defense if that is what he would like to do.

Your honor, Mr. Wade clearly introduced this line of questioning in two distinct ways in his examination of the witness: one he made him a direct witness to what happened in the motorcade and the exact location of the lead car when the first shot rang out and secondly by characterizing Chief Curry as part of the investigation, he surely has knowledge of the events. He obviously has firsthand knowledge of his own thoughts during the motorcade, and the door was opened by the prosecution.

Overruled, Mr. Wade. I will allow this questioning. Mr. Wade you clearly opened the door and I'm going to allow a very broad leeway in this matter. Chief Curry you may answer the question.

Curry looked pale as he thought of his answer. Cavendish stepped toward him. Murmuring commenced in the audience.

Chief Curry, perhaps you would like to have some more water, Cavendish said handing him the glass. The water was moving about in the glass as Curry's trembling hand raised it to his mouth. He attempted to set the glass on the rail beside the witness chair but it tumbled off and shattered on the hard floor.

Mr. Smith moved quickly toward the broken shards of glass that littered the courtroom floor.

Let's take a five minute recess. Mr. Wade you might wish to steady your witness.

The Judge stood from his chair but instead of stepping down and going out the chamber door he moved closer to the witness chair and whispered something to Chief Curry. Curry lifted his hand dismissively and nodded his head. Cavendish heard him tell the Judge he was fine, but he asked him if he had to answer that last question. The Judge, inflamed by the broken protocol immediately exited the courtroom.

After the glass had been cleaned up from the floor and order restored, Judge Brown reentered the room and took his position. His face was noticeably red.

I am instructing the witness that he must answer the last question. The court reporter will read the question.

"And in your estimation, where did you think that shot had originated?" she read back the words as asked by Mr. Cavendish.

Chief Curry hesitated and then quietly answered, *from somewhere up in the rail yard.*

Since his answer was barely audible, Cavendish asked him to repeat it louder.

From somewhere up in the rail yard. The crowd was now abuzz.

Order, Brown gaveled.

Cavendish walked over to the diagram still on the easel. He pointed to an area behind the picket fence. *Are you referring to this area?*

Somewhere about there, yes.

Isn't it true, Chief Curry that you got on the horn on your way to Parkland and commanded that officers get up there to investigate?

Yes, sir. I did. But it was just in case there had been anyone up there. I didn't know for sure that we had secured that area.

Your honor, Cavendish appealed lifting his hand palm pointed up toward Chief Curry.

The witness will just answer the questions.

But now that you have mentioned it, Chief Curry, had any of the buildings or grounds of Dealey Plaza been secured for the President's visit?

I had supposed that the Secret Service did a sweep.

But you don't know that for a fact, do you sir?

No.

Now back to that first shot.

In your professional opinion, having been around gunfire and having investigated a number of murders, when you heard the first shot, where did you think it had originated?

Objection, asked and answered.

Overruled.

Where did you think it had originated, Chief Curry?

Somewhere near the Triple Underpass perhaps behind the picket fence.

The commotion began in the very back of the room with numerous persons speaking loudly to each other. Judge Brown, who appeared stunned by what he just heard, shook his head and began banging the gavel. But the uproar just continued to spread causing the judge to go intense in his rebuke.

I will clear this courtroom if I have to do so. Mr. Cox, where do you think you are going? The pool reporter was moving back away from his station toward the exit in the back. He quickly took his position again near the jury.

Just stretching, your honor, he faintly responded.

The judge ordered a 15 minute recess. Before Chief Curry could even get down from the stand, Wade had him by the arm pulling him toward a side door. Cavendish had no doubt as to how that conversation would go. He smiled at Lee as they led him to a holding cell in the back of the building. For the first time, Lee returned the gesture.

Most spectators headed for the exits to go outside, perhaps some to puff a cigarette or two, but Cavendish knew as soon as the pool reporter got to a phone, within half an hour CBS would be broadcasting that last answer around the nation.

Donelson moved over to the chair beside Cavendish satisfaction glowing on his face. *Well, that was the shot heard round the world.*

Literally.

Do you think they will have him recant what he just said?

Well, Cavendish rubbed his eyes a bit thinking about the question, *I suppose they will attempt to explain it away, but I'm not finished with Chief Curry. He can always say that was his initial thoughts but he changed his mind after more evidence came in.*

But of course, that doesn't change the testimony of the 22 or so witnesses we have lined up willing to testify that at least one of the shots came from the grassy knoll or the some 20 police officers willing to attest that they went up the stairs of the grassy knoll because they were certain it was from there that the shots came.

Sylvester we have to be ready to deal with how they will bring in sound experts to try to confuse the jury. Echo effect is what they are calling it.

Do you really believe police officers would be fooled by echoes?

Just wait until they put Sorrels on the stand. I need to run to the men's room. I'll be back.

I'm going outside and burn one real fast. I'll be back.

The men's bathroom was around the corner and far back into the hall away from the Courtroom 7 being used for Judge Brown's trials. The bathroom was empty as he stepped to the trough and unzipped his pants. *People couldn't wait to get to the pay phones,* Tom thought as he relieved himself.

Blood flew from his nose as his face crashed into the wall in front of him. He could feel liquid running down his leg and a sharp pronounced pain gripped his right quad. He tried to twist to see who was assaulting him. He could taste the blood as he opened his mouth gasping for air.

Don't try to turn to see me or I will kill you right here. Oswald is guilty. And he is as good as dead. Back off or you all die, the husky voice said drawing close enough to his ear that Cavendish could feel the heat of his breath. That was the last thing he felt before hitting the floor and darkness overwhelming him.

****

Sylvester was sitting at the table and stood when Judge Brown reentered the courtroom. Chief Curry again was standing in the witness stand. Numerous spectators were trying to file back into the crowded room. Mr. Cox was not yet back in position and the Judge looked over at Mr. Smith wondering why his courtroom seemed to be turning into a circus quickly. He took off his glasses and rubbed his forehead. He walked back out the back door followed by his bailiff who seemed in hot pursuit. Their raised voices could easily be heard. Donelson was wondering why Tom was taking so long but figured he probably went downstairs to use the pay phones to call the office.

His concern grew frantic when he heard a lady in the back let out a piercing scream. He turned just as Tom was collapsing near the door his face a crimson mask. Judge Brown walked back through the door observing what had happened and ordered the officer stationed in the front to call an ambulance. Even General Wade rushed to the back to render aide to Tom. In less than ten seconds Tom was surrounded by those trying to help him. Oswald was escorted by another officer back to the cell. Since the jury was not in the courtroom as of yet, the Judge told Mr. Smith to secure the Jury room and station a guard there.

When the medical personnel arrived with the ambulance, they began to treat Tom Cavendish on the courtroom floor. His coat was removed and they could clearly see that he had been hit in the back of the head, a knot visibly rising on his scalp.

His nose is broken, the attendant announced and he pointed to a gash on his leg where his trousers were torn. A slight stream of blood was coming from the wound. They worked quickly to stop the bleeding, placed him on a stretcher and took him to Parkland Hospital. There he was treated and released. Sylvester brought him back to the office where Tom's wife was waiting.

The judge has ordered a three day continuance. Chief Curry has announced there will be an investigation into the brazen attack.

He could have easily killed me in that bathroom.

I know. Do you have any idea who he might have been?

All I can tell you is that he was about my height, extremely light of foot, and was strong as an ox. Hell, I wrestled in high school and I've never been up against anyone with that type of muscle.

Professional?

I'm betting so.

But why? Donelson looked at his colleague and realized the danger they all faced. *Oswald's telling the truth, isn't he?*

Why else would someone be trying to stop this trial?

Why not just try to kill Oswald?

He's a patsy; that's what they generally do. How do we know they haven't already tried to do so? Remember what Curry said about the transfer?

What was that guy's name he said tried to crash the party?

They both thought hard for a moment, but Cavendish was in so much pain that the name escaped him. Donelson was no better.

Your wife should take you home, Tom. You really look like you've been run over by a freight train.

Thanks. I feel even worse.

Curry sent over a couple of police officers. He wants someone with us around the clock. County has doubled the guard on Oswald and put him in isolation. They are guarding Wade as well.

We've got to find out what the meaning of this is, and why someone would attack a defense attorney over it.

Are you kidding me? You mean you can't understand what is going on here?

Tom was expressionless.

God bless, Tom, they have killed the President. Oswald didn't do this. Someone is trying to make this all go away.

But who?

Indeed! Who!

Chapter 10- The Trial Continues

A week after the attack on Tom Cavendish, the trial was set to continue. Sore and still nursing a couple of loose teeth, Tom was ready to do battle. He had broken more than one pencil in frustration as he prepared notes for his continued questioning of Chief Curry. There were only a couple of other areas he wished to probe. As he sat at the defense desk that morning waiting for Oswald and Donelson's arrival, he gritted his teeth even through the pain. *We're going to get these bastards if it is the last thing I do,* he thought to himself.

All rise! the clerk announced as the Judge returned to the bench.

I want to make a statement before bringing in the jury and I want everyone to listen carefully. First, Mr. Cavendish welcome back to my courtroom. He looked over his glasses and down to the table where the three sat stoically. *I am thankful that you have survived this vicious and horrendous attack. I promise if there is anything that I can do to facilitate the apprehension and conviction of this coward, I will. Second, I am mandating that security into the courtroom be greatly increased. This means people will be searched. Bags will be searched of everyone. No one will be allowed into this courtroom without being searched. This I realize will delay our start each morning, but I am prepared to take these measures in order to provide for the safety of each person involved in this trial. Mr. Oswald, I am committed to making sure that you are safe and that you receive a fair trial.*

Oswald looked at the judge then hung his head and just shook his head back and forth. *You'll never be able to do it,* he muttered.

Excuse me, Mr. Oswald. What was that?

Oswald stood suddenly and looking at the judge and said loudly, *you can't protect me! They will kill me!*

Judge Brown hit the gavel and ordered Mr. Oswald to be seated and reprimanded Mr. Cavendish in a gentle voice about controlling his client.

I'm sorry, your honor. I will attempt to do what I can to control these types of outbursts. But under the circumstances, I think it is obvious that there is a great deal of emotion going on here.

Bring in the jury, Mr. Smith. The bailiff opened the door to the jury room and disappeared for a few seconds. When the door opened again, the 12 members of the jury filed back into the jury box. When they were seated many of them turned and looked in shock at the bruised face of Mr. Cavendish.

I will ask the jury to please concentrate on the task at hand, this trial. Mr. Cavendish had a bit of an accident, and this is why we have not been meeting. But I charge you to remember why we are here.

Mr. Cavendish, would you like to continue your cross examination of Chief Curry?

Yes, your honor I would, the counselor responded standing and walking forward to the witness stand. It was as if it was the prior week in the afternoon session that had been interrupted.

Chief Curry, good morning.

Good morning, Mr. Cavendish. I hope you are feeling better.

I'm fine, sir.

Now when we last met, Chief Curry, you testified, and I quote, in regards to your belief about the origin of the first shot, you said, "Somewhere near the Triple Underpass perhaps behind the picket fence." Is that correct?

That is what I said sir, but...

And in saying that, you actually ordered police officers to go up there to check it out, correct?

Yes sir, I did. But I...

And is it still your belief that there was a shot or shots fired from the area of the rail yard?

Well, Mr. Cavendish...

Yes or no, Chief Curry.

No! There were three shots and they all came from the Depository. That is what the evidence says! Curry's face was turning red and a vein in his forehead was bulging.

Let's stick with what is in evidence at this time, sir.

The last statement of the witness will be stricken from the record and the jury is advised to ignore it. Chief Curry, no evidence has yet been presented having to do with the Depository. Please stick to just answering the questions.

Chief Curry, I'm going to ask you this again, and I would like for you to give me your professional answer based on what you actually did that day.

Objection, he's badgering the witness.

I'm going to allow some leeway here. This witness has become somewhat hostile, so I believe it is appropriate. Your question, Mr. Cavendish?

When the shots rang out, did you believe based on your professional ability that any of the shots had come from the grassy knoll or rail yard area?

Yes. Yes I did and I still do. There. Is that what you wanted?

Sir, I just want the truth. Based on your investigation, if a shot had come from the rail yard, the picket fence, the grassy knoll area, could Mr. Oswald have been responsible for that shot?

If indeed a shot was fired from any other place other than the Depository, I do not believe it would be possible that Mr. Oswald could have fired that shot.

How many shots did you hear, Chief Curry?

Objection your honor, not in evidence?

You opened the door by asking about any shot, I believe that gives me the right to ask this witness regarding his experience from the time he turned into Dealey Plaza until he reached the hospital.

Overruled. Continue Mr. Cavendish.

Chief Curry, how many shots did you hear?

At the time I believe that I clearly heard four shots.

You say at the time.

Yes, that was my thinking at the time of the shooting was that I had heard four shots.

And you believed that at least one of those shots may have come from the front right of the motorcade, correct?

Yes, from somewhere in front although I was unsure of where.

Did you have any idea as to the origin of the other shots?

The Depository.

So you thought at the moment of the assassination that the other shots were coming from the Depository?

Well, not at the moment. At the moment I wasn't sure where else they were coming from just that they seemed to be coming from somewhere in the back of the motorcade from that direction.

So at the time you weren't sure whether the shots were coming from the Depository or the Dal-Tex building or the Corrections Center, isn't that correct, sir?

Well, that's probably correct.

Moments after the shooting, you ordered officers to the grassy knoll, correct?

Correct.

Did you order any officers to go into any of the buildings?

No sir, when my attention became focused on getting the President to the hospital, I left it to others at the scene to do what they believed best.

So when Officer Marion Baker, for example, went into the Book Depository, that wasn't on your order. Is that correct?

That would be correct.

You testified Chief Curry that you did not personally question Mr. Oswald, is that correct?

It is.

But you did oversee the investigation of the assassination of the President and of the shooting of Governor Connally, correct?

Yes, I oversaw all aspects of the investigation.

Was there a point at which the Dallas Police Department stopped investigating the assassination?

Well, of course, yes sir.

Were you finished with the investigation when that happened?

General Wade was on his feet again objecting to the question. *I fail to see where this is going?*

Do you have a point Mr. Cavendish?

Yes, sir. I intend to show with this witness that the investigation was never completed, and why that investigation was prematurely ended.

Well, your honor, I object to such a question, because there is no foundation for it on cross.

Your honor, the prosecution asked regarding the role Chief Curry played in the investigation, whether he had questioned Mr. Oswald, etc. I believe he opened the door to asking about the investigation by the Dallas Police Department.

Well, Mr. Cavendish, I'm not sure that opened the door for you to continue down that road endlessly. General Wade, if I recall merely asked about his questioning of the defendant.

My intent, your honor is to show that the investigation into this crime was never completed by the Dallas Police Department because of interference.

Chief Curry was squirming in the witness chair moving first his left foot over his right knee and quickly reversing it. He cleared his throat in an apparent signal to the defense for help.

Your honor I must stringently object to this question being asked.

Well, I must admit Mr. Cavendish, you have my curiosity going now. I believe I will allow the question.

Your honor! I object!

Sit down, counselor! I've made my ruling! Judge Brown demanded raising his voice frightening most of the spectators and even causing the court reporter to jump in her seat in front of the Judge's bench.

Wade sat down in a huff.

Do I need to repeat the question, Chief Curry?

I must respectfully decline to answer the question, Mr. Cavendish due to National Security.

Do what?! Cavendish yelled.

Mr. Curry, the judge enjoined, *you must answer the question.*

Had you finished the investigation at the point at which you stopped being in charge of the investigation? It is a very simple question. How could this possibly have anything to do with National Security?

Chief Curry, you must answer the question. You are an officer of the court. You are sworn with an oath to tell the truth and all the truth. Judge Brown's face was now the color of a cardinal.

No, Mr. Cavendish, the investigation was not at an end when we ended the investigation. We were not finished, but I had no choice.

What happened that caused you to end the investigation by the Dallas Police Department?

Chief Curry turned to the judge, pleading with his face for an escape from answering the question.

Answer, Chief Curry, the Judge ordered.

I received a phone call ordering me to end the investigation and was told that it would be handled by the FBI.

And from whom did you receive this call?

The chief looked down to the floor appearing to seek asylum underneath the chair in which he was sitting. He mumbled.

I'm sorry Mr. Curry. We cannot hear you.

He slightly raised his head but once again said something underneath his breath.

Mr. Curry, the Judge ordered, *you need to speak into the microphone and speak directly.*

The call was from President Lyndon Johnson.

Your honor, that is all the questions we have for this witness at this time, but we would reserve the right to recall this witness later.

So noted. You may step down Chief Curry. Next witness Mr. Wade. Order in the court, he ordered banging his gavel hard. *I will have order in this courtroom.* A hush fell over the audience.

The state calls Forrest Sorrels.

Forest Sorrels, please come forward, the bailiff announced.

When he had been sworn in, General Wade approached the witness stand and asked him to state his name and occupation.

Forest Sorrels. I am the lead agent for the Secret Service in Dallas, Texas.

And you were present in the motorcade on November 22, 1963, is that correct?

Yes, sir.

I want to ask you some questions relative to preparations, threats, etc. First, let me ask about the President's car. Was the Lincoln Continental he was riding in furnished by the locals or was it a White House car?

It was one of the Presidential cars from the White House.

And is it true that it has a bubble top that generally is on the car.

It has a couple of tops that can be placed on the car, but I cannot reveal more than that because of security considerations.

Of course. So on this particular day it was reported that the top had been on the car when it arrived at the airport, at Love Field that is, and that it was taken off. Is this true?

It is. It had been raining earlier in the morning so the top was on. When we got to Love Field, the sun had come out so the top came off.

Who makes that decision?

Oh, President Kennedy. It was a standing order that any time he was to be in a motorcade and the weather was OK, he wanted the top off. The President made that decision.

What goes into deciding what route is safe in a motorcade, Agent Sorrels?

That depends on where we are going?

What was taken into consideration in regards to this particular motorcade?

President Kennedy wanted to go through downtown realizing that there would be a large crowd of people available to come out onto the street from all the businesses and office buildings. He believed strongly that the people who elected him should be allowed to see him clearly and not through a plastic shield.

OK, continue, what other factors went into the choice of this route?

The logistics were simple. We wanted to go through downtown so we selected the most direct route from Love Field to get us to downtown. Once we got downtown, we naturally selected Main Street for its central location and because there was a way we could get to the Trade Mart from the end of the route.

It had originally been announced in the paper that the motorcade would pass under the Triple Underpass by way of Main Street. Is that correct?

Yes, I believe so.

And when was the decision made to turn onto Houston and then Elm taking the motorcade by the Book Depository?

I believe it was made that morning.

And who made that decision?

I made the decision based on a recommendation by Chief Curry.

And why was that recommendation made?

Chief Curry pointed out that it was impossible to enter the Stemmons Freeway from Main Street. Only Elm Street has a ramp onto the freeway.

And Agent Sorrels were you in the motorcade?

Yes, sir, I was in the back seat of the lead car being driven by Chief Curry.

So you were directly in front of the President's car?

Correct.

When you heard the shots ring out, do you recall what you did?

Yes. I looked up on the terrace there.

At any point did you turn around to look at the President's car?

Yes. When I heard I guess two shots, I turned around in the seat to look back behind me.

Can you tell the court what you recall seeing?

I could tell from the commotion going on in the car that someone had been hit by the gun fire. I saw Mrs. Kennedy rise from her seat and attempt to crawl out the back of the car. I also noticed that Agent Clint Hill was quickly approaching the car and attempting to mount the back of the car.

Did you accompany the Presidential car to Parkland Hospital?

I did.

Did you remain there?

No sir, I almost immediately, I would say around 12:45, I got a Dallas Police officer to take me back downtown to the Texas School Book Depository.

You specifically mention that building. Is there a reason that you mention that building?

I went there because I had been told the Dallas police were searching that building and had witnesses claiming they saw a man in a window with a gun.

How long did you stay in Dealey Plaza?

Not very long. I entered the back of the Depository and spoke with Mr. Truly. I asked if anyone saw anything and he led me to talk with Howard Brennan and Amos Euins. I took them to the Sheriff's department across the street and questioned them.

Did you go back over to the Depository?

Things got so confusing after that, I really don't recall very well what I did after questioning these two witnesses. I don't believe I went back to the depository immediately.

No further questions.

Cross, Mr. Cavendish?

Yes, sir.

Mr. Sorrels, good day, sir.

Yes sir.

You say you were in the backseat of the car being driven by Chief Curry, is that correct?

Yes.

You said when you heard the first shot you looked up on the terrace. Can you point out on the map where the car was located and where you looked?

Sorrels stepped down from the witness stand, took the pointer from Cavendish's hand and pointed at a position on Elm Street just past the beginning of the picket fence approaching the Triple Underpass. He pointed to the picket fence area of grass just before the stairs on the grassy knoll as the area to which he referred.

So let me make sure I understand, you looked up on the grassy knoll area of the plaza instead of looking back toward the Book Depository. Are you saying you believed the first shot came from in front of the President's car?

At the time, it was my first impression that the shot had come from the right and in front of the President.

So when you came back to the Plaza, why did you go to the Depository instead of the Plaza?

I had been told that police were searching the depository and that a couple of witnesses came forward saying they saw the shooter in the window of the sixth floor. I had also been told that police had searched behind the picket fence in the rail yard and had found nothing?

You say that officers had found nothing behind the picket fence, correct?

That is correct. They found nothing.

But sir sn't it true that when these first officers reached the picket fence, in fact jumping over the fence they were met with a man identifying himself as a Secret Service agent?

I've heard that one officer said that, but I haven't been able to corroborate that statement.

To your knowledge were there any Secret Service agents stationed behind the picket fence that day or in the rail yard?

To my knowledge there were not, and since I was the agent in charge of the local office, I believe I would have known were there any agents behind that fence.

You testified, Agent Sorrels that the route had been slightly adjusted just that morning from going down Main Street to turning on Houston and Elm and going under the Triple Underpass on Elm to the Stemmons Freeway, is that correct?

Yes sir. Well, the change was made that morning at the insistence of Chief Curry but we had talked about it even the day before?

In your opinion, would there have been any way for Mr. Oswald to have known about this change?

Well, I suppose not.

Did you ever go up to the sixth floor of the depository that day to help in the investigation?

No sir. I do not recall having done so.

No further questions.

You may step down, Mr. Sorrels. We will adjourn for the day. Court is in recess until 9 tomorrow morning, the Judge gaveled and left the court moving quickly through the door while the audience noisily stood.

Chapter 11- Oswald in the Depository

Cavendish knew that it would be difficult to overcome the testimony of those who placed Oswald in the Depository and so he used the time before the next day to review the initial depositions of the witnesses listed to be called over the next couple of days. One of the key witnesses would be Howard Brennan. But first the state would call one of the detectives who had searched the building. Taking the list as being absolute, the state was entering into a series of very iffy witnesses. They would call Seymour Weitzman, Roger Craig, Howard Brennan, Captain Will Fritz, and a couple of the guys who worked in the *depository*. Billy Andreous, the firm's chief investigator, discovered that the four officers who discovered the gun among the boxes were telling different stories about what they found. He wagered that the ones testifying were willing to claim what they were told to claim. But all four had signed brief affidavits just hours after the killing assuring the fireworks would be intense.

Boss, I'm certain these guys found a Mauser in that building but it seems they paraded a Mannlicher only after they determined that Oswald owned one.

I'm just not sure how one finds a rifle and it changes type within a matter of hours. Billy, as far as you know, were there any pictures of the rifle taken in the depository where the gun was found?

I am told there were not.

Were any pictures taken of the bag Oswald allegedly brought the gun into the depository in?

No sir. They only released a picture with an arrow pointing to the area in the sniper's nest where the bag was allegedly found.

Tell me about the picture of the cartridges on the floor.

Not much to tell. It was not taken authentically as it was found.

You mean to tell me they moved the bullets around and then took the picture?

Worse than that, boss. A reporter was allowed to go into the depository with the police as they were searching. He came on the sniper's nest and there were three cartridges on the floor. He was trying to photo them from over the top of boxes. He attempted to get the picture, but Detective Fritz was making sure he did not get inside the perimeter they had set up around the window. So he claims Fritz picked them up and held them in his hand. No picture had yet been taken of the area, so the evidence was compromised. The reporter said Fritz put them in his pocket.

I'll file a motion to have the evidence of the cartridges thrown out then. The evidence was tampered with and there is no original proof of the condition in which they were found. We can subpoena the reporter. So give me some names.

According to my notes, Deputy Sherriff Luke Mooney discovered the cartridges. But I don't have the reporter's name. I'm sure it has to be part of the record somewhere.

But you said Detective Fritz picked up the cartridges.

Yes, that is what this reporter is supposed to have said. But Mooney is credited with having found them.

I don't know. Chief Curry told some guys that there were so many reporters in the TSBD that the police didn't even know half the folks in the building while they were doing the search.

But boss, that is perfect for us, then isn't it? We plant the seeds of doubt in the jury's mind. We tell them that there could have been evidence planted in all the confusion. You know what I'm saying?

It would appear logical, but the police will come back with all of these police officers saying they didn't do anything to the evidence, that it was what they found. And then there are the pictures they took. They could easily just say these were taken during the investigation. No come back for that to my knowledge.

Well, perhaps yes. Look at this picture of the casings. You can clearly see out of this window in the middle, correct?

Cavendish took the picture.

Let me see that second picture.

He took the second picture purporting to show the arrangement of boxes in the sniper's nest.

Why does the second window on the left appear to be blackened out as though it were night? Cavendish asked.

I believe it is because the picture was taken at night and to fake the appearance of it being that same afternoon, this window, Billy said pointing to the larger of the two parts of the window, *was made to look as though it is that afternoon. Obviously if the reporter is correct in saying the police officer just picked up the cartridges and put them in his hand for him to take the picture, and there had not yet been any pictures taken, then the police picture is staged.*

I've got to have that reporter's name.

I'm on it, Billy said walking out of the office.

This might well be the darnedest case I've ever worked, Cavendish mumbled under his breath.

****

The trial resumed the next morning, security around all the participants being extraordinary. Cavendish and his team felt claustrophobic with the armed police presence. But they knew it was for their own safety. Shortly before the day was to begin, the bailiff handed Cavendish a note that Oswald wished to speak to him in private in the conference room. Mr. Cavendish and Mr. Donelson removed from the courtroom walking the short distance to the conference room where a guard stood watch. He patted them both down before allowing entrance. Oswald was sitting at the table dressed in a large suit and looking perplexed.

This thing seems to be moving really slowly, Mr. Cavendish. Can't you make it go faster?

Lee, this is just the way the process works, he responded sitting in the chair across from the defendant. Donelson remained standing.

So who will they call next?

We believe they will call Detective Fritz.

Oswald's head hung low.

What is it, Lee?

I don't trust that man. He questioned me for hours. He was just making all kinds of things up I guess hoping I would cave in and admit to something I didn't do.

Lee, did you shoot the President? Donelson asked.

Lee's face turned dark with anger and his fist doubled. *For the last time, I did not shoot anyone that day. Why won't they believe me?* He appeared to be asking the wall.

Cavendish reached over and touched Lee on the hand that was lying on the table. It occurred to the lawyer that either he had just touched the hand that changed history or this young man was indeed a patsy.

****

Call your next witness, Mr. Wade, Judge Brown ordered.

State calls Detective Will Fritz.

Fritz entered the courtroom his trademark White Stetson in his left hand. He approached the bench, swore his oath and took his place in the witness chair.

Good day Detective. I just have a few questions for you.

OK.

On the day in question, November 22, 1963, were you stationed in the Presidential motorcade?

No sir. I was not. Originally I was asked to be in the car, I believe, behind the Vice President.

What happened to change that?

I received a call the night before from Chief Stevenson asking that I work the Trade Mart detail.

OK. What did you do at the Trade Mart?

No more really than check the speakers stand and stage area.

And at some point that afternoon did you become aware that something had gone wrong in the motorcade?

Oh, yes, sir. We heard through radio transmissions that shots had been fired at the motorcade in Dealey Plaza.

Were you in charge of any other officers at the Trade Mart?

Directly with me were Detectives Sims and Boyd.

They are both homicide officers?

Yes.

And you are the head of homicide?

Yes, sir. I have been head of homicide for some thirty years.

Impressive. So you have investigated any number of murders in Dallas, is that correct?

Numerous.

Would you check your notebook that you have with you and tell us, if you can, at what time you heard that the President had been shot?

According to my notes, he was shot at 12:35.

Was that when you heard about it?

No I have in my book that is when it happened.

How did you hear of the tragedy?

From two sources at the same time. One of the Secret Service agents got the news immediately on his transistor radio, I guess it is. And Chief Stevenson came and told us as well.

This was at 12:35?

No, it was just moments later.

What did you do?

Sims, Boyd and me got in a police car and went over to Parkland Hospital. We got there just shortly after Chief Curry and the Limo carrying the President and Governor Connally.

Continue.

Chief Curry was standing at the curb and I asked what he wanted us to do.

And what did he say?

He said he thought it best to get to the scene of the crime.

Is that what you did?

Yes sir, I don't even think our car stopped moving. We left the hospital, got back on the Stemmons Freeway and maneuvered to the Texas School Book Depository.

And what time did you arrive there?

We arrived at the hospital at 12:45, if you want that time, and we arrived at the scene of the offense at 12:58.

So you arrived at the Book Depository at 12:58, is that correct?

Your honor, I object. Both Donelson and Cavendish were on their feet in protest.

Cavendish sat down allowing Sylvester a moment in the spotlight of the proceedings. Beside it had been agreed that Donelson would lead on the cross of this witness. He had spent a substantial amount of time investigating the TSBD scene and had a great deal of information.

And what is your objection? A perplexed Judge Brown peered over his glasses.

Your honor I object to the witness' portrayal of the TSBD as "the scene of the offense." There has been no evidence put forward at this moment giving rise to such a categorization.

We are getting there, your honor, if you will allow me a bit more time with this witness.

Overruled, but the witness is reminded that he should stick to the facts as they are presented and refrain from prejudicial statements.

Yes, sir, Fritz said casting a bit of a glare toward Oswald. His mouth contorted slightly as a smirk crossed his face.

So when you arrived at the scene of the Texas School Book Depository did the three of you go inside?

Yes sir.

And what did you do next.

Well, before going inside I was told by Officer Marion Baker that he had checked the building and could find nothing unusual. He suggested that witnesses saw a man with a rifle in the window near the top.

Can you identify on the picture here on the chart board which window the witness alleged to have seen a man with a gun?

Oh yes, it would be the 6th floor end window facing Elm at the corner of Houston Street.

Did you already know that information when you entered the building?

Oh no, sir. When we entered the building we thought there could be a possibility that the killer could still be in there.

And the search of the building turned up what, Detective Fritz?

Next to that window we found what appeared to be a sniper's nest. Boxes were stacked in a certain way. We found a brown paper bag wrapper in the corner and spent cartridges on the floor.

How many cartridges did you find?

Three.

And was there anything else that was found at the scene?

Yes, a little later in our search we found a Mannlicher-Carcano rifle in the opposite corner near the stairwell and elevator.

Is it your hypothesis Detective Fritz that whoever shot the gun then went to the opposite corner, hid the gun and then took the elevator downstairs?

Donelson was on his feet immediately. *Objection, prosecution is testifying.*

Sustained. Mr. Wade restate in proper form, please.

Yes, your honor. Captain Fritz based on your examination of the crime scene and your years of investigation experience, have you reached any conclusions about how the scene developed?

I have.

What do you believe that is?

It is my professional opinion that the person who fired the rifle used the sniper's nest as the point of fire and as witnessed by the finding of the cartridges and then walked to the other side,...

Objection, your honor the witness doesn't know whether the person carrying the gun walked, skipped, or crawled to the other side. This is clearly stating facts not in evidence and is a blatant attempt at creating a scenario instead of presenting the facts.

I would tend to agree. The witness should rephrase.

Of course, the person then went to the other side of the building where the gun was hidden in the boxes before escaping down the elevator.

Donelson started to stand but decided against doing so.

You wished to say something, counselor? Judge Brown asked Donelson.

No your honor, I'll address this on cross.

Continue Mr. Wade.

At what point did you return to the police station?

Soon after 2:00 when we received word that Oswald had been captured.

And is it true, Captain, that you were the main interrogator of Lee Oswald?

I questioned him for a number of hours on several different occasions.

What was Mr. Oswald's attitude when you questioned him?

He was very jittery, belligerent, and verbally abusive. I'd say he was uncooperative.

Have you seen this type of response in many people you have questioned?

Occasionally.

And in your professional opinion, what has been your observation about suspects who act in this manner?

They generally have something to hide.

Donelson knew better than to object to the line of questioning because Oswald's team knew better than anyone else that Oswald was hiding something. They were just hoping it wasn't his guilt.

In your investigation did you find that Mr. Oswald owns two guns in question in this case?

We did indeed.

Your honor, Wade said to Judge Brown approaching the bench with a piece of paper, *the state wishes to submit People's Exhibit One.*

So ordered, the Judge responded.

Wade also handed a copy to Captain Fritz.

Now Captain Fritz, I have handed to you exhibit one being an ad for guns from Klein's in Chicago, Illinois. This was found in Mr. Oswald's possessions at the Ruth Paine residence where Lee Oswald sometimes stayed and where his wife Marina was living at the time of the assassination. Would you tell the jury what you are looking at as my assistant presents copies to the jury?

Yes, Mr. Wade. This is a copy of an ad we found for guns. There are two circled on the ad. One is the 6.5 Mannlicher-Carcano we believe was used to kill the President and the .38 special is the gun we believe was used to kill Officer Tippit.

How did you ascertain that Oswald had purchased these guns?

Well, sir, the guns were ordered at two separate times in the name of A. Hidell, but both were signed for when picked up by Lee Oswald.

Your honor we submit the following paperwork: the order form submitted to police from both of the places where Oswald purchased these two guns. And we also submit the receipt where he signed for them.

So ordered.

OK, Captain, can you tell the court the dates on which the orders were placed?

The Smith and Wesson, that's the pistol, was ordered on January 27, 1963. He had to pick it up directly from REA Express since the company would not mail to his PO Box which he had opened the previous October under the assumed name Alek Hidell. The rifle was ordered from the Klein Company in Chicago on March 12, 1963 and was to include a mounted telescopic sight. By coincidence, both guns were sent to Oswald on March 20 and were picked up on March 25th.

Were these guns examined for finger prints?

They were by Captain Day's team.

And what were the results of the finger prints?

There was a partial palm print found on the rifle that was determined to be Lee Oswald's.

In your interrogations of Mr. Oswald, did the defendant ever acknowledge shooting President Kennedy, Governor Connally or Officer Tippit?

No sir, he vehemently denied doing so. In fact he denied even being on the sixth floor of the depository.

Did Mr. Oswald ever give you any reason for why he was at the Texas Theater?

No sir. He did not.

I have no further questions, your honor.

Mr. Cavendish, I believe it is time for a short recess. Let's take 15 minutes and then we will have the cross examination of this witness.

38 Special alleged to have killed Tippit

Chapter 12- Fireworks in the Courtroom

The courtroom was buzzing with anticipation, the chatter being just short of the roar more generally associated with an elementary playground. Both reporters and observers believed that the scene was set for the defense to play some needed cards. Numerous strands of the picture had now been put down. It was time to see what the defense really had.

Donelson took the floor.

Captain Fritz, you have been on the Dallas police department for how many years?

I've been on the police department since 1921.

Wow, that is an incredibly long time. You started as a patrolman, did you?

Yes, I did. Was there for a couple of years before transferring to homicide.

And you have in those years investigated any number of homicides?

Several hundred I would say.

And when did you become head of homicide?

Oh, I think it was about '32 or so.

So you have been Homicide Captain for some thirty years, correct?

Yes.

And in that time would you say this has been the most high profile murder that you have investigated?

By far. It isn't an everyday occurrence, thank God.

Now I would like to take you back through the testimony you have given and make some comparisons and some clarifications. Are you alright with that?

Well, yes. Fritz's face contorted in puzzlement wondering just where this young lawyer was going.

Now you stated that you came back to Dealey Plaza from Parkland at the insistence of Chief Curry, is that correct?

Yes sir. He was standing outside the emergency entrance when we drove up, real near the President's car. They were just finishing putting the top back on the President's car, I think, but he waved us on and hollered for us to get back to the Plaza.

So you went back to the plaza, but you testified that you drove to the Texas School Book Depository and, in fact, you called it "the scene of the offense." Had you been told that the shots were fired from the Depository?

I might have been. I don't really recall. There was a lot of pandemonium and chatter on the radio. We saw police officers standing outside the building.

When you stopped at the TSBD, were there officers in the building?

I don't really know if there were. There were officers outside the building.

Did you communicate with anyone standing outside the building?

Yes, one of the officers asked if I wanted the building secured and locked down.

And.

I told him yes.

So the building was locked down. Had anyone searched the building prior to your arrival at approximately 1:00?

No, I do not believe there had been any police officers in the building.

Donelson walked to his table where Mr. Cavendish handed to him several folders of materials. Oswald closely observed the handover of documents and looked at his lawyer, slightly turned the corners of his eyebrows upward. Cavendish smiled slightly.

If it pleases the court, we would like placed in evidence the depositions of Officer Marion Baker and of Mr. Roy Truly, Superintendent of the Texas School Book Depository building.

Mr. Wade.

We would have no objection but would like to know for what purpose this unusual request is being made?

Certainly Mr. Wade. We believe that Captain Fritz may not be aware of the actions at the Depository in the half hour before he arrived and we would like to make him aware of those actions from those who were there.

Seems fair enough. So ordered. In fact I am so inclined to order the entry into evidence all depositions made for this case in a wholesale fashion. Otherwise, I have a feeling we will be doing this on a continuous basis. How many depositions have been taken?

All the lawyers looked at Mr. Wade who then looked at his assistants for help. There are over 200 I believe, your honor.

Oh that is undoable. Ok, we will take them as they come. These two are entered. Let the record show, however, that even if the witness has not been called to the trial, this court wants their deposition entered into the official addendum of the trial and the jury will be given access to those.

Objection, your honor, Mr. Wade frowned at the lawyer. *Do you believe that will be necessary? There well may be some witnesses who were deposed that have little bearing on the trial itself and will only become fodder for the doubtful.*

Then perhaps they should not have been deposed, Mr. Wade. This is no ordinary case, may I remind this court. I will not break the rules of conduct in the proceedings but I will not demur from bending them oh so slightly. Let's move on. Objection overruled.

Captain Fritz, let me ask you a couple of questions about the thoughts you were having as you drove with your colleagues to Dealey Plaza from Parkland. You knew at that point that the President had been shot, correct?

I had only been told that he may have been hit. Yes sir. I think I did.

You did know?

Yes.

Did you know that Governor Connally had been hit?

Yes, I did know.

Did you know whether anyone else had been shot?

I had been told that Vice President Johnson might also have been hit. Possibly even Mrs. Kennedy.

So as you drove to Dealey Plaza, did you have any idea where the shots had come from?

There was a report that several officers had run up that grassy area of the Plaza toward the fence. Like toward the rail yard behind the Depository.

In fact, did you know at the time that as soon as the cars cleared Elm Street headed for Parkland that some 20 uniformed officers ran up the grassy knoll?

I did not.

Did you know that of the witnesses closest to the President's car, most every one of them said one of the shots came from behind the picket fence? Did you know that?

I knew that a few of them did, but you know echoes and all make it tricky.

Yes sir, I'm sure. Did you know that of those who believed a report to have come from that area, both Chief Curry and Secret Service Agent Sorrels have both testified in this courtroom already that they initially believed that the first shot had come from that area?

Which area?

From the rail yard, behind the picket fence or somewhere up there on the grassy knoll.

No, I was not aware of that.

Yet, didn't you just testify a few moments ago that you were in contact with the chatter on the air?

Yes. *Did not Chief Curry request via the police frequency to get men up there to check it out?*

Perhaps. I don't know that I heard that request.

But yet, when you go to Dealey Plaza you immediately go to TSBD, correct?

Yes.

Why?

The Captain looked around the room as though looking for a hidden answer hiding amongst the spectators all of whom had eyes riveted on him. His face reddened. *Because I saw officers standing outside the building and someone from* headquarters had radioed me that a person was saying they saw the gunman in the window.

Did you think that the gunman might still be in the building?

Perhaps.

Now it is your testimony that when you arrived at some 1:00, some thirty minutes after the shooting and at about the same moment the President was being pronounced as dead, that not one of the officers had been in that building. Is that your testimony?

Yes, it was my understanding that no one had been in the building.

Yet, Captain Fritz, isn't it true that Roy Truly, the superintendent of the building told you and Chief Curry that Officer Marion Baker had entered the building not even one minute after the shooting and that he and Mr. Truly went through the building floor by floor?

If I was told that by Mr. Truly, I do not recall it. And what he told to Chief Curry, you will have to ask Chief Curry. I don't know, didn't know that Baker had been in the building.

Do you know Officer Baker?

No, I do not.

Do you know Mr. Truly?

I know the name, but I don't know if I could pick him off the street if I saw him.

So you did not know that Officer Baker and Mr. Truly actually saw and signed depositions that they saw Lee Oswald in the second floor lunch room drinking a bottle of pop some two minutes after the shooting?

Beads of sweat had now formed on Captain Fritz's forehead threatening to run into his eyes. He pulled out a white kerchief and dabbed at his forehead before placing it into his coat's breast pocket.

Do I need to repeat the question? Donelson offered after adequate time had transpired.

No, I heard the question. I might have heard something about that. Didn't really pay any attention to it.

Now, Captain Fritz, you were all over that building that afternoon, is that correct?

Sure. We were.

And not for another hour did detectives come up with something, is that correct?

It was about that long, I suppose.

And why was that, Captain? You testified that you went to that building in part because someone had told an officer that they saw a gunman in a window, correct? Didn't they tell you which window? Why didn't you just go to that floor and that window right off the bat?

We believed it best to go floor by floor in the event that the assailant was hiding on another floor.

Is that right?

Objection, your honor, the counselor is badgering the witness.

Sustained.

When you are executing a search of this nature you want to be thorough. It wasn't long before Detective Mooney radioed that he had found something on the sixth floor.

And what was that?

Shell casings near that very window where the witness had seen the man.

Before we go up there to the sixth floor, let me ask you another question, Captain. How many people were in the Book Depository during this search?

Oh, that would be hard to say, Mr. Donelson. Fifty. Sixty. Maybe more.

Did you know who they all were?

Oh no, not at all.

Mumblings filled the air with the surprise of that announcement. The gavel banged slightly, even the judge seemed taken aback by the admittance.

Did I understand you correctly? Brown asked the witness. *Did you just say you didn't know who all the people were in the building?*

No your honor I did not. As you said, this was a special situation. There was a great deal of excitement and things were quite out of control.

So could you give us an idea of who some of the folks were?

Police officers, of course. There were about 20 of us in there, perhaps. All the Texas School Book Depository employees were still there except for two, Oswald and another guy, I forget his name. Mr. Truly. Chief Curry was in and out. Lieutenant Day from our forensics team was there at one point. There were numerous reporters there.

Reporters! Are you serious?

Yes, there were reporters in the building.

Did you know any of them?

Oh yes. I knew most of them, in fact. The one that I was with mostly was a Tom Alyea; he is a photographer for WFAA-TV here in Dallas. I invited him to document our search.

Actually, I'm so glad you mentioned that because I was about to ask you about something he said in his deposition.

What?

When you were called by Mooney, you know you said you got a call from Mooney that he had found some cartridges. What happened after that?

I went to the sixth floor. Alyea was trying to lean over some boxes to take a picture of something on the floor. Mooney said the spent shells were back of those boxes. I reckoned that Tom was trying to get a picture of them.

What did you do?

Well, we got him in a position where he could.

Did you disturb any of the evidence?

Not to my knowledge.

Have you read the deposition of Tom Alyea?

Counselor you know that I haven't. That would be a violation of the law.

When Tom Alyea tried to get that picture of those shell casings, they weren't under the corner window, were they?

Well, sure they were, at least two of them were right there beside the boxes where the assassin was at.

The Carcano is a bolt action rifle, is that correct?

It is?

When the gun is engaged and the shooter is moving the bolt manually, isn't it true that the discharge is rather dramatic?

I'm not sure I understand your meaning.

Let me make this rather simple. When the Carcano is being fired, it depends on a bolt to load the new bullet while ejecting the spent casing. Isn't that correct?

Yes.

And when that action is engaged the spent bullet generally is propelled rather energetically into the air, isn't that correct?

If it is as most bolt action rifles, that would be correct. I have not fired a Carcano so I wouldn't know personally first hand.

Of course. But what I'm not understanding, and your honor, if I may ask for the admission of these two photographs. We would like for them to be marked according to the prosecutions marking as Peoples 2 and 3 if Mr. Wade has no objection.

None, your honor.

So ordered.

Mr. Donelson waited while the pictures were placed in a bag, marked clearly and handed back to the lawyer by the clerk.

Now, if you will please look at these two pictures. They both show the shell casings, correct?

The color drained from the witnesses face. He reached for a glass of water that was setting on the bar beside the bench. He took a gulp of the water.

Sir, are you OK?

Oh yes. I'm fine. What is your question?

These pictures both show the shell casings, correct?

It would appear so.

One of these pictures was taken by Lieutenant Day, I believe and the other, as attested by Mr. Alyea, he took himself. Except the picture by Day, the official picture is time stamped later than the picture taken by Mr. Alyea. Isn't that correct?

Well, there must be some mistake.

According to the deposition signed by Mr. Alyea, he was attempting to take a picture of the spent cartridge shell casings that he claims were close together and behind the boxes right in clear view of the opening to the sniper's nest behind this second window, not the corner window. And he claims because you would not let him walk back there, you walked back there yourself, picked up the casings and held them in your hand while he took the picture. Is that correct, Captain?

Absolutely not!

Is that your hand in that second picture? Donelson walked over to the jury box and handed the foreman the pictures who then began passing them around. One by one the jurors all began looking at Fritz. Noses wrinkled. Foreheads furrowed. Cheeks turned red.

That is not my hand, and if that man claims it to be, he is just out and out lying!

Alyea also claims that after he took the picture you placed the shell casings in your coat pocket, is that correct?

I never picked up the casings.

Turning to another part of your investigation, do you believe that the assassin left the sixth floor, if indeed the shots came from there, by the elevator or the stairs?

Oh, I'm sure it was the stairs.

And why are you sure?

Because a group of men had come down from the sixth floor to go watch the motorcade and they all reported leaving the elevator on the first floor. One of the men, in fact, says he left Oswald on the sixth floor because he didn't get over there fast enough and then Oswald asked him to send it back up.

Did he?

Says he didn't.

So if it were Oswald, what you are saying is that he would have had to fire three shots off in about 6 seconds, walk across the diagonal of the building, hide the rifle and then take the steps down four flights to the second floor, go just about across the building again to the lunch room, buy a pop which he is then drinking when Officer Baker and Mr. Truly encounter him, and do all of that in less than two minutes. Is that your conclusion?

Objection.

Sustained. Mr. Donelson, you are getting mighty close to a line that I would hate to see you cross. Now can we ask some proper questions?

Sorry your honor. Captain Fritz, is it your conclusion that Lee Oswald fired the gun that killed President Kennedy?

Yes.

Based on your investigation, how many shots were fired from that window?

Three.

Based on your investigation approximately how much time elapsed between the firing of shot one and shot three?

Based on the investigation, I believe it would be between 6 and 8 seconds.

Again, based on your prior testimony, you then believe that Mr. Oswald walked across the diagonal portion of the floor, from corner to corner, hid the gun and then walked down two, excuse me, make that four flights of stairs. Is that correct?

I'm not too sure he would have been walking at that point, but that is correct. That is what our investigation uncovered.

And let's stop there, for a moment.

Do you have any witness or witnesses who actually saw Lee Harvey Oswald pull that trigger?

Well, ah...no sir. I can't say that we do.

Do you have any witness that saw him walk, run, or skip across that sixth floor and hide that gun in the boxes?

Ah, no.

Do you have any witnesses who saw Lee Harvey Oswald go down four flights of stairs?

He was hanging his head sheepishly by this time realizing he wasn't doing his side any good at all. *No sir. I do not.*

Captain Fritz, so you have no witnesses to any of those things, is that what you are telling this court?

I suppose that would be correct?

Then if you have no witnesses to any of those things, how can you be so sure that any of those things happened?

The evidence, son, the evidence. It all points to Oswald!

Well, let's see about that, now. Captain Fritz, what type of evidence would one look for in investigating this type of crime?

Ownership of weapons found, for one. Fingerprints at the scene for another.

So those are the things that would be of importance. Who on the Dallas Police Department was responsible for investigating those forensic aspects of the case?

That would have been Lieutenant Day.

You have spoken in regards to the ownership of the guns in question, the Carcano rifle and the pistol allegedly used in the murder of Officer Tippit. Is it correct that the FBI was asked to investigate the forensics of the rifle?

That is correct.

And what conclusions if any did they come to in regards to the Carcano being the murder weapon?

Well, outside of the one bullet that was found on a stretcher at Parkland and a couple of fragments found in the President's car, they did not have a great deal of ballistics to work with in the case of the rifle.

But did they arrive at any conclusions?

I do believe they did.

Do you know what those conclusions were? As to whether this was the gun used to assassinate John Fitzgerald Kennedy, what did the ballistics show?

According to the ballistics report, their results were inconclusive. The grooves created were consistent with the Carcano type rifle but it was inconclusive as to whether this particular rifle had been used.

And why was that, do you know?

Lack of bullets, I would say.

I will want to come back to that line of questioning throughout the trial as we learn more, and your honor, I will reserve even at this time the right to recall this witness.

Are you finished for now?

No sir, your honor, I just wanted to make note of that for the record, because I do believe the ballistics will be an important aspect of the trial. I want to move to another aspect of the evidence, the finger print evidence. Let's start with the depository. You testified that there was a partial palm print matching Oswald on the rifle, is that correct?

Yes.

Where was that palm print?

Again the witness paused and grabbed the glass and this time downed about half the contents. The top portion of his shirt collar was darkening with the perspiration.

The palm print was on the underbelly of the barrel where it sits atop the stock.

Am I correct that in order for that to have been placed at that position, it would have to have been placed there when the gun was unassembled would that be an accurate statement?

Yes sir, I do believe it would.

And would such a palm print be consistent with the ownership of a gun?

It would.

Were there any other prints on the rifle?

None that we could find. There were some small partials that we couldn't lift, some smudged impressions that might have been prints.

But no other prints?

None.

Do you find that odd?

That there were no other prints?

Yes.

Not necessarily. He could have been wearing gloves?

Ah, gloves. Did your investigation and search turn up any discarded gloves anywhere in the depository?

Not that I'm aware of.

Did any witnesses to your knowledge report seeing Oswald wearing gloves that day?

Not that I'm aware of.

Were any found on the bus he rode a couple of blocks?

No.

How about in the taxi he rode to his boarding house?

None.

Did you find any in the room at his boarding house?

No.

Did he have any gloves on his person when he was arrested at the Texas Theater?

No sir, he did not.

So do you think it safe to say that he did not wear gloves that day when he allegedly committed this crime?

I don't know that I could say one way or the other.

If he were not wearing gloves, how do you explain the lack of finger prints on the rifle?

I don't know maybe he whipped it off.

What do you think he whipped it off on—a shirt perhaps?

I don't know.

Did you find a towel or rag or something? Anything?

No sir.

Did you check his clothes for evidence of having fired a gun and whipping it off on maybe a shirt?

We did paraffin tests.

Oh really. Sylvester abruptly turned to his co-counsel and placed his palms toward the ceiling in a gesture of question.

Your honor, Cavendish was on his feet, I don't believe the state has furnished us with those findings.

Mr. Wade.

It should have been part of discovery. If not I apologize for the oversight and will have it in their hands within the hour. Wade looked at an assistant who immediately got up and left the courtroom. There was little doubt that the assistant wasn't going to the bathroom.

Thank you, Mr. Wade, Cavendish responded sitting back down in his chair.

A rumble of chatter disrupted the solitude of the crowd and they began to become restless until gaveled back to order by Judge Brown.

Now sir, can you share the results with this court? Your honor, may the report of the paraffin test be placed into evidence at this time if it has not already been stipulated in pre-trial.

It is listed, Mr. Donelson, as People's exhibit 95. Stipulated in pre-trial, General Wade volunteered.

And so it is. I do see it on the list. So Captain Fritz, if you please. What were the results?

The results were negative.

Negative?

Yes sir, negative.

Can you explain to the court, sir, what it means when the paraffin test is negative?

It means that we found no evidence, based on this test, that Mr. Oswald had fired a rifle that day?

The courtroom exploded in conversation as the roar seemed like a sudden touchdown had been unexpectedly scored by a football team. Judge Brown was so stunned by the admission that he momentarily forgot to pound the gavel to restore order.

Interesting, Donelson remarked when the crowd calmed. *So let me ask you concerning some other forensic activities in this investigation since it seems you are batting a 1000.*

Your honor! Mr. Wade was about to pop every button on his stiffly starched shirt.

Counselor, that was uncalled for. I'm fining you fifty dollars for that. You've been warned. I'm not going to tolerate rude and inconsiderate behavior.

I apologize to the court and to the witness. May I continue?

If you can do so without the sarcasm, by all means, go ahead.

I understand that Lieutenant Day also dusted three or four of the boxes in the sniper's nest, is that correct?

Yes, I ordered him to dust for prints the boxes nearest the window that would have been in direct contact with the assassin.

And what were the results?

Oswald's partial palm print and one index finger were found on two of the boxes.

And was there any way of telling when they were left there? Of course, keeping in mind that Lee Oswald was an employee of the Depository and as his job would have been touching the boxes, isn't that correct?

Well yes, but... well in any case, only one of the palm prints was recent. According to the test it had been placed in the last three days, but the others were older.

And were there any other prints on those boxes?

Fritz paused again and his hand reached for the glass. But it was empty.

Need more water, Captain?

The clerk came over with a pitcher and refilled his glass. When he was satisfied, he placed the glass back down on the rail and looked directly at Oswald.

Yes sir, we found a few more.

How many prints did you find on those four boxes?

Approximately twenty.

Again Judge Brown pounded the gavel.

Order. Folks, we will have order in this courtroom.

How many did you say? Even Sylvester Donelson nearly choked on that piece of information which again they had not been given.

20 fingerprints.

You mean prints from 20 different people?

Yes, sir. That is what I mean.

And have you identified all these prints?

Yes, all but one.

So 19 prints have been identified, is that correct?

Yes.

And these were employees?

Yes, the 19, including Oswald's were all employees.

Well that leaves you with one set of prints unidentified, correct?

That is correct.

And do you have any idea to whom those prints belong?

We do not?

I think I do...I think they belong to the killer. No further questions.

Your honor, objection.

Counselor, Judge Brown looked at Wade over his glasses, *I bet you do object. But I'm overruling the objection. Court will stand in recess until tomorrow morning.* BANG!

Chapter 13- The Remainder of the State Case

That was absolutely brilliant! Cavendish praised Donelson when he walked into the office less than half an hour after his performance in court. The lead attorney stood at the conference table applauding. A couple of interns and a secretary also stood at the far end of the room, smiles lighting their faces. They had worked so hard to uncover the evidences Donelson had used against the state today. And while he had introduced evidence during his cross it went directly to subjects first broached by the prosecution. And their hypothesis had started collapsing.

This changes the lay of the land, Sylvester.

The lawyer leisurely entered the room, a concerned look interrupting the joy of the moment.

What's wrong? one of the interns asked.

It is sure that we have deflected enough of the case on the Kennedy killing that we would hope the deck of cards would collapse, but we still have to move the charges on Tippit. And I'm just not sure how we dispute the evidence. We could say they had no eye witnesses to the Kennedy Assassination even in a building filled with people. But in the streets of Oak Cliff, there were witnesses and they are willing to say they saw Oswald kill the Officer.

Well, Tom smiled, *I have a few surprises for them on that front as well.*

****

The call came to the nightstand phone beside his bed. It was barely past 10:00 but Tom and his wife had gone to bed early to enjoy the extra time they had with the children staying at the grandparents. Both worked punishing hours and rarely did they have time with each other without the children. Five boys could make a house crazy, but they had turned off the television when the boys had piled in the station wagon and headed off to Grandpa Cavendish's house across town. Tom's wife had unplugged the phone for a couple of hours before they finally retired to bed.

Tom heard the ringing and first thought it was in a dream he was having, but when he also heard the pounding at the door, he realized something was wrong. He quickly turned to answer the phone while his wife put on her housecoat and left the room to go see who was at the door. Tom could hear the voice on the phone but he was still groggy. When he detected the clear voice of Sylvester in his living room, he knew for sure that there was trouble. Now he put the receiver down on the black phone having heard what the caller said but not believing it. He wanted to hear the message from his partner.

He grabbed his robe and walked down the hall still brushing back his unruly hair.

Oh Tom. It is terrible. We have been trying to call you for hours. Oswald has been shot.

The color drained from Tom's face and his legs felt wobbly. He sat down on the plush brown sofa. *What happened?* he asked softly the sleep causing his voice to crackle.

When the guards were taking him from the courtroom after we met with him, there was a guy waiting down in the garage. He pulled a .38 and pumped two shots into Oswald.

What's his condition?

One of the shots grazed his arm barely missing an artery. The other hit him in the chest and is near his heart. The doctors believe he will survive. They have him under heavy guard.

Did they get the guy who did this?

Oh yes, and you aren't going to believe who it was.

Who?

Jack Ruby that night club owner who tried to get into the basement when they did the transfer.

Why'd he do it?

Says he was just totally distraught about Kennedy's killing. Thought it would spare Jackie from having to testify and all.

Oh that's bull! I want the whole staff on this. I want to know everything there is to know about Jack Ruby and I want to know it now! His face grew red. He closed his eyes and tried to calm himself. He couldn't lose Lee. He just couldn't.

****

But we can't conduct a trial without the person charged being present, Cavendish heard himself saying. He knew better, but offered the statement in an effort to delay going forward with the trial until Lee was healed.

General Wade didn't waste a second pummeling the defense team with case after case where the courts had ruled that a defendant could indeed be tried in absentia.

The Judge looked concerned that the incident would disrupt his court beyond repair.

And we should just continue with the trial as though nothing has happened? Doubtless these jurors have heard that Oswald has been shot. How could they have helped it? Everyone is talking about it. Donelson was resolute; Cavendish had taken a seat in the judge's chamber realizing their arguments were reaching a dead end.

Well, gentlemen, Judge Brown interrupted their argument. *I'm quite concerned the impression that such a knowledge would have in tainting the jury's judgment. Let's face it, we all are wondering what the real story is behind this attempt. And that it is Ruby's second attempt to get at Oswald smacks of subterfuge in this affair.*

Perhaps he was just passionate about it, your honor, as he says, General Wade offered. *I questioned him the first time during the transfer, and he seemed genuinely upset with Kennedy's death. He says he was a big fan of Kennedy.*

Is that right? the judge moaned. *I'd like to know where Mr. Ruby was during the motorcade.*

Well, we know where he was during some of the questioning, your honor, Cavendish responded. *We all saw him on television during one of Curry's press conferences correcting*

Chief Curry on the name of some organization of which Oswald was affiliated while in New Orleans.

And how would Mr. Ruby be privy to information regarding Oswald's actions in New Orleans? the Judge asked.

The look on Wade's face indicated that he was seriously contemplating something. *Your honor, would it be appropriate to have a closed session without the jury and put Ruby on the stand and question him?*

The judge thought about the request.

Well, Judge Brown, if we allow such a disruption, will it not indicate that we believe there is more to the story? And if so, then will that not tend to prove that there has been a conspiracy in the murder of the President? Donelson had hit upon a good point. Giving too much press to this matter could be great for their case, but work a hard hand against the justice system.

Gentlemen, I'm in an extreme situation here. If we have him come in to a closed session, I'm assuming it would be because we do not know what he might say and we do not want to taint the jury. Is that correct?

I would think so, your honor, Wade responded.

How long is Oswald expected to be out?

At least a month, Judge Brown, Cavendish answered. *I don't really have a problem with continuing I suppose, but I'm concerned that his absence will bring more speculation on the part of the jury toward his guilt if they don't know what has happened. I believe that they should be told by Judge Brown that Oswald has been shot. They can be charged not to read anything into the incident. However, I would be willing to venture a guess that they are going to believe that others are involved. It will give greater credence to the defense position.*

And you would love that, would you Cavendish?

Why, General Wade, I suspect that this event has even shaken your belief in his guilt, if you were to tell the truth.

Let me make something plain to you. I believe without any doubt that Lee Oswald, your client, shot and killed both President Kennedy and Officer Tippit and wounded Governor

Connally. And I aim to prove it with evidence. We have already presented his guns and I'm not through with the rest of that. By the time we are finished putting on our case, even Lee Oswald will believe he is guilty.

Yeah, right. And in the meantime, the problem remains, do we continue or not?

Gentleman, I'm going to err on the side of the state. I would like to continue with the trial. I'm going to go back to the jury room and let the jury know what has happened to Mr. Oswald. I will carefully remind them that they should not read anything into the event as it impacts this trial. However, I certainly cannot guarantee that it will not impact their thinking. They are human less we forget.

Yes sir. And I also think, Cavendish added that it would be appropriate to remind all us attorney's that we should not in any way use the attempt to murder Oswald to move the jury unless evidence comes forward that Ruby is somehow involved in a conspiracy to kill the President.

A knock at the door interrupted the conversation. The judge looked irritated as the clerk of the court poked her head through the now opened door.

I'm sorry, your honor, but Billy Andreous said it was urgent.

Show him in. Billy stepped through the door holding what appeared to be a large blown up picture.

Mr. Andreous what is so urgent that you are willing to divert our attention off of what we were discussing? Billy smiled warmly at the judge who was obviously not pleased.

Well, sir, I apologize for all of that. But I've been up most of the night looking through every picture I could find that has been presented and I found something so important that I thought it would be of interest to both Mr. Cavendish and Mr. Wade.

And what would that be Billy? Cavendish asked.

Boss look at this picture. It was taken during the motorcade. That is the front door of the Texas School Book Depository.

So, General Wade grunted as he glanced over at the picture being held by Tom. *This was worth the interruption.*

Billy handed the two counselors another picture. This one was of Jack Ruby's mug shot. They again looked at it and placed it on the table in front of them for Judge Brown to also examine.

Mr. Andreous, I would ask that you get to the point, the Judge demanded.

Yes, sir. If you look at the first picture closely, you will see a gentleman standing to the right of the door with sunglasses on. Sunglasses! He really stands out in the picture, correct? Look at the hairline. Now look at the mug shot. I'm 100 percent sure that the man standing beside the building entrance was Jack Ruby.

Well, I'll be, the Judge looked closer examining it lifting his glasses to his forehead. *I believe you are correct, Billy. OK, Mr. Cavendish, I believe that I'm going to go with your suggestion. We are going to have a closed door with Mr. Ruby. I want to know what he knows about all this, and particularly I want to know what he was doing at the front door of the depository during the assassination.*

Mug shot of Jack Ruby- Dallas Police Department

Chapter 14- The Prosecution Is On!

When Judge Brown returned from his discussion with the jury, a discussion that took the balance of an hour, he seemed perturbed. He slammed a legal pad on his desk and ordered everyone to leave his chambers for five minutes. When they returned he was just finishing a cigarette and a small glass of golden colored bourbon was being raised to his lips. The smoke hung heavily in the air.

Gentleman, have a seat. I don't mind telling you that this is the darndest thing I've ever witnessed. In all my years I've never had a defendant shot during a trial. I did have a lawyer shot once by a jealous husband a few years back. Now that was a case, mind you, he continued lifting the glass toward them. When he had gulped the final mouthful, he put the glass on a cabinet behind his desk and turned toward the lawyers who had reassembled.

So here is what we are going to do. The jury is very upset about this turn of events. I think it best to get them focused on the trial quickly before they lose their composure. Understandably they are concerned about their own safety. Already we have had a lawyer beaten up and now the defendant has been shot. They sense that there is something larger going on here, and there is nothing I can say one way or the other that will reassure them otherwise. I'm not even sure at this point of what is going on myself. But I know we aren't going to declare a mistrial, so Mr. Cavendish, don't even think of asking. What I have done, however, is to ask that Lieutenant Governor Smith set up a military guard around this courthouse, and around both Ruby and Oswald. There will be no more shootings or beatings happening in conjunction with this trial. Why the New York Times is having a field day with their coverage saying that Dallas is part of the Wild, Wild West and that we will be lynching Oswald by the end of the trial. We are going to show them New York liberals that we can run a trial in this city.

Your honor, with all due respect, how do we go from here? Donelson felt uneasy at asking the question but it was certainly the elephant in the room.

Mr. Wade, who are you calling next? That is, I do recall Mr. Donelson that you were finished with Captain Fritz, correct?

Yes sir, I...

If it please, I would like to redirect on Fritz, interrupted General Wade.

Of course, General Wade. You have that right. So after you have redirected on Fritz?

My plan is to call Officer Mooney and then Lieutenant Day.

OK, well, let's head into the courtroom and continue on. Then on Tuesday of next week, I am going to schedule a closed-door hearing with Jack Ruby.

Your honor, Wade began. But the judge already had his hand up.

General Wade, I know what you are going to say. Save it. I am determined that I'm going to question him on the stand and find out what he knows about all of this. I know it is unorthodox, but it is going to happen. The record will be held, the jury will not hear it, and only you gentlemen and the recorder will be here to witness it.

I suspect, Cavendish interjected, *that if the feds get wind of it, they will demand to be present as well.*

Bring them on. The Judge walked down the hall away from the lawyers who were to enter the courtroom from a side door while the judge entered from behind. When the *All Rise* was shouted by the bailiff, the lawyers were about mid-way to their places in the courtroom. The judge hurried to his seat and then asked for the jury to be shown in.

You may call your next witness.

Your honor, the state would like to ask Captain Fritz back to the stand for redirect.

Captain Fritz came forward to the stand.

You are still under oath, Captain Fritz, the Judge reminded.

Yes sir.

Captain Fritz, I just want to clarify a couple of things about your testimony. When you left Parkland to go to Dealey Plaza, did you have an idea as to where you needed to go?

No sir, none whatsoever. We were hearing a great deal of chatter on the police line and most of it was indicating that they were to go to the School Depository Building. I had also heard that a search had been conducted of the train yard and nothing had been found.

So your choice of the TSBD was based on what you were hearing, is that correct?

Yes.

And when you arrived there were officers standing in the front of the building?

Yes. Numbers of officers, probably two dozen.

And your testimony is that no one had yet searched the building, is that correct?

No sir, I misunderstood your question. When we arrived the search had already commenced in the building. I merely ordered it to be sealed and for them to report to me any information on any finds or if they found a shooter. I'm sorry for my mistake.

So the hunt was already underway?

Yes.

And at some point Officer Mooney sent word to you that the spent cartridges had been found and you went to the sixth floor.

Yes.

OK, thank you sir. I'm finished.

You may step down Captain Fritz. General Wade you may call your next witness.

The state calls Deputy Sherriff Luke Mooney to the stand.

Luke Mooney, the bailiff repeated.

The Deputy Sherriff walked through the door wearing his uniform complete with his sidearm.

Will my security guard remove the firearm from the Deputy Sherriff?

Your honor, Mooney started to protest.

Cavendish looked up instantly as though slapped in the back of the head. He turned to Donelson and whispered, *there's something about his voice that sounds familiar. I just can't place it.*

Deputy, you know the rules. No witness is allowed to wear a gun while in the witness chair. Now give the man your weapon and come be sworn in.

Mooney obliged the order and reluctantly handed Officer Daniels the gun. Before going into the chair, he raised his hand, placed the other on the Bible and swore to tell the truth. As he began to sit in the chair he glanced over at Cavendish and nodded his head in his direction. Cavendish twisted in his chair the discomfort overwhelming him instantly. He couldn't get out of his head the idea that he knew that voice.

Officer Mooney, we have had testimony from Captain Fritz that you were the person who discovered the shell casings on the sixth floor of the depository. Is that correct, sir?

Yes, he said with an east Texas drawl that made President Johnson sound like a Yankee.

And would you tell the jury how you came upon these spent casings?

Sure. We was up on the sixth floor and we began near the stair well and went to the left. There was large amounts of boxes in der, so we just took our time.

You say we, who else was present?

They was a television reporter with me, Tom Alyea, he is. He was with me and they was two other police officers from Dallas City up thar. They went to the right and we went to the left.

Was there anyone else up there?

I think they may have been a couple of employees up thar and them Secret Service agents. It were real crowded downstairs and I don't really remember everythang from that day. You know it were very emotional and all.

Yes, sir. I understand. So you started around to the left, continue.

We looked through them boxes to see what we could find.

Let me ask you this before you go on. Who had sent you into the building to search?

When Captain Fritz came to the building around one, I had taken up a position just in front of the door. I had heard about the shooting and walked over from da Sheriff's office, you know.

Yes, it is directly across from the Dal-Tex building, is that correct?

Yes.

Did you hear the shooting inside the building?

No sir, I did not.

So you are in front of the TSBD building front door when Captain Fritz comes up. He orders the building secured and asked if you would help in searching the floors. Did he seem to be the officer in charge?

Captain Fritz?

Yes, did Captain Fritz seem to be the officer in charge?

I believe he were.

Did anyone suggest to you that they had seen anyone in the window of the building with a gun?

Yes, there were an officer Miller said two witnesses seen a man with a gun on the sixth floor in the winder.

And so you are making your way toward that window, correct?

Well, yes, but you see, this building is like a big warehouse. It is large. I mean we didn't just walk over to that winder. We didn't know as to what the killer was still thar? So we are searching behind practically every box.

Did you find anything between the staircase and the area that has commonly come to be called "the sniper's nest?"

Lots of boxes. Didn't find nothin' until I came on them shells.

How many were there?

They was three casings.

Did you see Tom Alyea attempting to film the casings?

No. I can't say I did.

What did you do when you found the casings?

Well, I let everybody know that I had found something. I sent word down to Captain Fritz that we'd found somethin' on the sixth floor.

But you never saw Alyea trying to video them?

He had da camera runnin', but I never seen him make any effort to get over the barricade of boxes. It was pretty tight in thar. Hardly enough room for a person to walk.

Did you remain there?

No sir. When Captain Fritz came I left and went on searching.

So you did not see anything that transpired between Captain Fritz and Tom Alyea in regards to the bullet casings, is that correct?

I did not.

No further questions. Your witness.

Mr. Donelson arose quickly and walked directly toward the witness chair.

Deputy Mooney, have you watched the video shot by Tom Alyea?

I might have seen it on the television.

It is interesting because when we see you in the video, I do believe you are in it, it is around the finding of the gun. Were you present when the gun was discovered?

I were still in the building.

We asked the television station to make available to us the video. We have it.

Yes, I were thar, but I wasn't one of them officers that found it.

OK, and in regards to the finding of the casings. Alyea's video is pretty clear that there are two other officers there but neither appears to be you.

Yes sir. I were thar. I'm in the film.

So you say.

Objection your honor. Mr. Donelson is badgering this witness. Is there a point to be made from this cross?

Clearly, your honor, there are contradictory stories going on here. The witness claims that he came over to the depository and is sent in by Captain Fritz, and in Mr. Alyea's deposition, he claims they went in before Fritz arrived. I'm just trying to arrive at the truth.

Badgering the witness when he had answered your questions isn't getting us closer to the truth. You say you have the video.

No I said we requested the video.

Do you have it?

We do not. It was requested and even subpoenaed but they refused to turn it over.

Well, let it be known that we do have a copy of it and we can gladly end this discussion by showing the video, with the court's permission, of course.

I do not want to show it at the moment, Mr. Wade, but when we want to do so, we will remember that you have it and didn't provide a copy in discovery.

Properly noted, interjected Judge Brown. Now continue, please.

Thank you, your honor. So it is your testimony that you discovered the spent casings even though Mr. Alyea states in his affidavit that he and Fritz discovered the casings. Is that your testimony?

Objection, your honor, asked and answered.

Get on with it Mr. Donelson.

Yes sir. I am going to show you a picture that was taken in the so called sniper's nest. Could you please tell the court if this was the position where you found the casings laying on the floor?

He hands the picture to Mooney who glances at it, and then looks even closer as his eyebrows bunch up together toward the center of his forehead.

This is not at all where them casings were located according to my recollection.

If it pleases the court, this exhibit has been marked People's 10 and is identified as the official crime scene photo of the casings. Now Mr. Mooney, if you could tell the court what the difference in placement is between this picture that I have shown you and your recollection of their placement.

Well, the location is all wrong. They have that one bullet over har in front of the second winder by itself and they was all in that immediate area, not just the one.

There were none of these by the wall or that close to the boxes, is that your testimony?

Exactly, Mr. Donelson. I know what I seen. They was within inches of that box that formed the upper end of the barrier line of boxes. But over toward the first winder just a tad bit more. It was really kind of hard getting close to dem without going inside the barrier. That's what I recollect. But anyhow, I could be off just a bit on exact location, but I do remember dem being bunched up together like.

In fact, Mr. Mooney, in his deposition Mr. Alyea states they were close enough together to fit within the top of a bushel basket. Does that sound accurate?

Sure.

No further questions at this time your honor, but we do reserve the right to call this witness again.

You may step down. The judge glanced at his watch, ordered a short fifteen minute break and then scurried out the back door.

I think Judge Brown is as nervous about this trial as we are, Donelson suggested to Cavendish as they sat at the defense table. Out of the corner of his eye, Donelson noticed a heated confrontation happening between General Wade and a clerk that showed up with a message.

When Wade had finished his dogging of the clerk, he turned to the defense table with the intent of sharing some information.

Trouble in paradise, General? Tom asked.

Wade walked over to the table, laid a file down on the table and squatted down in order to reel his words in close and not be overheard.

Gentleman, here are a couple of other discovery pieces that were inadvertently left out of the process, with my apologies, of course. I also need to let you know a couple of things that have transpired. This case is just driving me crazy. We had subpoenaed the doctor from Bethesda who did the autopsy on Kennedy to testify at the trial. Seems the Justice Department has rescinded the summons citing national security. They will only make his findings in the report known but will not allow him to be questioned on the stand.

Can they do that?

He is military. I don't believe I can compel him to testify if the government forbids his participation. Even I'm beginning to wonder if something is being covered up. But oh well. We'll use the autopsy to prove the point.

Day is up next, correct?

Yep.

All rise, the bailiff announced.

Defense calls Lieutenant J. C. Day.

After Day was sworn in, he sat In the chair twitching first toward the prosecution table then toward the jury, then back at center. He was already perspiring before Wade had asked the first question.

Would you state your name for the record?

Lieutenant J. C. Day.

Now Lieutenant Day, you work for the Dallas Police Department, is that correct?

Yes sir.

And how long have you been employed with the police department?

Some twenty-two years.

And what is your current position in the Dallas Police Department?

I am the head of the Investigative Unit.

This is like a crime investigative team, is that correct?

Yes sir.

And what are your responsibilities within this unit at a crime scene?

It is our responsibility to gather evidence, to ascertain it is properly gathered, labeled and that a chain of custody is followed and carefully documented.

In the particular case under our consideration, where were you at the time of the assassination?

I was in the basement of city hall. Around 12:45 we heard that the President had been shot. I immediately returned to my office on the fourth floor and listened on the radio. Around 1:00 I was summoned to come to the Texas School Book Depository on Elm Street.

What did you do when you arrived?

I was told by an Inspector at the front door that I should report to the sixth floor and see Captain Fritz, that they had found some bullet casings.

So you went to the sixth floor. Were there a large number of people in the building?

Oh yes, there were lots of people in the building?

Did it concern you to see such a large number of people in the building?

Not really because I knew the crime scene was being secured.

So you went to the sixth floor, continue.

My team went up the stairs to the sixth floor. We couldn't figure out how to use the elevator so it took us a few minutes to get up there with all our equipment.

Who was with you?

Officer Studebaker was with me. He generally is the person in charge of photographing the crime scene.

OK, so when you got up to the scene of the 6th floor, what did you do?

We went over to the northeast windows—I mean southeast windows, you know the windows facing Elm Street, the corner window on the sixth floor, it would be the corner of Elm and Houston but facing Dealey Plaza.

OK. Continue.

We took pictures of the three shell casings.

Your honor we have three pictures we would like marked as Peoples 2,3,4. General Wade handed the pictures to Judge Brown who handed them off to the clerk for marking. *If you would look, Lieutenant Day, at these three pictures. Are these the three pictures taken at that time?*

They are.

And you took these pictures, is that correct?

Oh no. They were taken by R. L. Studebaker.

OK, but these are the pictures taken by Officer Studebaker for your criminal investigative team, correct?

Yes, they would appear to be the pictures.

How many shell casings are in the picture?

Well, you can see two, actually just the point of one of the others in this picture, and in this picture you can clearly, well, almost clearly see all three. Day's face turned reddish.

Picking up a baggie from the table in front of the bench appearing to contain three shell casings, General Wade walked in front of Judge Brown and asked that the evidence be marked People's exhibit 100.

So ordered.

Are these the shell casings that were found on the sixth floor of the Texas School Book Depository?

The witness looked very closely at the shell casings and when he saw something on one, looked up at General Wade, smiled and acknowledged that they were.

And how were you able to ascertain that they are one and the same as those found on November 22, 1963?

One of them has my last name written on it.

So you marked them.

Oh yes, we always mark such things so that we know that they are the authentic article found at the scene. It is common practice.

Did you also dust the boxes in the area for fingerprints?

We dusted four boxes in the vicinity of the window, what we call the sniper's nest, for fingerprints.

And were Lee Oswald's fingerprints found on any of those boxes?

Yes sir. We found a palm print on two of the boxes and the imprint of his index finger on the corner of one of the other boxes.

Officer, you also were involved in the finding of the gun about an hour later, is that correct?

Well, not in the finding so much as the processing.

OK, so do you know who found the gun?

At the time the gun was found there were four officers in the area. I am assuming that one of them spotted the gun. It was well hidden.

Was it in the same area as the shell casings?

No sir, it was actually in the opposite corner near the elevator and staircase.

Do you know the names of the officers who were looking among the boxes in that area?

Yes, I have them written in my notes here. If I may? he asked holding up a small pad of paper.

Certainly.

According to my notes it was Weitzman, Deputy Sherriff Boone, and Deputy Sherriff Craig that actually discovered the rifle. I was in the area when the discovery was made and I was the person who took the gun out from behind the boxes.

Did you dust for finger prints in this area?

I dusted the gun.

Were there any fingerprints found on the rifle?

There was a palm print eventually found on the rifle but only smudges or what appeared to be some fingerprints were found but none that could be identified.

I am now going to show you another picture that was taken by a reporter just moments after the shooting on November 22 from the street below. We have blown up the picture...

General Wade, is this picture in evidence?

Oh, I'm sorry your honor. We would ask this picture to be marked People's 5.

Done.

Lieutenant Day, as I was saying this was taken by a reporter and we have blown it up to show floors five and six of the depository building just moments after the shooting of the President.

Yes.

Now in this picture you can clearly see the two colored employees in the fifth floor windows.

Yes sir. I believe they were both questioned by police that afternoon.

Oh, yes, indeed they were.

And now, if I may direct your attention to the sixth floor? You can clearly see that there is a box sitting somewhat askew in the widow setting, correct?

Yes, that was part of the boxes that had been stacked up we believe by the assassin.

And was that box in that position when you arrived at the scene?

Yes.

And is that the same box that you examined for fingerprints?

Yes.

And is it the same box that appears in Peoples 2, 3, 4 that you previously examined that were taken by Mr. Studebaker?

It would appear so.

Now I want to ask about the other box in the window. What other box?

The one that appears in the window of the reporter's picture. Do you see it?

Well, I see something that appears as a box, but I believe that what you are seeing is the boxes that are stacked behind there some 2 ½ feet from the window.

So you are saying there is no box in the window other than the box on the sill?

That is correct.

Could it be that boxes were moved before you arrived on the scene?

I was told by Detective Sims that nothing had been touched because they were waiting for my team to arrive.

OK, thank you Lieutenant. I have no further questions. Your witness, Mr. Cavendish.

Would the defense like to cross examine this witness? Judge Brown asked.

Most definitely, responded Sylvester Donelson as he hurriedly approached the witness stand.

Government Exhibit 115

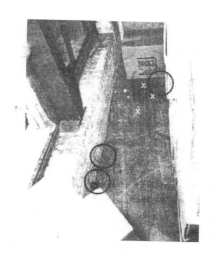

STUDEBAKER Exhibit 1.

STUDEBAKER Exhibit 2

The Studebaker Pictures

Chapter 15- Somebody is Lying

Good morning Lieutenant Day.

Good morning.

Earlier this court heard testimony relative to the happenings in the Depository between the time of 12:32 when Marion Baker first entered the building looking for an assailant and the arrival of Captain Fritz at 1:00 approximately. Are you aware of any of that testimony?

Perhaps some.

Would pandemonium be a word that would aptly describe what was going on in and around the Depository?

Objection your honor. General Wade's second chair, David Arnough, who had been reasonably quiet up to this point, rose slowly to his feet. His distinguished look showed a touch of gray at the temples and a finely tailored black, pinstripe suit tightly fitting an apparently hefty body.

And what is your objection, Mr. Arnough? Judge Brown asked looking over his black-framed glasses.

Your honor I'm merely getting at the seeming confusion in the testimony and why it is important for the jury to understand the state of things inside that building.

Mr. Arnough studied for a moment before sitting down. *Withdrawn.* The daunting task of filling the shoes of General Wade, who had momentarily stepped out, overwhelmed Arnough. Wade, the seasoned veteran, would have torpedoed through the objection whether he really understood a purpose for doing so, but the novice Arnough was out matched.

Would that then, Lieutenant Day, be a reasonable description of things inside the TSBD on November 22, 1963?

Yes sir. I would say bedlam would be accurate. The Secret Service were climbing on top of boxes and throwing things around. The police were searching everywhere for whatever they could find. By the time I arrived there must have been twenty people on just the sixth floor.

Did you know all the people on the sixth floor?

Why heavens no!

Can you give us an idea of the people there?

I know there were Secret Service agents there, and Mr. Alyea, the television reporter was filming things to chronicle the search, and Captain Fritz and his team and Sims, and my team, and police officers and deputy Sheriffs. It was pandemonium.

So in your testimony, you have said that you were told at the front door to go to the sixth floor because they had found shell casings, is that correct?

Yes.

And about what time would you say that would have been?

It was about 1:15 or so. I really didn't look to check.

But it was definitely before 1:30 was it?

Oh yes.

And did you know by then that the President had died?

I'm not certain when I learned that; I knew he had been shot. I knew also about officer Tippit, and I knew that the shots were thought to have been fired from the TSBD.

You mean the shots fired at the President's motorcade?

Yes, the shots hitting the President and Governor Connally.

So you have said that when you arrived, you went up to the sixth floor and spoke with Captain Fritz, is that correct?

Yes.

And he took you to the location of the spent casings?

He pointed to where I would find them.

And you mentioned that Mr. Alyea was present.

Yes, he was filming around the large area that was being searched.

Now you have testified that nothing had been moved from the time of the assassination to the time you arrived, is that still your testimony?

Certainly.

And just how did you know, do you know now, that nothing had been moved?

I was told by Captain Fritz that nothing had been moved.

But isn't it true that Captain Fritz only arrived at the scene at 1:00 some thirty minutes after the shooting?

If that is what he has said, then yes.

And indeed that is what he has said. So how would Captain Fritz know that nothing had been moved?

I don't know, but that is what he told me.

Well, I believe that is what he told you, but I'm wondering if it is true. Let's take for example that picture that General Wade showed you a short time ago, the one taken by the reporter from the ground level. It would appear to the casual eye that there are two boxes in that window, one closest to the corner alleged to have been used by the gunman and then one near the center post separating the two windows in the section. Wouldn't you agree that it appears that way?

No sir. I explained that the second box is about 2 ½ feet back from the window.

And just how many boxes are back 2 ½ feet from the window, Lieutenant Day?

There were probably 15 or so of them. They are stacked about 5 feet high almost like a pyramid with a middle box on top of the pile.

So you are saying there were approximately 15 boxes forming what a barrier, would you say?

A hiding place. It meant the sniper's nest was hidden from view from anyone else that was on the floor.

OK, so there are some 15 boxes piled up, stacked up some 2 ½ feet from this box that is in the frame of the window, correct.

Yes, I would say that is about correct.

But only the one box is at the window that is the one in the window frame, is that correct?

That is correct. That is how I found the area.

So why then can we so clearly see this second box, in the same type of light as the first box if it is 2 ½ feet from the window?

Oh, it is undoubtedly because the sun is striking the box.

You think? Kinda like the sun is striking the two colored fellows in the window below?

Perhaps.

But then, they are right at the windows, aren't they, not 2 ½ feet back, isn't that correct, Officer Day?

I suppose. Day looked down toward his feet and then gave a quick glance over to the prosecution table where General Wade had his hand up to his forehead leaning into the palm of his right hand blocking his view of the witness stand. Day glanced quickly over to the jury. Then he sat up and looked right at the defense attorney.

But them colored boys are on a different floor. The lighting might have been different.

Or there was a stack of boxes on the right side of that first window that had been moved by the time you got there, isn't that a possibility?

I suppose it could have been.

Mutterings rippled through the audience. The judge gaveled them quiet once again.

I am going to show you a picture that is time stamped. It has already been entered into evidence. Can you tell me what you see in the picture?

It appears to be someone holding the three spent shell casings.

Now Lieutenant Day, after Officer Studebaker photographed the scene, did you pick up the casings and bag them as evidence?

That was eventually done, but not by me. I was later handed the bag with the spent shell casings.

Did you put any markings on the casings?

Yes, I did, I wrote my name and I think date on the casings. It was very plain to see.

Now look again at this picture. You have already told us that someone is holding the shell casings in their hand while they are being photographed. You see the time stamp on the picture. It is before you arrived, isn't it?

Well, it says that it is, but I believe that must be a mistake.

Look at the picture closely, sir. Do you see your markings on any of those spent casings?

It doesn't appear so, no.

Mr. Alyea states in his affidavit that he took that picture before you arrived and that the hand holding those casings is Captain Fritz.

That can't be so! Day slammed his hand down on the wood arm of the witness chair.

Why is that, Lieutenant Day? Why is it that it can't be true, because Captain Fritz told you nothing had been moved?

He told me nothing had been touched!

But Lieutenant Day, you said in your earlier testimony even just a few moments ago that the Secret Service agents were, and I quote, "throwing things around." By your own testimony, sir, you have contradicted what you are now saying. Things were moved around, weren't they? Things had been moved. And that means the supposed crime scene had been compromised, doesn't it?

I don't believe those spent casings had been moved! His voice was getting high and loud.

Then how do you explain Mr. Alyea's picture?

I don't know. Maybe it was doctored?

Maybe it was doctored? How about maybe the Dallas Police Department destroyed the original scene and restaged it, would that be accurate?

What are you saying?

I'm saying that someone is lying!

Objection your honor, Mr. Wade had now returned to the courtroom was on his feet and his face was beet red. He is blatantly badgering the witness!

Overruled, but Mr. Donelson, be careful here.

Yes your honor.

Let me ask you further about the fingerprint dusting you did. We actually can see you dusting the rifle in the video. Is it correct that you dusted four boxes in the so-called sniper's nest?

Yes I did.

Why just those four?

Because after finding the shell casings it was determined that those four boxes would have been in direct contact with Mr. Oswald while he was firing.

Your honor, I ask that the last part of that answer be stricken from the record. It has in no way been established that Mr. Oswald was even on the sixth floor.

Would the witness like to reword the answer please?

I dusted those four boxes after the casings were found there because it was felt that the shooter would have been in direct contact with those four boxes.

And could you tell us about your findings?

I found a palm print on the box that we believe the assassin would have been sitting on. It matched Oswald. I also found a palm print on the box we figure was used to rest the gun on. It matched Oswald. We found on the corner of one of the other boxes an index finger matching Oswald.

So in all, you checked four boxes and found Mr. Oswald's palm print on two boxes and a single finger print on the corner of one box, is that correct?

Yes.

And it is the belief of the investigators that the assailant moved these boxes into their positions, correct?

Probably so.

How much would you say these boxes weigh apiece, Lieutenant Day?

Oh, they are pretty heavy. I'd say a good 30-50 pounds for the most part. You know they are textbooks.

Yes, indeed. Now do you think you would be able to move one of those boxes, let's say by just putting your palm and an index finger on the boxes and lifting them that way? Is that a normal way of moving boxes?

Well, I don't really know. I suppose one could lift them any way they wished.

But it seems a bit odd, doesn't it, Lieutenant, that you claim that Oswald moved all four of these boxes into this position but yet his finger print is only found on one and a palm print is found on two, and nothing on one other from Oswald. Is that a correct disposition of the facts of the fingerprinting?

That seems to be correct.

So did that fourth box just move itself?

Well it could be that it was already there.

Well, I guess it could be. Let's talk for a moment about the finger and palm print. In the analysis that was done on them, was it possible to determine how long those finger and palm prints had been on the boxes.

Day's face suddenly drained of color and his Adam's apple bobbed in his throat as he glanced over to the defense table a look of bewilderment in his eyes.

Should I repeat the question, officer?

No, I heard the question. A, a, the fingerprint and palm print do have a general range of time that one can read from the testing.

And in this particular case, sir, what were you able to ascertain in regards to these three prints lifted from the boxes that matched Lee Oswald?

Day put his hand to his forehead as though trying to suppress an oncoming headache and gently shook his head from side to side.

Lieutenant Day?

Yes, well, I was able to determine that one of the palm prints had been left on the box, the one which the shooter might have sat on, within the previous three days.

And the others?

They were older.

The loud mumblings of the audience disrupted the proceedings once again. Judge Brown picked up his gavel and a hush fell over the room.

You do know, don't you Lieutenant Day that Lee Oswald worked in that building, correct?

Yes.

Would it be unusual for a person who has been working in the building for the past two months to have prints found where they work?

I suppose not.

So you didn't check any of the other boxes in the area to see if Mr. Oswald's prints were on any of those, correct?

That's correct.

Oh, by the way, Lieutenant Day, just out of curiosity, is it correct that some twenty prints were found on those boxes?

Day let out a guttural sound clearing his throat.

A, a, a, yes, we found other prints.

And how many of those prints were from employees of the depository?

Nineteen, including the defendant. So you were able to identify all of the fingerprints and palm prints on the boxes as employees of the Texas School Book Depository, correct?

Well, yes except for one.

Wow, those boxes were touched a great deal, would you say?

Seems that way.

So you mentioned that there was one set of fingerprints you were unable to identify as an employee's, is that correct.

Yes.

And to whom do those belong?

We could not determine that?

So there is a set of fingerprints on those four boxes that do not belong to any employee of the Texas School Book Depository. Could you tell how old the prints were?

Yes. Within three days.

So you have 20 sets of prints, one of which you can't identify, and because Mr. Oswald's prints were lifted, even though he too was an employee, you immediately reach the

144

conclusion that Lee Oswald must have been the shooter, is that about right?

It certainly indicates that he touched those boxes.

As evidently did eighteen other employees. We have a saying in argumentation: that which proves too much proves nothing. Would you agree in this case that those fingerprints prove nothing?

No, I would not agree. Oswald's fingerprints were found there and his gun was found across the room. I believe logic would say we have the right shooter.

Or someone is being framed for the shooting, perhaps. So let's talk about the gun and the shooting, sir. When you arrived on the scene, did you check for the smell of gunpowder?

What do you mean?

Sylvester walked over to the defense table and picked up a book and opened it to a page he had marked with a blue ribbon. He turned and walked back to the lectern, placed the book on it and looked up at the jury. He sensed they were intrigued by his line of questioning and were deeply interested in where he was going next.

In this textbook on forensics, the author states that proper investigative techniques involved in a shooting investigation are, may I quote: "1. smell for gunpowder 2. check for evidence on the alleged assailant that the suspect has fired a gun 3. look for residue of gunpowder on clothing and surfaces 4. check the gun to see if it has been recently fired." End of quote. Now, Lieutenant Day, you have been investigating shootings for a number of years, yes?

Yes.

And would you agree in your experience that these are the things one should do when investigating a shooting?

I would.

So I again ask, did you smell for gunpowder?

I can't say that I did.

So you are there in that building where the police claim three shots originated within what forty minutes of the *shooting, and you can't tell us whether you could smell gun powder?*

I don't recall smelling for gunpowder.

You don't recall attempting to smell for gunpowder, or you don't recall smelling any gunpowder?

Neither.

Well, then, let's move to the second thing our book tells us. Did you check Mr. Oswald to see if there was any evidence of his having fired a gun?

Yes, we did conduct a paraffin test on Mr. Oswald.

And what were the results of that test, Lieutenant Day.

It was negative, he mumbled.

I'm sorry. I don't think the jury heard you, Lieutenant Day. Could you repeat...?

It was negative! he yelled loudly.

Let's go to the third thing in our book, Lieutenant Day. Did you check the surfaces on the sixth floor of the depository, the boxes, the window sill, Mr. Oswald's clothing for the presence of gun powder?

A, a, no sir, we did not.

Why did you not follow procedure and do that?

Well, I guess we forgot.

You forgot?

Yes.

Now in regards to the fourth thing our book tells us should be done. We see in the video of Mr. Alyea, that you immediately on the finding of the rifle dust for prints. What did you find?

We found a palm print from Mr. Oswald.

Would this be uncommon if it were a gun owned by Mr. Oswald?

I suppose not.

Where did you find the print?

A, a, well, I'm not sure I recall at the moment.

Let me refresh your memory. On initial investigation you found no prints on the outside of the gun that were identifiable, isn't that correct?

Perhaps.

And on further inspection by the FBI, they found a palm print on the underbelly of the barrel of the gun where it fits onto the stock, isn't that correct.

I believe so.

So let me ask you this. How does a right handed person generally hold a rifle?

Well, it has been my experience that the right hand goes near the trigger with the palm flat against the stock and the left hand goes just somewhere near the head of the stock underneath.

Would you demonstrate that? Oh here. Let's use the gun we have here, it is in evidence, correct, your honor?

Yes, I believe it is. Exhibit 201. I believe.

Ok, Donelson picks up the Carcano for the first time and hands it to Lieutenant Day. *Would you show us generally how a gun such as this Carcano would be held?*

Day handles the gun and then proceeds to stand, holding the gun as a shooter would pointing it over the heads of the audience.

Thank you sir. Day hands the rifle back to Donelson who places it on the evidence table. *Now can you tell us how a shooter could possibly shoot a gun and not leave fingerprints on the gun?*

He would have to have been wearing gloves.

Oh, there go those gloves again. It has been suggested before. But let me ask you the same thing I asked Captain Fritz. Did your search of the depository turn up any discarded gloves?

No I don't believe so.

How about the bus Mr. Oswald rode?

I don't know that we looked for anything on the bus.

In the cab that he took to the boarding house?

Again, I don't believe we looked for anything in the cab.

How about in the room at the boarding house where Oswald went?

We did not find any gloves there.

Yet you have fingerprints on the boxes but none on the gun is that correct?

Yes, it is.

And in checking the gun, let's talk now about ballistics. Would you have been in charge of the ballistics tests?

I was in charge of seeing that ballistics tests were done on the rifle. The actual tests were conducted by the FBI.

OK. Let's start with the finding of the rifle. It is my understanding that a rifle was found about 2:00 or so, some hour and a half after the shooting? Is that correct?

That is approximately the correct time.

Was there a reason that it took so long for all those men to find the gun?

It was well hidden behind a row of boxes.

Now on the video, you are clearly the one who brings the rifle out from behind the boxes, correct?

I was. I haven't seen the video you are referring to, however. But I was the one who brought it out.

How did you bring the rifle out from behind the boxes?

I was able to grab the strap that was attached to the gun.

So, Lieutenant Day, who originally found the gun?

I believe that was officer Weitzman and Deputy Sheriff Boone.

And are you familiar with their affidavits concerning the finding of the gun?

No sir, I am not.

Donelson walked over to the desk and picked up a file folder. He handed two sheets of paper to Judge Brown. *Your honor these are the sworn affidavits of Officer Seymour Weitzman and Deputy Sheriff Eugene Boone. I believe that with the other affidavits they are already part of the record, but we wish now to refer to them with the courts permission.*

So allowed, Mr. Donelson.

Would you, Lieutenant Day, read to the jury the short affidavit of Officer Weitzman? He handed the page to the witness who took out a pair of reading glasses from his inside coat pocket. When he had positioned them on the bridge of his nose, he commenced to read.

"Yesterday November 22, 1963 I was standing on the corner of Main and Houston, and as the President passed and made his turn going west towards Stemmons, I walked casually around. At this time my partner was behind me and asked me something. I looked back at him and heard 3 shots. I ran in a northwest direction and scaled a fence towards where we thought the shots came from. Then someone said they thought the shots came from the old Texas Building. I immediately ran to the old Texas Building and started looking inside. At this time Captain Fritz arrived and ordered all of the sixth floor sealed off and searched. I was working with Deputy S. Boone of the Sheriff's Department and helping in the search. We were in the northwest corner of the sixth floor when Deputy Boone and myself spotted the rifle about the same time. THE RIFLE WAS A 7.65 MAUSER BOLT ACTION EQUIPED WITH A 4/18 SCOPE, A THICK LEATHER BROWNISH-BLACK SLING ON IT. The rifle was between some boxes near the stairway. The time the rifle was found was 1:22 pm. Captain Fritz took charge of the rifle and ejected one live round from the chamber. I then went back to the office after this. Seymour Weitzman".

So let me understand something here. These two officers found this gun in the boxes of the sixth floor of the depository. Is that correct?

Yes. That is my understanding.

And according to Officer Weitzman, the time was 1:22. He was pretty exact about the time. And this would have been about the time that you were...oh; this would have been just shortly after you supposedly arrived, correct?

About that time, I suppose.

So what we see in the video from Alyea dated around 2:00 is not the original finding of the gun, is it?

I believe there is a mistake in his affidavit. He must be confused.

But he wrote this one day after the assassination, Lieutenant Day. You believe that his recollection of what happened is inaccurate?

It must be.

Why, because your recollection of the events all these month's later is inerrant?

I am telling you, I took that gun out of those boxes just like you see on the video.

But I thought you hadn't seen the video, Lieutenant Day?

I didn't mean that I have seen the video; I mean based on what you said earlier was on the video, I pulled that gun out of those boxes.

So you are saying that when Officer Weitzman and Deputy Boone found that gun, they did not pull it out of the boxes? Is that your testimony?

No.

And when Officer Weitzman states that the gun was a Mauser, he didn't accurately identify the gun?

No, he didn't. He just glanced at it.

In the affidavit, Officer Weitzman seems pretty sure of the identification even remarking the size and the type of scope. He sounds pretty sure of himself. Are you saying he was wrong about that just like he was perhaps wrong about the time?

He was wrong. Everyone knows that it was a Mannlicher-Carcano rifle that was found.

Everyone except Officer Weitzman. And when he says that Captain Fritz quote "took charge of the rifle and ejected one live round from the chamber," was he again mistaken?

The gun was not a Mauser! He was wrong about that.

Was he?

Yes.

Or perhaps there is something else going on here, something far more sinister. Were you aware of the fact that Officer Weitzman owned a sporting goods store that sold guns?

No.

Let me ask you about the ballistics. Were tests conducted on the rifle to determine whether it was the rifle that had been used in the assassination of the President?

Yes, those tests were conducted by the FBI.

And did they have bullets from the assassination?

There were two small fragments from the car and a bullet found on a stretcher at Parkland hospital.

OK, we will get to the Parkland bullet in a moment.

When the tests were done on the rifle in comparison to the bullets, what conclusions were reached?

The FBI concluded that the striations of the bullets were consistent with having been fired from a Carcano rifle.

Could they reach an absolute conclusion on whether those bullets were fired from that gun? he asked pointing to the Mannlicher-Carcano rifle at the exhibit table.

Day sighed loudly before giving a perceptibly anguished negative response.

Now concerning that bullet as you have mentioned from Parkland, when did you learn that this bullet had been found, on what, I believe a stretcher, was it?

Yes, on a stretcher. I was told later that day by a Secret Service agent that a bullet had been found at Parkland.

Did you ever examine the bullet?

No sir.

You mean to tell this court that you are the lead investigator of this case for forensic evidence and you have not seen a bullet that supposedly, according to the FBI caused seven different wounds in President Kennedy and Governor Connally and may be one of the few things connecting this gun forensically with the shooting?

I was never allowed to see it. It stayed in the possession of the FBI in Washington.

Have you subsequently seen a picture of the bullet?

I have not.

General Wade, Judge Brown interrupted, *where is that bullet today?*

General Wade quickly stood up, taking his glasses off his nose and tossing them on the table looking quite startled. *Your honor it should be sitting on that table.* He walked over to the table and quickly looked through the collection of evidence but found nothing corresponding to the bullet. He looked back at an assistant sitting in the row behind his prosecution table. The assistant immediately rose and motioned for Wade to come close to him. He whispered something in his ear. Wade's face grew red and then pale.

Your honor it would appear that in the rush to prepare for trial, we failed to secure that bullet. It is, in my understanding, in the possession of the FBI in Washington.

I will immediately sign an order for it to be brought to Dallas for this trial. It is primary evidence. And I am holding you in contempt of court and fining you $500 for failure to serve discovery. And if there is any other lapse that shows up, General Wade, I will be making moves with the state board to pull your license. Do I make myself clear?

Yes sir.

Mr. Donelson, continue.

Your honor, I have no further questions for this witness, but would like to recall for rebuttal purposes Captain Fritz for just a moment.

Captain Fritz, would you please take the stand again?

The captain was now sitting in the back of the courtroom and looked as though he had been personally beaten by the previous questioning.

The witness is reminded that he is still under oath, the judge admonished.

Captain Fritz, you have heard the conflicting testimony in regards to the boxes, gun powder, fingerprints, the rifle, etc. We need some clarity because the one person who seems to be connected with all the testimony is you. In the course of the search of the sixth floor, were boxes moved anywhere on that floor?

There were a number of boxes. This is a huge warehouse. These boxes of books were stacked up in rows as many as six cases high all throughout the room. There were but narrow paths to walk through them. We had to move boxes out of the way in order to check out smaller openings in the rows of boxes. That is actually what led to the discovery of the gun. When a box was moved, the butt of the rifle was exposed just enough to know it was a gun.

And who exactly found the rifle?

Weitzman and Boone found the gun just as Day said. Craig was in that group of men, but they spotted it at about the same time.

And was the gun taken from its hiding place between the boxes before Lieutenant Day removed it?

It was.

The audible disapproval of those in the room hit one's ears at the same exact moment like the sudden explosion of a lightning strike. General Wade was again tending his forehead with his palm as though he were trying to rub something in or remove a stain. One could only imagine the immense pressure of this prosecution and having at stake not just one's reputation but perhaps even a career.

And did you engage the bolt action and discharge a live round from the gun?

I did indeed.

We have the three empty casings, Donelson began, holding up the bag containing them, but we don't seem to have the live round?

Last I heard it was in the hands of the FBI and I don't believe it was given back.

I will also order it so, Brown interjected.

OK, and as to the identification of the rifle. Both Weitzman and Boone identified in their affidavits that the gun that they pulled from the boxes was a Mauser 7.65. Yet later in the day of November 22, 1963 Lieutenant Day is showing off a Mannlicher-Carcano. As one having handled the gun at the scene, was the gun that was shown to the press later that day the same gun from which you had discharged a live round?

I believe that it is?

Then why the day after did two officers, both of which had seen the gun and handled it, identify it as something else?

I have no idea. You might best ask them. The gun I handled in the depository was the Carcano.

And you are absolutely sure without fear of contradiction that the gun you took from the boxes and discharged a live round from was the Carcano?

Absolutely, 100%.

So let me ask you to look at a picture please, Sylvester Donelson went over to the desk and retrieved a picture. *Your honor, we have given a copy of this picture to the prosecution and we would ask that this be marked for evidence, and stipulate that it be marked as Defense Exhibit 1.*

Your honor, this evidentiary movement is a bit unorthodox.

Indeed it is General Wade, but I'm going to allow it, ruled the Judge. *I believe they have the right to present contradictory evidence in cross.*

Thank you, your honor. Captain Fritz, this is a composition of three pictures taken from three different pieces of information. The first picture is Lieutenant Day holding up a rifle in the hall way of the Dallas Police Department among the throng of reporters. The second picture is the official picture of the Dallas Police Department of the rifle. And the third is a picture furnished by the FBI of the gun they have in their possession which gun is supposed to be the gun sitting right over there on the evidence table. Now I want you to look at these very carefully and I'm going to hold up the rifle on the table.

And what do you want me to do?

That's simple, Captain Fritz. I want you to tell me first if you see anything different in these three pictures?

Well of course I do. They are obviously not the same gun.

A whisper from the spectators pierced the air. Gavel.

So you are telling me that the gun that was held up by Lieutenant Day on November 22, 1963 in this now well-known picture is not the same as the FBI have in their possession, in fact this gun that I'm holding?

Now let me look closer. Are you trying to confuse me? How do I know that these pictures haven't been doctored?

Seriously? Doctored? Now imagine, who do you think would do a thing like that? And why? So let's get serious here Captain Fritz, look at all three pictures and at this gun and tell me what you notice that is different.

Well, obviously this third picture has a much longer stock butt than the others. This first one appears to have a sling attachment that is much shorter than the second and it appears to be underneath where the other appears to be on the side. The scopes don't sink either by size. The stocks on these first two are very different models.

So, I believe you have very well stated the case of the guns' differences, Captain, now I have but one more question for you.

What's that?

He was holding up the rifle that had been on the evidence table. How can we even be sure that this rifle was even the one that the Dallas police believe was used to kill our President?

Captain Fritz just sat starring at the photographs and shaking his head.

Your honor, I have no further questions of this witness. At this time, the defense moves that the bullets and the rifle be excluded because not only are they tainted, but the chain of custody of this so called evidence cannot clearly be established either in the depository or after it left the depository. The fact is that if this is indeed the crime scene, it was horribly corrupted by the very officers of the court that are sworn to protect it.

General Wade, I assume you have somewhat to say about this?

Wade stood at his table, his glasses in his hand tapping the edge of a legal pad, his knees nearly buckling.

Your honor, I stand here totally baffled at what we have heard and seen. I must stringently object to this motion.

While I understand there are some legitimate questions that have been raised here that bears further investigation by I believe an independent board of inquiry, and if in its findings the defenses' charges of impropriety are accurate, then disciplinary measures should be taken. However, having said that, I must quickly add that the defense, while giving rise to doubts over how it has been gathered, have yet to show that the casings weren't found there, that the gun wasn't found there, and they have done nothing to show conclusively that the defendant was not involved in the assassination as the shooter.

And equally, your honor, the prosecution has done nothing to show that my client was even on the sixth floor during the assassination.

Gentlemen. Come to order counselors. Now listen, I'm taken with the evidence of improper handling of the evidence. General Wade, you need to give me one reason why I shouldn't grant this motion. The silence in the room was deafening.

I'll have my ruling in the morning. I believe we are at a good place to stop for the day, gentlemen. Until in the morning, we stand in recess.

The jury was shown out while Judge Brown asked both teams of attorneys to gather in chambers. In his office, the judge took the prosecution to task explaining how he believed they were failing miserably in presenting their case against Oswald.

General Wade, let me tell you something. If this was all the evidence that I thought you had against Oswald, I'd go back out there and throw this case out. You have nothing; do you understand what I'm telling you? But I believe you have more to present. You've only presented not even half a dozen witnesses, but the defense has been more than ready for the challenge in each of those cases. Now as to the motion, Mr. Cavendish, I feel like I have to bring it in, but I'm going to do so with a great deal of suspicion. I just don't know how in this high profile case I could possibly exclude what the prosecution believes to be the murder weapon. Can you tell me how I can do that?

I'll tell you how, Judge Brown, began Tom Cavendish, *until the prosecution deals with the aspect that we have at least three different rifles that have been depicted in official government documents, I can't believe at all in the veracity of that gun as the murder weapon.*

General Wade.

You've caught me totally by surprise on this Tom. I don't have an answer for you. If one merely glances at these, they look the same. But the analysis you have done shows that there are depicted three different guns. I have to hand it to you I don't have an answer for that one, your honor. You'll have to do what you feel is the right thing to do.

Ok, fellows. Out of here. I've got a great deal of thinking to do. And I want you two to know that I realize how important this case is. This is the trial of the century.

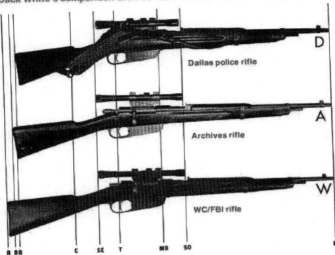

Jack White's comparison of three Mannlicher-Carcano rifle photos.

SAME GUN? The 6.5 Mannlicher-Carcano rifle said to have killed President Kennedy is shown in three different photos. Gun "D" is the Dallas police department official evidence photo. Gun "A" is now in the National Archives (photo courtesy JFK researcher Fred Newcomb of Salem, Oregon). Gun "W" is pictured in the Warren Report. The photos were made under similar studio conditions with the camera lens axis perpendicular to the approximate center of the gun, so that minimal foreshortening exists. The photos are printed so that *metal* parts of the guns are the same length. Thus muzzle (M) to trigger (T) distance is same on all. Yet the *wooden* stocks do not correspond, as seen in the location of the butts (B). Notice how exactly pictures "W" and "A" match for *more than four-fifths of the length*, at scope objective lens (SO), mounting bracket (MB), scope eyepiece (SE), and comb (C). Can four-fifths match without the other one-fifth corresponding? (Photo analysis by Jack White, Fort Worth Texas.)

Jack White's analysis of the guns found in three different government locations. Which is the gun found in the depository?

Chapter 16- The Judge Rules

The news from the hospital about Oswald was promising. Cavendish and Donelson went by the hospital and visited with Oswald for just a short time. They assured him that things were going well. He told them that Marina had been allowed to visit for a short time that afternoon.

Back at the office the messages had piled up, but one caught Donelson's attention. It was from FBI agent James Hosty's office. Hosty was a Dallas agent who was somewhat acquainted with Lee Oswald, but not in a good way. He asked that Donelson call him. The phone rang but four times before Hosty answered.

Agent Hosty.

James Hosty this is Sylvester Donelson returning your phone call.

Yes sir. Thank you for calling. I understand that you hit some strong hits in the courtroom the last couple of days.

Well, we will see.

You know he did it, don't you?

I don't believe he did, Mr. Hosty, and I don't believe the government including you, believe he did either.

Ah but we definitely do. I've known of Oswald for several months. Tried to locate him before the assassination to ask him some questions about the attempt on General Walker's life. We thought a nut case like Oswald might try something like that. That's why he has been under surveillance.

Well, that is some surveillance if you let him kill the President, wouldn't you say?

Couldn't find him, Hosty said indifferently.

Really? You didn't know he worked at the Depository? He tells me that you've been stalking him.

Oswald said that?

Yep, even told us that he went to your office and wrote you a note to stay away from his family and stop harassing them. Except you didn't tell any of this to the Dallas Police, did you?

Y'all in over your heads. The line went dead.

Sylvester dialed over to the DA's office and asked David Arnough if they had secured the file on Oswald from the FBI Dallas Bureau.

Told us they didn't have a file on Oswald.

Well, that would be an out and out lie. I just talked to James Hosty. Oswald told us that this agent was harassing him and his family.

Why would the FBI have any interest in a low life like Oswald?

Because I don't believe Oswald is who the government is trying to get us to believe he is. Think of this David, they won't give us access to his military file saying it is classified. Now why would it be classified? Local FBI tells you they don't have a file on Oswald when they are making efforts to question him. They did question Marina, and in fact, Oswald went to the FBI office to confront Hosty about that. But of course, Hosty is denying it.

How would Oswald even know Hosty if there wasn't something to it, Sylvester? It isn't as though one can just casually find out the name of a federal agent.

For the first time Donelson was sure the prosecution was having some doubts.

Can you try to see what you can find out?

Sure. I'll get right on it.

And it is probably best that no one knows that you and I talked, especially not General Wade.

Sure, he responded with more of a question that an affirmation.

****

Gentleman, before I bring the jury in, Judge Brown began the next morning, all eyes affixed to him expectant of the ruling he was about to make, *I am going to make a few statements that I want everyone to hear before I make my ruling. I've been a judge for a few years now and in this courtroom I've heard a number of cases. None of those cases have risen in importance nationally as has this one. We are* talking about the murder of our President and the attempt to murder our Governor as well as the killing of a Dallas Police Officer. This is an important trial. The world is watching, and the picture being presented to them at this moment is very troubling to me. It is both obvious and disconcerting that mistakes were made in the gathering and examination of evidence. Of importance in this decision particularly are the admissibility of the shells and the rifle reported to have been found in the depository. Honestly if this were any lesser of a case, I would have no choice but to throw them out, but this case is different in many ways. I believe these must come in. It is the job of the prosecution to define their importance and their true value and of the defense to disprove those claims or to raise an element of doubt as to their veracity. Having said that, I am denying the motion of the defense to have this evidence excluded. Also late yesterday, Mr. Cavendish submitted a written motion to throw out all charges based on lack of evidence. Mr. Cavendish, since we have heard only a fraction of the evidence the prosecution claims to have, I am denying this request as well.

May I ask, your honor, before the jury is seated, the status on the Parkland bullet? Cavendish asked rising from his seat.

General Wade.

We served a subpoena for the bullet yesterday afternoon through a district court in Washington, DC. We were told that the FBI would respond to our request within thirty days.

What? Judge Brown, Tom Cavendish, David Arnough and Sylvester Donelson said in harmony.

Judge Brown rose from the bench, motioned for the bailiff and court clerk to follow him to his chambers. No one dared speculate what Judge Brown was going to do, and since none of the lawyers were asked to join, it could only mean the judge was extremely upset. In a few moments the main attorneys were called into the Judge's chamber.

Gentleman, I just put in a call to Attorney General Bobby Kennedy. I was told by Deputy Attorney General Nicholas Katzenbach that the bullet was in the evidence box at the FBI being guarded by none other than J. Edgar Hoover. He has put in a request that the bullet be brought to Dallas to the office of General Wade by 8:00 this evening. He has included in the file the FBI findings concerning the bullet. He apologized for the oversight and has guaranteed that they are going to look through all the things they have to ascertain whether any other evidence has been withheld from the trial.

Fair enough, replied General Wade.

Your honor, my office has processed all the materials now from discovery. I am aware that an autopsy was performed on the President, but it was not a part of the record. We also did not see the ballistics on the pistol or on the shell casings found near the crime scene where Officer Tippit was killed. The prosecution has also not furnished to us any manuscripts relative to police calls or reports made in and around the shooting of Officer Tippit.

We will be glad to share what we have, but we have also not been given the autopsy report. Judge Brown, we served a subpoena on Dr. James Humes who performed the autopsy on President Kennedy, but it is being blocked by the feds who claim that since he is a Navy doctor, he is protected under executive privilege and according to the White House he will not testify beyond the submission of the autopsy report based on National Security. They are attempting to arrange an affidavit to be presented with a Washington lawyer questioning him.

Your honor, I strongly object. Our government is surely attempting to obstruct justice in this matter.

And who would you have me charge with such a crime, Mr. Cavendish? Judge Brown asked sarcasm dripping from his tongue like melting chocolate. *You want me to send my bailiff up to DC there and arrest J. Edgar Hoover? Or maybe you would prefer us handcuff President Johnson?*

Cavendish decided that silence was the better part of discretion.

And while we are talking about supplanting of justice, I have tried to arrange for Jack Ruby to appear in this court on Tuesday of next week. Through his lawyer, Mr. Ruby has declined our offer of an appearance. In part the lawyer responded in writing, and picking up a letter laying on his desk, I quote "it is the view of Mr. Jack Ruby that he will not appear in a court in Dallas, Texas as he feels his life is in jeopardy if he were to talk to the court as to what he knows about this matter. Now if the court can arrange for Mr. Ruby to appear in a venue perhaps in Washington, D.C. or at some other place where his safety can be guaranteed, then he will gladly reconsider testifying." End of quote. And there you have it.

Your honor, the response itself says a great deal about the situation, don't you think?

It could be, Mr. Cavendish, or it could be merely a ruse for publicity.

You could order his testimony, your honor, General Wade added. Why not do so? You bring him in with plenty of guards, seal the courtroom, and perhaps he sheds some light on this. There are certainly a great number of rumors making the rounds of Dallas.

Like?

Well, I'm hearing from some of my people, Wade explained, that Ruby and Oswald were acquainted. If one goes back and looks at some of the footage broadcast from the assassination, Jack Ruby was all over the place. We also have noticed that several witnesses have described a person fitting Ruby's description in their reports of what they saw in Dealey Plaza. I'm certainly not saying that Jack Ruby is the person that they are describing, but it is not a coincidence, I believe. Your honor, I'm confessing something here in confidence, ok? OK, Tom?

Certainly.

Sure, General Wade, what is on your mind? The judge looked at General Wade his face haggard with heavy lines of worry sketched across his face.

I believe that Lee Harvey Oswald had something to do with all of this, but I do believe there may have been others. I can't accept the report of the FBI that Oswald acted alone. And it just could be that Jack Ruby holds the key to unraveling this whole thing.

Tom thought seriously about what he was hearing. *You do realize that if there was another person involved, then it may well be that there were any number of people involved. Are you prepared to go there?*

If I have to.

I believe gentleman that we have a case to try.

The judge had called his meeting to an end and stood abruptly giving silent invitation for the two lawyers to take leave of his chambers.

Chapter 17- A Cavalcade of Witnesses

Newspaper articles and media stories were filled with speculation that the defense had scored numerous points and that the defense team had turned in a remarkable performance. One story even remarked how the prosecution was blowing a slam dunk case to a stubborn defense team. But things started looking badly for Oswald with the next several witnesses. The prosecution decided not to call Weitzman and Boone, but did call Craig to confirm the information they wished to present about the finding of the rifle. Craig confirmed that there had been confusion as to the make of the rifle, but that it was just the three officers reacting too quickly. Craig confirmed that the gun was indeed a Mannlicher-Carcano. On cross, Donelson showed him the picture of the three guns. The only damage Donelson could do on Craig's testimony was getting Craig to admit he was unaware of the origin of the other pictures, but he repeated confirmation that the rifle on the evidence table was the same rifle they had found among the boxes. Donelson decided then and there he would add Weitzman and Boone to the defense witness list.

General Wade decided next to go for the juggler by calling eye witnesses who identified Oswald. First he called Charles Givens who testified that he had returned to the sixth floor to get his cigarettes and that Oswald was there. When asked for the time, he reported that the time was 11:55 some thirty-five minutes before the assassination. Since Oswald worked on that level, Cavendish asked on cross, would it be strange that he was there. *Does that prove he pulled the trigger?* asked the counselor.

Of course not.

It could have been you, correct?

What do you mean, I didn't shoot nobody!

But if you saw Mr. Oswald on the sixth floor, that also means you were on the sixth floor. And I was just supposing that if being on the sixth floor meant one was the assassin, well then, it might have just been you as much as it might have been Lee Oswald. Doesn't that stand to reason, Mr. Givens?

Hell no! I didn't do nothing.

You will watch your language in my courtroom Mr. Givens or you will find yourself in jail, Judge Brown warned.

Sorry, sir.

Oh, by the way, is it true, Mr. Givens that on the day of the shooting, Cavendish asked walking away from the witness stand, *you also, along with Lee Oswald, left the depository and were later picked up by the police because you have a police record?*

A... yes that is true.

And what was the nature of the charges?

Drug charges.

Next up was Bill Shelley, who also had been serving on a crew that was laying a new floor on the sixth floor.

At 12:30 you were standing outside on the steps of the depository along with Lovelady and others, isn't this correct, Mr. Shelley?

Yes.

At the moment of the shooting, did you see Lee Oswald?

Well, I can't say that I did.

On cross, the story expanded.

At the time of the shooting, were there numerous employees on the steps of the building?

Yes.

Was Lee Oswald one of those employees?

I can't be sure, there were several. I don't really know all the employees. Lee might have been there.

You had seen him on the sixth floor before coming down for lunch, is that correct?

Earlier in the morning I did. When I came down for lunch, I saw Lee on the telephone on the first floor.

When was this?

Probably about 12:15. I don't know that I looked at a clock or anything.

Certainly.

The prosecution next called Howard Brennan.

Mr. Brennan, you witnessed the assassination of President Kennedy, is that correct?

I did, saw the whole thing.

Where were you standing during the motorcade?

I was standing at the corner of Elm and Houston Streets on the retaining wall at the pool across the street from the Book Store.

Now when you say Book Store, you are referring to the...

Texas School Book Building.

Yes. Of course. And at some point while you were there you looked up into the windows of the building, is that correct?

Well, I heard a noise that sounded like a firecracker, and I thought someone was throwing firecrackers from the Book Store building. I looked up and I saw a man in the window on the sixth floor of the building holding a rifle. I looked up just as he was taking his second and last shot. After he fired that shot, he withdrew the rifle to his side.

How much of the man did you see?

At one point he was sitting in the window sill so I saw from his hips up.

Where was he positioned when he was firing?

He was kind of standing up with the gun tilted down.

And when he was firing the rifle, how much of him could you see?

From his belt up.

What was he wearing?

Khaki colored clothes. Light color

How would you describe him?

Oh, a man in his thirties, kind of thin about 5', 10" tall. I'd say he weighed about 160-170.

Were there any other people in the windows on that floor?

I did not see anyone else in the windows.

Did you see anyone else in windows on any other floors?

Yes, just below that on the fifth floor, there were two colored guys in the windows.

Were you asked to identify the man in a lineup at police headquarters?

Yes.

Did you tell the police that you thought Lee Oswald the defendant might have been the person in the window.

I did.

Thank you sir. Your witness, counselor.

I just have a couple of questions, Mr. Cavendish rose at his table, *Do you recall whether you saw anything else in the window beside the gunman and the rifle?*

Nothing else that I recall.

You did not see any boxes in the window, perhaps boxes that the shooter placed the gun on?

I don't recall seeing any boxes, and I sure don't remember seeing the gun resting on any boxes.

You mentioned, Mr. Brennan, that you took part in an identification lineup at the police station, correct?

I did.

And were you able to positively identify Lee Harvey Oswald as the man you saw in the window?

I said he might have been the guy.

Let me ask you this. You have testified that the person you saw was about 5'10" tall, correct.

Yes about that.

Are you aware that Lee Oswald is approximately 5'8" tall and weighs about 140 pounds?

No sir.

And you reported the person in the window was in his 30s, correct.

That is accurate.

Are you aware that Mr. Oswald is 24 years old?

No sir, I am not.

So sir, let me just ask you plainly, can you positively affirm that Lee Oswald was the person you saw in the sixth floor window of the depository?

Brennan looked around an expression of defeat on his face. *No sir, I cannot positively say that.*

The crowd burst into very loud talk. Judge Brown pounded his gavel ordering that his courtroom come to order. But this took several seconds.

I noticed sir that you wear glasses. Eyes are weak, are they?

I have bifocals.

What were the guys on the fifth floor wearing, Mr. Brennan?

Couldn't tell you.

How much of them could you see?

I don't really remember, just recall seeing their faces. I don't know, they may have been squatting down or something.

I'm going to show you a picture that was taken from the ground looking up shortly after the shooting. He hands Brennan the picture. *What can you see in the sixth floor window?*

Oh, all I see here is just the...

Boxes?

Yeah.

How about on the fifth floor?

Well them colored boys didn't seem like they was standing in the window like that when I saw them. I'm telling you I saw a man in the sixth floor window holding a rifle.

Perhaps you did, Mr. Brennan, but can you swear that it was Lee Harvey Oswald?!

NO, I suppose not! He lowered his head realizing he had done nothing good for the prosecution. He wanted so much to help.

Mr. Brennan, I'm going to show you another picture. Your honor this picture is a frame from the Zapruder film which is already entered into evidence. In this picture sir, we see the area where you were sitting on the wall. Do you see yourself?

Yes, I'm right back there.

And as you can see the President appears to have been hit by the first shot. Is that correct?

Appears that way.

Do your recall this moment?

Brennan lowered his head and began to silently weep.

I know this is disturbing to remember Mr. Brennan. But it is important.

I can't forget it. It was so horrible.

And look carefully at the picture. Approximately six seconds from this moment is when the President was struck in the head. Did you see that?

Oh, dear God. Yes, I saw it.

You were looking as in this picture directly at the President weren't you?

Yes.

Did you ever actually look up at the Depository window?

Objection, your honor.

Withdrawn. That's all, your honor.

Mr. Brennan slowly walked from the witness chair across the floor, head lowered. He stopped at the table and looked over at General Wade.

I'm sorry sir. I did see him.

General Wade just smiled gently and reached over and patted his arm and turned back to his legal pad allowing Brennan to walk through the gate separating the proceedings from the audience. He turned and sat in a seat on the back row in the old church pew that lined the back wall.

Arnold Rowland was the next witness called.

Sir you were present at the time of the tragic events on November 22 of last year?

Yes sir I was.

And you have told investigators that you saw a man in the window of the sixth floor, is that correct?

Yes sir, it is.

And could you tell us about what you saw?

Well, there was a man standing back from the window I'd say about 15 feet or so from the window, holding a gun to his side, like in the military.

Could you describe him?

He was slender in proportion to his height with dark hair.

Did he appear to have a receding hair line?

No sir. He had a full head of hair.

Was he Black or Caucasian?

I would say he was either Latin or Caucasian.

What type of gun did he have?

It was a high powered rifle. I say high powered because it had a scope on the gun.

You were asked to do a lineup by the police, is that correct?

Yes, I did.

Could you identify anyone as the man you saw in the window?

Not positively.

What time did you see him in the widow?

Oh, I'm not exactly sure of the time. It was several minutes before the President's motorcade came through.

No further questions.

Mr. Rowland, did you see boxes in the windows?

No sir can't say that I did.

Did you see anyone else on any other floor?

No.

I'm going to show you a picture taken from the ground looking up at that window just moments after the assassination.

Can you tell me what you see in the sixth floor window?

It appears to be maybe some boxes.

In fact, sir, there are a row of boxes some 5 feet high stacked literally just 2 ½ feet from the window running approximately from near the corner to beyond this second window here (pointing to the second window in the section). Now you say you saw this man who was holding the rifle standing back some 15 feet from the window, but that isn't possible, now is it? Would it have even been possible to see 15 feet into the window at all?

I know what I saw.

Sure you do. You really didn't see anything did you?

Objection, badgering the witness.

Withdrawn. No further questions.

Gentlemen, we will stand in recess for lunch until 1:00 this afternoon.

Rise.

The judge left out the back door leaving the two teams of lawyers to gather their belongings and head to wherever they could pick up something to eat. Donelson seemed in a trance.

Sylvester, what you thinking so hard about?

I'm thinking that we just missed an opportunity?

About what?

I just remember reading Rowland's statement he gave to the police. I'm not sure why the prosecution would risk putting him on the stand, but it didn't occur to me to ask about his other testimony.

What other testimony?

That he saw another man in the window with the shooter. Just like Carolyn Walther. She even described the guy as wearing a suit.

Zapruder frame showing wall where Brennan was located just before the first shot was fired

Chapter 18- The Witnesses Stack Up

The trial resumed after lunch with Cavendish and Donelson looking for the perfect opening into the second shooter. Donelson decided to be very direct.

Your honor, before the prosecution calls their next witness, we would like to ask permission to recall Mr. Rowland.

Your honor, people thought they were finished with their cross of Mr. Rowland. This seems very unorthodox.

But General Wade, Judge Brown interjected, *they only finished just an hour and a half ago. Isn't it reasonable that during lunch they may have thought of something they forgot to ask?*

But, your honor...

Now, now, General Wade, I believe they are within reason on this request and I will grant it provided that Mr. Rowland is still present.

Rowland stood up in the back of the courtroom.

I see that he is still here. Would you come forward, Mr. Rowland? And I remind you that you are still under oath in this matter.

Mr. Rowland, this will only take a couple of moments, Donelson began. *In your prior testimony you spoke concerning seeing a man about fifteen feet from the window, isn't that correct?*

Yes sir. I did say that and that is what I saw.

In your affidavit, which I read again at lunch, you say you saw more than that, didn't you?

I'm not sure what you mean?

In your affidavit, didn't you testify, similar to eyewitness Carolyn Walther that you saw two men in that window?

Yes sir, I did.

And is that still your recollection of what you saw?

It is.

And why didn't you mention this earlier today?

Well, I don't rightly know.   Just didn't come to my mind, I suppose.

So let me make this very clear. Some several minutes before the arrival of the Presidential motorcade, you saw two men in the sixth floor window of the depository and one of those men was holding a rifle. Is this correctly stating your testimony?

It is correct. That is what I saw.

Thank you sir. Nothing further.

Redirect, General, if you like, Judge Brown called out.

We have nothing, the General responded eliciting a snort from Tom Cavendish as he stifled a laugh.

Next witness then, General Wade.

State calls Amos Euins to the stand.

Amos Euins approach the front, called the bailiff.

There was a bit of a murmur through the crowd as the witness entered the courtroom and it was realized that the next witness was not only a teenager but was also black. After he was sworn in, the witness, who nervously twisted about in the seat, sat up straight and prepared for the questioning.

State your full name please.

Amos Lee Euins. Amos clearly stated his name the s of his last name carrying on a bit longer than necessary.

And just how old are you Amos?

Sixteen.

And what is the date of your birth, young man.

I was born on January 10, 1948.

Are you a student in High School?

Yes sir. I go to Franklin Roosevelt High School

How are your eyes, Amos, you see well?

They are alright.

Can you see good at a distance?

Yes sir, I can see real good at a distance, but can't see good up close.

Like when you are reading?

Yes sir. He slouched down in the seat just a tad as he responded.

So can you read without glasses?

Oh yes sir. I don't have glasses.

So how are your grades in school, Amos? You make good grades?

I guess they are average.

All right, now I want to ask you about the morning of November 22, 1963, last year, Amos. Do you remember what you were doing that morning?

Yes, sir. I got up and went to school.

And what happened later in the morning?

Our principal announced that if we wanted to go see the President we could come to the office and get an excuse. So I did and my mama took me downtown.

What time was that when you left the High School?

It was about 11:30 that morning.

And where did you go?

Downtown.

Where downtown, Amos?

I went to the area around the county jail, in that park right near the pool of water.

Do you know the name of those streets?

No sir.

So if I told you Main Street, Houston Street or Elm Street would that help you remember?

It was near the freeway.

Alright, here is an aerial picture of the area, Amos. Can you point out where you went?

Amos pointed to a spot on the picture.

Please let the record indicate that Amos is pointing to a point at Elm and Houston Streets by the fountain.

It was just at the street there by the Book Depository building right there on that corner.

The Texas School Book Depository, is that correct?

Yes, sir.

Would you just take this pencil and put an X on that building.

Amos took the pen and placed an X on the School Book Depository Building.

So you saw the President's motorcade coming down which street?

That one right there.

The record will show that he is pointing to a street previously identified as Main. And when the cars got to this corner they turned right, is that correct?

Yes sir.

And what did they do from there?

They turned there on that street in front of the Book Depository.

Elm Street.

I suppose so.

So what next?

Well, I had been standing on the corner there by the fountain. There wasn't hardly anybody at that spot and I waved at the President as he went by. He saw me and waved back.

And then what happened?

As they were turning that corner there, pointing to Elm and Houston, *I noticed a pipe or something that looked like a pipe sticking out of that window up there in that book building.*

Would you place an X on the place, the window where you saw the thing you thought was a pipe?

Amos again took the pencil and placed an X on the 6th floor window closest to the Houston corner of the building.

Let the record indicate that young Amos has placed an X on the sixth floor window, the one closest to the northeast corner of the building, the corner closest to Houston. When the car turned the curve and you saw this pipe sticking out the window, what happened next?

I wasn't paying a lot of attention to the building and was looking toward the car and I heard this low crack that sounded like a backfire. I looked around like everyone else. Then I looked up at the window and he fired again?

What did you do?

I jumped behind this wall keeping my eye on the window.

That concrete wall that is there by the fountain? Is that where you hid?

Yes sir.

And what happened next. There were a couple more shots. I could see the guy's hands on the pipe, the gun trigger, you know.

So you could see the man?

Just his hands. But he tried to look out the window and I could see a bald spot on his head.

Did you see him pull the gun inside the window?

Yes, he pulled the gun inside and then I couldn't see him anymore.

What did you do after that?

I went up to one of the police officers that was headed toward the depository building and I told him what I saw.

Can you describe the person in the window?

No sir. I can't. I didn't see anything but his hands and the bald spot.

So what color was he? Was he black or white?
I don't know.

OK, your honor. I think we are finished with this witness for now. But I may want to recall him later.

Cross, Mr. Cavendish? the judge asked.

Yes, sir. Hello, Amos, he greeted the youth as he walked toward the witness chair. *I sure appreciate you being here today. I just want to ask a few clarifying questions.*

Ok.

So when you heard this first loud crack, you had the wherewithal to duck for cover. Did you recognize that a shot had been fired?

I thought it was the moment I heard it.

So you look up to that window in the depository building, correct?

Yes.

And you were behind this pillar in the pool wall, correct, kind of peeking out over the top, is that right?

Yes sir. I was afraid that it was just someone firing off a gun, and I didn't want to get hit. So I looked up at the window where I saw the pipe.

Did you know immediately that the pipe looking thing you saw was a gun?

No sir. Not until he fired another shot. Then I knew it was a gun and that the shots were coming from there.

And how many shots did you hear?

I heard four shots.

You heard four shots?

Yes.

Are you sure you heard four shots?

Yes, two of the shots were very close together.

How close together?

I'd say maybe a second, two at the most. They almost sounded like the same shot.

And when you were looking up in the window, did you ever get a good look at the gunman?

No sir. The only thing I saw was the hands and the bald spot.

So after the gun is withdrawn, I'm sure there was chaos, correct?

Oh yes, sir. There were people running everywhere. Women were crying. I walked over to a police officer who was near me and told him what I'd seen.

That was a good thing to do, right?

I thought so.

And when you talked with the police officer, did you at any time hear anyone say anything again about a person with a bald spot?

Objection, your honor. Foundation.

You brought this in during direct, General Wade. The young man said he saw a bald spot on the shooter. I'm just merely inquiring as to whether he heard further about such.

Overruled.

So did you have an opportunity as you were with the police to hear anyone mention anything about this bald spot again?

Yes sir. There was this police officer who came up to the group of officers around me ...

And how many officers were around you?

About half a dozen, I'd say.

OK, continue.

This officer came up and said he had been on the back side of the depository and that a man told him a guy ran out of the back of the building. When he asked him to describe him he said he had a bald spot. I paid attention to that because I figured it might have been the same person I'd seen in the window.

Do you have any idea of what happened to this man?

No sir. I don't have any idea.

So if you had a series of people in a lineup, would you be able to identify the shooter you saw?

No sir. I didn't see nobody. Just their hands and that bald spot.

OK, thank you, Amos. I hope you continue to do well in school.

Chapter 19- Finishing the Prosecution

The court was in recess for about an hour while the Judge took care of some other matters and the Jury was given lunch. Tom and Sylvester sat at a diner not far from the courthouse. They took a secluded table nestled in a corner in a second dining area for privacy.

And why hadn't we ever heard anything about this man with the bald spot? Sylvester asked.

Beats me, but it is obvious to me that while the cops were gathering at the front of the building the shooter was sneaking out the back door. And no one would have ever even known about it had it not been for the construction worker, the police officer and a young boy of fifteen.

You know Oswald has a bit of a high hairline especially on his left side, Sylvester reported. *You don't think the kid saw that and thought it was a bald spot, do you?*

Why the doubt in your voice? Tom asked.

I'm looking at all this stuff and not making any sense of it. Why in heaven's name would they keep putting witnesses on the stand that not only aren't solid, but are doing damage to their case?

Tom noticed for the first time in the trial that Sylvester's face was drawn and worn. He obviously had been working long hours.

Well, I don't know, but back to Amos' testimony, Tom requested. *Why didn't Marion Baker run into this guy?*

Perhaps he did, Donelson suggested.

What do you mean?

Wasn't Mr. Truly the one vouching for people? Perhaps in all the confusion of the moment... he may have even been having that momentary conversation with Oswald at the second floor lunch room while the real shooter slipped right on down the stairs. There were dozens of workers in that building. I don't know how many of the hundred or so people that were working in the building went back in the building after the shooting. Probably most of them. Certainly within a short time they were all back in the building because only two ever left by the time roll was called. Did the police ever investigate any of the construction workers that were working in the building?

Not that I'm aware of. They turned their focus on Oswald from the start. The description that went out was supposedly of Oswald, and that went out before Officer Tippit was shot. Supposedly the reason he stopped Oswald on the street was that he matched the description of the person of interest that had been broadcast to the police.

Something about that, Sylvester suggested as he took a bite of his sandwich, *that doesn't make sense to me. Why didn't Tippit call for backup as soon as he spotted him? He didn't call in anything. That breaks protocol.*

He patrolled in that general area, you think it was because he knew him?

I don't know, Tom, but it doesn't ring true. And I know they are about to call a bunch of folks on the stand who are going to say that it was Oswald that killed Tippit and most of them were a block away or so, and...

What?

I am not really sure as to whether he shot Tippit or not.

I'm not either, Sylvester. The evidence from the paraffin test is conclusive that he had fired a pistol. The bullets they took from Tippit came from that gun Oswald was carrying. That's pretty damning.

But how do you end up with different shell casing manufacturers than bullets?

Haven't figured that one out yet.

They finished eating their lunch and walked quickly over to their office before going back to the courthouse. At the office, Tom's secretary reported that Oswald had called about 10 that morning and was doing well enough that they were going to take him back to the jail that afternoon.

Hey Tom, Sylvester called from the door of his office across from the secretary, *I got a call from General Wade wanting to talk about the Ruby thing. Wants to meet this afternoon in Judge Brown's chamber to discuss the details. Says he has something new that just crossed his desk. Says he has two eyewitnesses that can place Ruby with another guy around Dealey Plaza the morning of the assassination. Says one is a police officer.*

Seriously?

Yep.

Well, let's do the meeting. Call over to the clerk and ask if we can meet in chambers before resuming.

Will do.

******

When all the parties had arrived in Judge Brown's chamber, things got heated quickly.

Gentleman, I've again requested that we be able to meet privately with Jack Ruby, but now the Dallas Police Department has denied our request saying they believe such would be inappropriate while an investigation is ongoing.

What are they investigating? General Wade asked? *Ruby shot Oswald right in front of police officers, court officers and television cameras.*

By the way, Cavendish interjected *Oswald has been taken from Parkland back to the county jail. I'm meeting with him this afternoon. He says he has a great deal to tell me. I think he may be ready to talk.*

Seriously? Judge Brown asked. *We get this far and now he wants to talk.*

A man comes close to dying, makes you think about things differently. So General Wade, you said you had some new evidence?

I didn't say it was evidence, but it is testimony that has come to our attention from two witnesses, that I wanted to share with the court and, of course with the defense team, he said smiling, *that could have a great deal of bearing on this meeting with Ruby.*

I'm just getting very confused, Donelson butted in. *What does Ruby have to do with this trial? Do you really believe that Ruby shot Oswald for any other reason than to shut him up? Seriously.*

And you don't know that! Wade yelled.

I believe I do know that, and I think you know it too! Why else would he lay in wait for him and shoot him like that? He's up to his eyeballs in this mess, and the state knows it. Sylvester seemed to be coming unglued, but Cavendish did little to stop him. Donelson was basically saying what Tom had felt all along, that there were others involved and they would do whatever they had to do to shut Oswald up.

Now look, Sylvester, I'm sharing this information with you and the court. I don't have to. I could have just sat on it.

And let an innocent man go to his death?

Innocent?! You still think Oswald is innocent?

Well you haven't done anything to convince me he is guilty!

Nor this court! Judge Brown confessed. *And I know I shouldn't say this, and it is totally off record at this point, but General Wade, you have done one piss poor job presenting evidence of Oswald's guilt. I'll about guarantee you that if the jury were polled today they would vote to acquit.*

Everyone sat stone faced, mouths agape at Brown's condemnation. It was rare that a judge would tilt his hand on how things were going, but this case was different from the get go.

So, General Wade, time is money. What do you have for us? The judge seemed immensely irritated. But then again this trial was wearing on everyone's nerves.

Your honor, colleagues, I received a phone call last evening from Chief Curry. He is concerned about some of the talk that is about having to do with the supposed presence of Jack Ruby in Dealey Plaza before the shooting. There have been two witnesses that have included in their testimony that they saw Jack Ruby that day. We don't know if any of their testimony is reliable or not. But they have all contacted the Chief after seeing a picture of Ruby on the news in connection with the Oswald shooting to say that he is the man they saw in Dealey Plaza before, and actually in one case after the shooting. I'm telling you this because one is a Dallas Police Officer. The others I'm not as convinced about, but the one seems pretty credible.

OK, tell us about it, the Judge ordered.

The police officer's name is Tom Tilson. He was with his daughter on Commerce Street coming toward Dealey Plaza at the time the President's motorcade came through the triple underpass. Tom saw a man sliding down the embankment on the north side of Elm Street. He saw him toss something into the car and then haul it out of there. Tom already knew about the shooting and thinking the guy might have thrown a broken down rifle into the car, he turned around and followed the guy who was heading toward Fort Worth. He got the license number of the car and got close enough to the car to see the guy. He has positively identified the guy as Jack Ruby. He was so certain that it had something to do with what had happened that he called it in as soon as he reached his home. He called it into Homicide. Get this. They reprimanded him for getting involved in something that wasn't in his department. I've asked the obvious. No record of the call was made.

So you said there were others, Donelson reminded.

Yes. One of the witnesses that you are scheduled to call also called back to say she saw him. She had been one of the people closest to the President on the final shot. Her name is Jean Hill. In her affidavit given on November 22, 1963, she said she remembered after that last shot seeing a man running from the TSBD toward the rail yard. Said he was shorter, wearing a suit and hat and was kind of heavy set. She said he was wearing sunglasses. When she saw the pictures of him on television after he shot Oswald, she called and said that Jack Ruby was the man she saw running from the Depository.

Any others? Cavendish asked.

There is one other, but we are uncertain of the reliability of her testimony. This lady, he began looking at his legal pad for her name, *Julie Ann Mercer reported seeing at about 12:15 a pickup truck that was on the side of the road down by the underpass. Said there was another guy with him that got out and got something out of the back of the truck that* looked perhaps like a rifle in a carrier, and he walked up the grassy knoll. We've talked to her several times and her story has changed a few times. However, when she saw the pictures of Jack Ruby she immediately called the police department to report Ruby as being the man she saw in the truck. I've also got at least five or six other people who reported seeing Ruby around the TSBD before the assassination.

So what are you saying with all of this? Cavendish asked.

What I'm saying is that I believe Ruby was an integral part of the plot to assassinate the President. I still believe that Lee Oswald was deeply involved and I'm positive he's going down for Tippit and on the Theater charges. But we need to get Oswald to talk. I'm willing to make a deal.

I'm listening.

We will agree to drop the assault charges stimming from the arrest at the theater. We will take the death penalty off the table on Tippit. He agrees to plead guilty on Tippit and to conspiracy to commit murder on Kennedy and Connally and he gets life in prison, no parole. And this is only if he gives us information and rolls on the others involved.

Sounds like a pretty fair deal, Judge Brown chimed in.

Well, it does except for a couple of things. You are assuming that Oswald had knowledge that the assassination was going to happen, who was involved and how it was planned. He is saying he was a patsy. He may well know some of the characters, but I don't believe for a moment that he is going to plead guilty on conspiracy charges when he believed he was being used by others.

But if he was being used by others, he knows who the others are, right?

Perhaps, Donelson responded. I think it sounds like a fair deal or the efforts of a DA who knows he doesn't have a case.

Look, I'm trying to determine what the truth is here. I believe there are many aspects of this situation that none of us are aware of nor do we want to be a part of.

No sir. I don't believe he will agree to it. But I'm going to go see him and, as you know, I must tell him of this offer.

You have 24 hours to respond.

I'll ask him.

Now gentleman, the Judge interrupted, *we need to get on with this trial until such a time as we have an answer; perhaps many answers. Shall we?* He asked standing from behind his desk and beginning to place on his robe.

Tom, can I see you in private for a moment?

Sure, General.

The men walked over to the office door and walked out and down to the adjacent conference room where just a few days before he had met with his client.

I have to tell you, Tom. There is a great deal of pressure coming down to end this trial.

You mean Mayor Cabell?

No, I mean higher than that.

Lieutenant Governor?

No, sir. I'm talking Washington. FBI, CIA, White House, Attorney General's office...

Bobby Kennedy is trying to get you to end this thing?

Look, this stays just right here on the fence post, you hear me?

Sure, General Wade. You are kind of giving me the creeps about right now. You mean to tell me these folks want this trial ended?

In the worse of ways. I don't know what all has happened here, Tom, but this thing is bigger than the both of us. Now I'm telling you. The feds are afraid that something is going to come out, national security, involvement of high ranking officials, hell I don't know what, but they are putting a great deal of pressure on and they won't let us have key pieces of information.

Such as?

They have refused to give us the autopsy report or the official autopsy pictures. They are prohibiting Dr. Humes and anyone else who was in the room at the autopsy from testifying.

Now they are telling us that what was left of the brain is missing. We are not being allowed to see the X-rays that were taken. We have very little. And they keep trying to feed us information about how things happened as though we haven't got the good sense to do our own investigation.

Seriously, this is happening behind the scenes?

Tom, I'm dead serious about this. You know something is up. You have already been attacked. Oswald was shot. We are getting death threats on a daily basis. Witnesses are being intimidated by FBI agents.

Well, my daddy use to tell me that when you are in the cow pasture, you best look down or else you will eventually step in a cow patty. Sounds to me like you done up to your waste in it.

I guess so.

We better head back to the courtroom.

******

Call your next witness, General Wade.

Your honor, if we might, the state would like to recall Lieutenant Day.

Certainly.

Lieutenant Day to the stand.

Day came through the door and walked to the stand. Wearing his glasses and holding a sizeable Stetson in his hand, he sat down in the chair.

I will remind you Lieutenant that you are still under oath.

Yes sir.

Lieutenant Day, I now would like to ask you in regards to the forensics having to do with the death of Officer J. D. Tippit. Did you also handle the gathering of that forensic evidence?

Yes sir. My office did and I supervised them.

Based on your study of the incident, how many shots were fired into Officer Tippit?

There were four shots fired at Officer Tippit from close range with a .38 special.

General Wade walked over to the evidence table and picked up a revolver. *Lieutenant Day, I am holding such a .38 special. Is this the gun responsible for the death of Officer Tippit?*

We believe beyond a doubt that it is.

And to whom does this gun belong?

It belongs to Lee Harvey Oswald.

And we spoke earlier of the paraffin test in regards to the rifle. Were there also tests conducted to see if Mr. Oswald had recently fired a pistol?

There was. We conducted paraffin tests on both the left and right hands of Mr. Oswald.

And what were the results?

The paraffin tests came back positive. It showed that Mr. Oswald had very recently fired a pistol.

Thank you sir, no further questions.

You may cross, Mr. Cavendish.

Lieutenant Day, were there bullets found on the person of Lee Harvey Oswald when he was arrested at the Texas Theater?

Yes sir, there were.

Can you tell me the manufacturer of the bullets that were in the possession of Mr. Oswald?

I believe they were Winchester-Western and Remington –Peters bullets.

Can you tell me of the four bullets taken from officer Tippit the number and make of each?

Three of the bullets were Winchester-Western bullets. The fourth was a Remington.

So what you are telling this court is that the bullets taken from Officer Tippit do match the brand of bullets Oswald had on his person when arrested, is that correct?

That is correct, answered Day allowing just the right corner of his mouth to curve upward.

During the course of the investigation of this homicide crime scene, were there any shell casings found?

Yes sir, there were four shell casings found lying in the grass nearby.

Can you tell me if there were any fingerprints found on the casings?

We did not recover any fingerprints from them, no sir.

And can you tell me of the four shell casings how many of those were manufactured by Winchester-Western?

Two.

And may we assume therefore that the other two were Remington?

That is correct?

And is it your belief that the spent cartridges are the four shots fired at Officer Tippit?

A—A, well, yes sir that is our thinking.

Now that's kind of odd, don't you think? Here you have three Winchester bullets taken from Tippit but only two casings, and one Remington bullet taken from the officer's body but two Remington casings. What do you make of that Lieutenant Day?

I wouldn't care to speculate about it, sir.

You wouldn't? I bet you wouldn't. You know what I think, Lieutenant Day?

What do you think Mr. Cavendish?

I think it's another tell-tell sign of a conspiracy to frame my client.

Objection, your honor.

Mr. Cavendish! Judge Brown was peering over his glasses, his face reddened, and an evil look of intent on his face.

Withdrawn. No further questions.

The courtroom grew silent as Day made his way out of the witness chair knowing that once again he had done damage to the prosecution case by admitting too much. The audience released their collective breaths when the Judge merely suggested that General Wade call his next witness.

The state calls Helen Markham.

Mrs. Markham, you live in the neighborhood where Officer Tippit was killed, is that correct?

Yes, I live about a block away.

And the afternoon of November 22, 1963, did you have occasion to witness the shooting of Officer Tippit.

Yes sir, I sure did.

Can you tell us what brought you to the corner of 10th and Patton that afternoon?

Sure. I was walking to the bus stop down toward Jefferson Street on 10th.

Where were you going?

I was going to work.

And where do you work?

I work as a waitress at the Eat Well Restaurant at 1404 Main Street in downtown.

So you were on your way to catch the bus into downtown. At what time would that have been?

I usually leave the house just after 1:00 because the bus runs at 1:15.

And where do you catch the bus?

At Jefferson and Patton.

That's what about a block away from where the shooting took place, is that correct?

Yes.

And what did you see that particular day?

I saw this man walking along 10th street. He was almost across Patton and I see this police car coming down 10th real slow close to the curb. He pulled alongside this man and stopped. He evidently called the man over because he went to the car and bent over into the passenger window. They talked for a few moments then the man straightened up and took a couple steps back. The officer opened the door and got out of the car. I didn't think much about it 'cause it seemed they was friendly and all. Then just as the officer got to the front left tire, the man shot him, bang, bang, bang.

And you saw all of this?

Yes.

What did the man do next?

He started in my direction. It liked to scare me silly. I thought he was going to shoot me. So I put my hands over my face, like this. She raised both hands flat palms against her face with fingers extended upward.

What did he do next?

Well in a few seconds I looked through my fingers and realized that he had turned and was trotting away.

Which way did he go?

He crossed over Patton toward Jefferson and took off around a house and then disappeared from my sight.

Did he still have the gun?

Yes, he was holding the gun in both hands fumbling with it.

Could you tell what he was doing with the gun?
Fumbling with it or something. I don't know.
Did you scream or yell or say anything to him?
Oh no.

What did you do when you realized he wasn't coming toward you?

I ran over to the policeman. I wanted to do whatever I could to help him, but I think it was too late.

Is it true Mrs. Markham that you have positively identified Lee Harvey Oswald as the man who killed officer Tippit?

Yes, I'm sure it was him.

No further questions. Your witness Mr. Cavendish.

Tom stood initially at the defense table to ask the questions not wishing to look as though he were attacking her.

So you have testified that he was across the street from you initially and then crossed Patton on the other side of 9th from you.

No tenth.

OK, the other side of 10th. You live on 9th, correct?
Yes.

So he was diagonally across from you and up the street on 10th just a little ways, correct?
Yes.

How far would you say it was between you and the squad car?

Oh, I'm not good at that sort of thing. I really don't...

Fifty feet maybe?

Oh, I just would hate to say. I'm not sure Mr. Cavendish, it might have been fifty feet or more even. I just don't know.

So you can't tell us how far the distance was between yourself and the man whom was killed?

It was just up a little bit from the corner.

How much is a little bit?

Well, I don't really know.

Cavendish walked over to the lectern.

And how many shots did you hear?

I heard three shots. I'm sure about that. Three shots.

And you are sure that you heard three shots even though the evidence shows that Officer Tippit was shot four times?

She paused, a look of doubt on her face. She bit into her bottom lip and looked over at the prosecution table.

How many shots, Mrs. Markham did you hear?

I am certain that I heard three. Crack, crack, crack. Just like that.

Now in your affidavit to the police, you described things a bit differently. For example, do you recall telling the police that you screamed and the assailant ran east on 10th across Patton and out of sight?

Perhaps I did.

Do you also recall telling the police that the assailant was short and somewhat stocky with bushy hair?

Well, I might have said that, but I was all tore up and so nervous by what had happened.

Oh, I'm sure you were Mrs. Markham, but you have to realize that a man is on trial here for his life and you have been one of the witnesses that have claimed to positively identify Lee Harvey Oswald as the man who killed Officer Tippit.

Yes, sir, I'm aware of that. And I've tried to tell the truth as I remember it.

So which is the truth, Mrs. Markham that you screamed or that you didn't?

I didn't.

So why did you tell the police you did? Which is the truth Mrs. Markham that the assailant was just across the street, or is it more to the truth that the assailant was standing some 150 feet, at least, from you when he pulled that trigger?

Oh I don't believe it was that far.

You don't? You reported to the police that the car was parked in front of 404 10th Street and that is precisely what the police report of the shooting also says. You said you were on the corner opposite at 10th and Patton. The police measured it. It is in their report. 150 feet. Is that correct or not?

Well, if they said so.

At the police lineup, you seemed very uncertain of the person who you had seen in regards to the people in the lineup. They showed you the clothes Oswald wore, and you said they were not the same color, yet you picked out Oswald (number 2) as the person who had killed officer Tippit. What did you base that ID on?

His eyes. I saw those eyes and knew it was the same man.

You saw his eyes at 150 feet and knew it was the same man, is that what you are saying?

Absolutely. Remember he was closer to me after the shooting. Just across the street on the opposite corner.

Yes, I remember you saying you had your hands over your face. Can you see with your eyes closed, Mrs. Markham?

Well, you are getting me all confused.

No further questions, your honor.

State calls Domingo Benavides.

Mr. Benavides, on the afternoon of November 22, 1963 were you in the vicinity of 10th Avenue where Officer Tippit was killed?

Yes I was.

What caused you to be there?

I work just down the street as a mechanic and I was assisting this guy who broke down on 10th Street. I was on my way to get some parts.

You happened upon the scene of Officer Tippit speaking with a man on the sidewalk, correct?

Well the police officer was in his car but was just getting out.

Where was the other man?

He was standing about at the windshield of the police car on the other side of the car.

And what did you see next?

The police officer was going around to the front of the car when the other guy pulled out a gun and shot him three times.

What did you do?

I pulled my truck into the curb and just watched to see what he was going to do. I wanted to go to the officer to help him but was afraid the guy would come after me.

How far away were you?

I was about two houses down from them.

So you were very close.

Yes.

Did you get a good look at the assailant?

The what?

The shooter?

Yes.

And what did he look like?

Well he was around 25 I'd say.

How tall?

How tall are you, Mr. Wade?

I'm about 5'11.

He was about your height.

How much would you say he weighed?

Oh I'd say probably about 170 or so. About the same as you?

Did he have dark hair?

Well it was dark.

Was it black?

Oh, no it wasn't black, perhaps, brown or a little lighter. But it was dark.

Was he dark complected?

No he was white but he was ruddier than me.

How close were you to the gunman?

When my truck came to a stop I was perhaps a car length away from the front of the police car. He was directly across from me.

You have positively identified Lee Harvey Oswald as the assailant in a police lineup, is that correct?

Yes. I did.

Do you still believe that Lee Oswald is the man you saw shoot office Tippit?

I am sure of it.

Your witness.

Mr. Benavides, you have testified, Tom began, *that you heard three shots, is that correct.*

Yes.

Even though Officer Tippit was shot four times, you only heard three shots, is that correct?

I don't know how many times he was shot, and all, I do know what I heard.

Now in your affidavit, your honor am I allowed to ask him about the affidavit?

Of course, Mr. Cavendish. It has been admitted. You are in fair territory if he covered it in his affidavit. Do you desire to ask him about something in the affidavit that was not just asked of him?

Yes, your honor. I want to ask him about his actions as he describes them after the assailant fled.

Objection your honor. We did not cover that in direct. He has no right to go there now.

But General Wade, you earlier stipulated the admittance of affidavits as evidence. Doesn't that give him license to go there if it is covered in the affidavit?

I do not believe so, your honor. But if it pleases your honor to allow it, I would certainly desire to redirect.

So ordered. Objection overruled. Proceed.

After the shooter fled, Mr. Benavides, did you attempt to get help for Officer Tippit?

I did. I tried to use the police radio to call for help.

Were you successful?

We got through.

You say we.

Yeah, me and this other guy who came up was finally able to get through.

And what did you do after that?

I walked toward where I had seen him throw casings out of his gun and picked them up and put them in a cigarette package I had.

You actually picked up evidence? What did you do with it?

I only found two of the shell casings and I gave them to a police officer.

Was there anything else that was disturbed at the scene?

Well the other guy...

Ted Callaway?

Yes, him. I looked over and saw that he was getting the gun out of the officer's hand. I didn't think he should do that.

What did Mr. Callaway do?

He left in a cab that was parked on the curb on Patton.

At the moment that the shooting happened, were you aware of anyone else being present at the scene?

Objection, foundation.

Sustained.

No further questions.

Next witness General Wade.

The state calls Officer Nick McDonald.

The tall officer walked down the aisle and took his place on the witness stand.

Officer McDonald, it is my understanding that you were with a group of officers who descended on the Texas Theater in Oak Cliff, is that correct?

Yes.

What brought the officers there?

We had received a report that the assailant of Officer Tippit was possibly in the area, and in fact, a person had entered the theater without buying a ticket. Based on the description we had been given, we thought he might be the shooter.

You went into the theater from behind the curtain in front, is that correct?

Yes. I had been given information that he was sitting near the back of the theater a few seats from the end and I was to approach him from the front.

What happened when you approached him?

I asked him to get up and he said "It's all over now" and drew his pistol.

What did you do?

I reached for the pistol and we scuffled to the floor in between the rows of chairs. He had hit me and I had hit him back just before we fell to the floor. When he tried to shoot me, I grabbed for the gun. The flesh between my thumb and pointing finger hit just as the hammer hit to fire the gun. That was all that kept me from being shot.

What happened then?

Two other officers helped subdue Oswald and bring him to his feet. It wasn't easy and they were injured as well.

How did Oswald act once you had him cuffed?

He was very belligerent and defensive. He was as we call it resisting arrest.

No further questions, your honor.

Cross Mr. Cavendish.

Cavendish rose at his table. Cavendish looked at the officer, started once not to ask anything about halfway to his seat, and stood erect again.

I only have one question Officer McDonald. As you approached Oswald at the theater, how would you characterize his behavior?

What do you mean?

Well, did he seem relaxed or uptight?

He was moving about like a cornered animal. He looked wild-eyed.

Thank you. Nothing further.

Mr. Wade, next witness.

Your honor, the prosecution rests its case.

The look of shock on Judge Brown's face registered with everyone in the courtroom. Tom Cavendish was looking at General Wade as though he had just slapped him. Wade sat down and began writing something on his pad that he slid over for his second to read. The second looked at him and frowned.

OK, Gentleman, since it is late in the day, we will end our session for the day and Mr. Cavendish will the defense be ready to go in the morning?

Yes sir, your honor, we will and Mr. Oswald will be joining us in the morning, if we could have special security in place.

Absolutely Mr. Cavendish.

Until tomorrow, we stand adjourned for the evening.

Dallas Police Cruiser driven by Tippit. When he reached the front left tire, the assailant opened fire with three shots and then a final shot to his temple.

Chapter 20- The Defense Begins

Mr. Cavendish, call your first witness, Judge Brown ordered as the morning proceedings started right at the 9:00 hour. The audience waited with baited breath as rumors abounded who that witness might be. Once more Oswald was sitting at the table looking somewhat gaunt and with guards setting around the table.

Thank you your honor. The Defense calls as its first witness the honorable Governor of the state of Texas, Governor John Connally.

The doors in the back of the courtroom opened and in walked the tall Texan carrying his trademark white Stetson. The crowd in the gallery immediately stood in honor of the man who almost lost his life along with President Kennedy. He was flanked by large security guards who walked to the gate entrance into the inner sanctum of the courtroom. He took his place at the witness stand, raised his hand to swear his oath and was seated.

Governor Connally, first of all, on behalf of the people in this courtroom, we are so pleased and thankful that you are with us this morning.

The Governor nodded his appreciation and smiled slightly. It was obvious from observing his movements that he was still healing.

Governor Connally, on November 22, 1963 you were present in the motorcade with President Kennedy, is that correct?

Yes, sir. I was in that car.

Who else was present in the car?

I was sitting directly in front of President Kennedy in a jump seat. Beside me was my wife, and beside President Kennedy was his wife. In the front seat were two Secret Service agents. Roy Kellerman was directly in front of me.

When the Lincoln made the sharp turn onto Elm Street, would you tell the court what was happening in the car?

We had just made the turn. Nellie had turned to the President just a short time before that as we left Main Street and said something like "you can't say Dallas doesn't love you Mr. President." And I was waving to the folks lined up along the sidewalk there in front of the Book Depository when I heard a loud crack. I could tell from the sounds behind me that something had happened to the President.

Did you hear him say anything?

No, I don't recall hearing him say anything.

I began to turn to my right to try to get a view of the President and because I felt the shot had come from behind me over my shoulder.

Were you also hit at that time?

No sir. I was not. I know the FBI has reported that I was hit by the same bullet but I am here to tell you that they are wrong.

Well, I would think you should know, sir.

You would think.

Did you see the President at that time?

No, I never saw the President during the whole thing.

At what point did you realize you were hit?

When I couldn't see well what was going on, I had decided I was going to turn back to the left to try to get a better view. That is when I felt the bullet hit.

Is it your belief that you were hit by a second shot?

Well, let me explain this to you. I heard the first shot. Clearly heard it. No mistaking it. I attempted to turn to my right to look over my shoulder both to see President Kennedy because I knew the shot was that of a rifle and figured immediately that it was an assassination attempt. I could not see the President nor could I see anything that looked unusual happening off behind us and tried to turn to my left. Within seconds of the President being shot I felt the bullet hit my back and I knew I was badly hit and since I had a chest wound knew it might be fatal. I collapsed in my wife's lap. Or rather, she pulled me down into her lap. Soon I heard the third shot and heard it hit. I saw brain and blood all over the car including on my pant leg. I was certain the President had been hit even though I never saw him. After that I passed out.

When did you regain consciousness?

When I arrived at the hospital. They had to get me out of the car before they could get to the President. I remember being removed from the car.

When did you know the President was dead?

I knew, Mr. Cavendish, the moment I heard that third shot hit and saw a sizeable portion of his brain about the size of my thumb on my pants.

In regards to the gunfire, what were your thoughts regarding how fast the gunfire was happening?

The shots happened so quickly my first thought was that there were either numerous shooters or that the gunman was using an automatic rifle.

You have read the report issued by the Federal Bureau of Investigation in regards to the shooting in which they state that President Kennedy was hit in the upper back and that the shot went through his back before striking you. Based on what you experienced, do you believe that it is possible that the same bullet hit you that had hit the President?

No sir. I do not at all believe it was the same shot. If you know about these things, you know that a man will never hear the shot that hits him. The bullet travels much faster than the speed of sound. If I had been hit by the same shot, it would have hit me before I even turned to my right and the shot would have hit me square in the back. In fact, if that had been the case, I don't believe I would have been here to testify.

Other than the bullet hitting you, what else happened that made you cognizant that you had been hit?

The bullet shattered part of a rib; the pain was rough. I had been holding my Stetson in my right hand and I dropped it as the bullet shattered my wrist. I felt a stinging sensation in my left leg and realized it had hit my thigh as well. I was very quickly covered in blood.

As you know some have suggested that you were not hit until after the shot that hit the President in the head. Is it *possible that you were covered in the President's blood instead of your own?*

Oh no. I'm certain of that. I know when I heard that shot.

And what was your impression as to where that shot originated?

Same place. From behind some place.

Elevated?

I suspected so. From one of those buildings behind us is what I thought.

Did you witness any bullet or fragment hitting the windshield of the limousine?

I am not aware of any such.

Were you aware of a bullet or fragment hitting the metal bar that was in front of you between the jump seat and the front seat?

No sir. I did not witness any such.

Were you aware of any bullet fragment hitting the cushion of the front seat in front of you?

No sir. I'm not aware of anything of the kind.

What if anything did you say during the shooting?

The only thing I recall saying was "Oh, no, no, no!" just after I collapsed into my wife's lap.

Do you recall Nellie Connally or Jackie Kennedy saying anything?

I do not recall my wife saying anything but "you are going to be ok." She said that to me. I did hear Mrs. Kennedy say "They have killed my husband." She said something else, but I would prefer not repeating it, please.

Certainly, I understand.

Governor, how many shots did you actually hear?

I heard the first shot that hit the President and the last shot that hit the President. I did not hear what would have been the second shot.

You believe then that there were but three shots?

Yes sir.

In the FBI report of the assassination, they suggest that the first shot missed the motorcade, hit a curb causing a piece of concrete to be propelled into the air hitting a James Tague on the cheek. Do you believe this could be possible?

No sir. I do not believe so. I heard that first shot and based on what my wife saw and what I recall happening, I believe this first shot hit the President in the back.

Could it be possible that two shots were fired so close together that it sounded as though there had only been a single shot fired?

I suppose that might be possible, but I'm not sure that I could testify to that because I don't believe that is what happened.

If I told you that all the doctors at Parkland Hospital described the wound in the President's throat as an entrance wound, would that impact your thinking about the direction or number of shots?

Well, if that were the case, and...

Objection your honor, Wade blurted out before Connally could finish his sentence. This calls for knowledge of such testimony that has not been placed in evidence yet.

The affidavits of the doctors are in evidence.

Mr. Cavendish, I understand where you are leaning with this question, but it is a bit presumptuous to believe that Governor Connally would be aware of the content of their affidavits. I will sustain the objection. I believe you should reword your question.

Yes sir. Tom Cavendish stood in front of the witness stand, looking square in the eyes of the most powerful man in Texas politics and thinking how he could word this question to provoke the correct response. If you were to be presented with medical evidence that proved the throat wound to be an entrance wound, would this impact your thinking of where the shots originated and/or how many shots were fired?

Objection, calls for speculation.

Overruled. I'll allow the question, but be careful Mr. Cavendish? Governor, you may answer the question.

First, I do not believe that such evidence will be forthcoming, so no, I don't believe that there was any more than one shooter and no more than three shots. That's what I heard, and that is what I believe.

But Governor, may I correct you?

About what?

You have testified that you only heard two shots. So if you only heard two shots but believe there was three fired, couldn't it be possible you didn't hear another shot?

I don't think so, Mr. Cavendish.

Governor, did your doctors leave any fragments from the bullets in you?

I'm told they left two small fragments?

Do you know if the total weight of these fragments is greater, less than or the same as that missing from the bullet found on the stretcher which the FBI claims to be the bullet that caused the back and neck wound of the President and your five wounds?

Actually, I do know the answer to that. The collective weight of the fragments taken from me and left in me greatly exceeds the amount of material missing from bullet 399.

Thank you Governor, I have no further questions.

General Wade didn't wait for Judge Brown's permission, but immediately moved to the rostrum. Governor Connally, I just have a couple of clarifications. How many shots were fired at the motorcade?

There were three shots.

And where did you believe those shots to have originated?

I believe the shots came from one of the buildings to our rear.

No further questions.

Redirect, your honor.

Of course, Mr. Cavendish.

Governor Connally you do not have any personal knowledge as to the exact origin of the shots with any amount of certainty, do you, sir?

No sir. I did not see where they were coming from exactly.

And thus, you have no personal knowledge of who fired the shots that hit you and the President, do you?

No sir, I do not.

Thank you, Governor. I pray you continue to heal well.

Thank you.

You may step down Governor. We all pray your continued health.

The Governor rose to leave the witness stand and everyone in the courtroom with the exception of Judge Brown and the two prosecution lawyers stood. Tom Cavendish looked over and even Oswald had gotten to his feet. As the Governor walked past the table he could not resist scowling at Oswald.

The bailiff walked over to the judge and handed him a note. Judge Brown looked over his glasses at Oswald. *Gentlemen, we shall take a recess for half hour. I have some business in my chambers I must attend to.*

All rise.

I wonder what that was about? Oswald asked Mr. Cavendish. *He looked at me like something he discovers.*

Cavendish hated it when Oswald broke into his Russian accent.

I don't know.

The officer came over to take Oswald back to the holding cell. Cavendish stopped him momentarily. *I'd like to meet with him back in the conference room.*

That won't be possible, Mr. Cavendish. It is in use. I've been instructed to take the prisoner to the holding cell.

OK. Lee, we will talk in a bit.

Sure. I have much I want to tell you. He smiled a nervous smile.

When Oswald had walked away, Cavendish turned to Donelson and they discussed how to go forward and what they thought might be going on. It was a good half hour when both teams of lawyers received word that court would not resume until mid-afternoon due to unforeseen events. What they could not see was that just on the other side of two walls sat Judge Brown speaking with Jack Ruby the man who had shot Lee Harvey Oswald. The meeting had been arranged through a "friend" of the Judge who was in good accord with Mayor Cabell.

Late in the afternoon, Judge Brown sent the bailiff to bring both law teams to his chambers.

Gentleman, I just spent the last several hours meeting privately with Jack Ruby.

What! General Wade blurted. *How did you arrange that?*

The Judge held up his hand for quiet. *I don't want to hear another word. I just need you to listen. Understood?*

The four expressed agreement, although Donelson wanted to know if the Judge had let anyone else know of this meeting.

Mayor Cabell is the only other person who knows of this meeting as well as Sheriff Decker. That's it, I promise. Decker brought Ruby here himself. Now Gentleman, I'm going to share with you what Ruby told me. I have a recording system in the conference room that can only be turned on by me. I recorded the conversation. Ruby does not know it was recorded. And no, you may not hear it, yet.

Judge Brown, where are you taking us?

I wish I knew the answer to that question.

Here is the gist of what Ruby has told me. He told me that he and Oswald did know each other and that they were part of a special group of guys.

Mob? Cavendish asked.

He didn't say. I took it to mean covert ops perhaps.

And, General Wade added impatiently.

Here is what he told me. He had a certain assignment having to do with the assassination of the President. He said that Oswald didn't do it. They set him up to take the fall while others, meanwhile, were assigned to get the real assassins out of the city. He said they were well hidden and slipped right through the police and no one suspected a thing. This is the part that is scary. He said he didn't know who was calling the shots, but that he assumed it was someone in Washington. Said they had trained under direction of some mob/CIA contacts down in New Orleans. Said they were so deep under cover that nobody would ever suspect them. Ruby said the assassination was planned in the summer and that everything had a connection.

This man is really weird. And wired. Very nervous character, but he knows something, gentleman. He said everything happened just exactly the way it was planned. He said that it was unfortunate that he had been unsuccessful in killing Oswald, but that it wouldn't stop until Oswald was silenced. He said that Oswald knew a lot about the operation because he was military intelligence.

Oswald, military intelligence? Donelson said, his voice reaching into upper octaves.

You must be kidding me, General Wade said. You aren't buying this bull, are you?

Well, Decker told me something was going on that seemed strange. That is how he was able to get the meeting. Decker found out that the night after Kennedy was killed Oswald had attempted to make a call to a John Hurt in Raleigh, North Carolina. Military man. What connection would Oswald have to Hurt and why would he call him?

Decker spoke with Agent Hosty of the FBI and Hosty, Decker said, turned white as a ghost. Wouldn't answer any more questions. Gentleman, we have a situation here that has put us all in danger. If Ruby is correct, there is no one safe in this situation. None of us.

What do you propose be done? You don't think that Ruby is telling the truth, do you, Judge Brown? General Wade was pacing the floor. I know I don't have all the answers, but I'm sure that Oswald killed the President as sure as I'm standing here, and I don't want anything to fowl up this conviction, because he is going down.

Oh shut up Wade, Brown snapped. Your case got torn to shreds in there, and you know it. You are going to get a conviction on the Theater incident, and that might be it. I don't believe this jury will buy any of the manure you have tried to shovel.

Judge Brown! I presented solid evidence. We have his gun, the shell casings, the eye witnesses ...

Who didn't really see anything of any value, Donelson added.

OK, Gentlemen.

So what else did he tell you? Did he tell you who was involved?

No. He just rambled on and on for two hours. But he knows something. He knows a lot. He started giving me meetings that he took with Oswald and others. The fact, gentlemen that they know each other, tells me something is wrong. He said we should get Paine and Mohrenschildt in here and ask them questions about their relationship with Oswald. I don't know. I don't feel like I know any more now than I did, but heaven help us.

What are you going to do? You aren't going to declare a mistrial, are you?

Oh no. I can't tip our hand that anything is wrong because if I do, I might be putting all of us in jeopardy. I want Mr. Cavendish to meet for the next couple of hours with Oswald and see if you can get him to talk. You have what six or seven more witnesses to go, Mr. Cavendish?

Yes, sir. About a dozen, I think. I don't know whether Lee is going to continue to insist on testifying or not.

Talk to him. See what you can get out of him. We will convene the court in the morning and finish up testimony. I want final statements the day after and the case to the jury by that afternoon. Is that understood? We have to finish this trial but do it quickly. If we can finish up and render a verdict, then hopefully there will not be collateral damage if whoever decides to go after Oswald again.

I don't like this a bit, Donelson said. Can't you see the mob is in this thing?

The mob, Cavendish restated. *You think the mob is involved?*

Yes. Who you thinking?

The government.

What? The government would never do anything like this. You can't be serious. General Wade was back to pacing again.

Wade! Wake up man. Who has been blocking us at every juncture since the moment it happened? They took the President's body so we couldn't do an autopsy. Now they will not give us access to the autopsy, or the doctors, or the pictures and x-rays. We can't get all the evidence back. There are all these different pictures of the rifle. Need I go on?

I know all the things you've said, Tom; I've heard them in the courtroom. You've clobbered me out there every time I think I've got something solid. This is the biggest mess I've ever seen.

How about the greatest cover up? Judge Brown said. *I just don't want to become a target.*

Me either, Judge Brown, General Wade responded.

Ok, gentlemen, let's do what we have to do.

******

For two hours Tom Cavendish sat in the conference room, the very room where just a few hours earlier Jack Ruby had spoken with Judge Brown and spoke to Lee Harvey Oswald. The stoical Oswald just sat and listened saying little. It was as though he had been told something.

Lee, a few hours ago Jack Ruby sat in this room and spilled the beans. He told Judge Brown everything. How the two of you know each other, about New Orleans, the plot to kill Kennedy, etc. He was supposed to kill you to shut you up, but it seems even though he didn't succeed, something is keeping you from talking. This jury is going to send you to the chair, Lee. You are going to die.

If not, I'm dead anyway.

Why not just come clean?

If I talk, too many people will be in danger.

I'm going to ask you some questions. Answer me if you will.

Oswald folded his arms across his thin chest and sat with a smirk across his face.

Are you military intelligence?

No answer.

We know you called an intelligence officer in Raleigh. Hurt, I believe was his name.

Oswald's eye twitched in recognition of the name. He looked down to the floor.

You didn't really buy that rifle, did you? Someone else bought it and hid it at Paine's house, right?

Nothing.

When you were walking down 10th toward Jefferson, you were headed to Ruby's house, weren't you.

Eyes blinking with recognition.   Touched a nerve, Cavendish thought.

You shot Officer Tippit when he told you he was there to keep you quiet, right? Why else wouldn't he call in seeing a man that met the description of the assassin of the President of the United States?

Looked down. Not going to tip his hand.

Were you supposed to meet a contact at the Theater?

Just went to see a movie. Didn't know what else to do?

Why because they screwed you over? They told you to kill the President but you didn't have the heart to do it, so you backed out, called out, and they said, we'll just screw him over. Make it look like you did it anyway.

Nothing again.

Who'd you call from the depository, Lee? Witnesses saw you using the phone.

Marina.

Why?

To tell her I loved her in case I didn't see her again.

What made you think you wouldn't see her again? Is that why you left your wedding ring on the dresser?

Yes.

You were supposed to do it weren't you?

No. I knew it would happen. I was just supposed to let the shooter in the building and get him out again without anyone seeing him.

OK.

They said no one would know where the shots came from. But when I heard the shooting going on and the police start charging in the building, I knew it was time to get out.

And what went wrong when you left?

They were supposed to have a car outside waiting for me, take me to the airport where a pilot was waiting with a plane. They were going to fly us out of the country.

Who was calling the shots, Lee?

What? Lee had that wild look in his eyes. *You think I'm going to tell you that? You think I even know? Mr. Cavendish, I don't know as much as you think I know. But I know enough to keep my mouth shut. I'm through talking.*

Were you intelligence in military?

Perhaps.

Did you shoot the President?

No.

Did you shoot Tippit?

Nothing.

OK, Lee. We will resume here in the morning. I've just got a few more witnesses. You still want to testify.

I cannot testify.

I thought you wanted to testify.

Silence.

OK man. I don't know what you have gotten yourself into, but I'll do what I can to keep you out of the electric chair.

Either way, I die.

 The Magic Bullet

Chapter 21- The Surprise Witness

The defense team had put together a listing of some forty witnesses. At the top of that list had been Governor Connally and his testimony had certainly added question to the government's theory that the same bullet had traversed both Kennedy and the Governor during the assassination. The Government's explanation of events required three shots fired from the Depository from presumably Oswald's gun or else there was immediately a conspiracy with multiple shooters. The defense knew the lone nut theory the FBI had offered, in fact, Hoover had offered the very afternoon of the assassination before the investigation was barely warm, was filled with spurious inferences and conclusions. Proving them as such was beginning to look like a task with insurmountable complications. The government not only played loose with the facts, but had outright invented facts from fiction. The greatest of these suppositions was the single bullet theory. Donelson had been hard at work trying to ascertain that the defense mounted a vigorous campaign to debunk it.

The defense calls Jonathan Pitts.

Jonathan Pitts to the stand.

Mr. Pitts was a government expert who had closely examined the bullets for the FBI. It had been difficult to get their cooperation in the investigation, but even more difficult to secure the testimony at trial. Mr. Pitts walked forward and immediately Sylvester Donelson questioned the wisdom of having called him. His quirkiness became apparent immediately as the twitches in his facial features and his thick glasses made him less than desirable as the ideal witness.

State your full name, please sir, Donelson requested.

My name is Matthew Jonathan Pitts.

Sylvester was stunned when he heard the resonance of his voice, a rich baritone that seemed strangely affixed to this otherwise bookworm of a caricature.

And what is your occupation, sir?

I am the head of ballistics and forensic science for the FBI's Washington bureau.

Sylvester liked the way this guy spoke with stellar clarity and authority. He noted that the jury sat up straight as the witness continued.

During the investigation of the assassination of President Kennedy and the shooting of Governor Connally, did you have an opportunity to examine the evidence having to do with the gun and the shooting?

I did. I in fact received all the evidence from the Dallas Police Department on November 23 and returned most of it to them by the 27th of December.

And I am particularly interested in only a couple of pieces of the evidence for which I need your expertise. First, to the matter of the bullet that was given to the FBI found on a stretcher at Parkland Hospital. Were you able to determine as to whether that bullet was a match to the Carcano rifle in question?

I was able to determine that in all probability that bullet did originate from that rifle.

Were you able to tell when that bullet was fired?

No sir, tests do not yield such data.

And according to the FBI, it has stated in its report that this bullet was fired from the sixth floor window of the depository striking President Kennedy in the lower cervical area just above the scapula and to the right of midline approximately 5.5 inches below the right mastoid process then entered Governor Connally' body just below the scapula near the right arm pit, exited his chest just below his right nipple, shattered his right wrist and then entered his left thigh just before the knee. Based on your examination of this bullet, is it plausible that this bullet caused all of those wounds?

I do not believe that it is possible. There is too much intact matter remaining in the bullet compared to the amount of fragments removed from the Governor and remaining in the Governor. A bullet having caused so much damage to bone would not be expected to be in this nearly pristine condition.

And I will also remind you that Dr. George Burkley, President Kennedy's personal physician and the one signing his death certificate, located the back wound as being about the third thoracic vertebrae, making it too low on this kind of trajectory to have exited his throat.

In your examination of the bullet in question, which has been classified as exhibit 399, could you detect any human tissue, blood, or even enzymes on the bullet that would indicate it had been shot into a human body?

None, sir, the bullet was clean.

And in your examination of this bullet 399, did you detect any fingerprints on the bullet.

None that were of any usage beside smudges and the like.

May I further ask you in regards to the nature of bullets used in a Carcano rifle?

Certainly.

Is it a correct characterization to say the Carcano bullet was intended to penetrate the victim remaining primarily intact?

The bullet generally can be characterized in that manner. They are full metal jacket bullets and unless they hit an extraordinary amount of bone will penetrate through soft tissue easily, usually quite intact.

So might it be surmised since the bullet hitting President Kennedy in the head disintegrated, that it was perhaps fired from another gun or was a different type of bullet?

That could be a possibility but isn't a necessary conclusion. It would be somewhat unusual that it did not just blast through the brain and exit in a direct line.

In which case, if the government is correct that the entrance wound for the President's head wound was the crown of the head would have exited where?

In a true trajectory, it would seem logical to expect the bullet to have exited the President's face.

Thank you, sir. No further questions.

Cross, General Wade? Judge Brown asked.

Yes, your honor. Mr. Pitts, in your testimony you stated that it would be impossible. Let me ask you about possibilities of this bullet. Do you have a general knowledge of this caliber of bullet?

Yes, sir, I am familiar with the Carcano rifle and the bullets generally used in them.

Then let me ask if with this rifle a person were firing from an elevated height of approximately 60 feet at around a 45 degree angle, and the bullet first hit an object passing through muscle and soft tissue but not hitting bone and then hit another person, would it be possible that the bullet could cause 7 different wounds in those two persons? Let's just get that much out of the way. Is it theoretically possible?

I suppose that under just the right circumstances a bullet of this nature could cause that many injuries to two people. What one would find, however, is that the laws of physics would soon catch up with the bullet slowing the momentum so drastically, especially after colliding with so much bone, that it would hardly have enough energy left to cause the wound to the thigh witnessed here. It would perhaps have merely fallen into the floorboard.

Do I recall correctly that these bullets are particularly made so as to penetrate straight through an object without falling apart or exploding on impact?

I do believe they were intended to do so, but that would depend greatly on what they have hit. For example, the bullet hitting President Kennedy in the head immediately disintegrated into dozens of fragments.

Ok, sir. No further questions. Thank you, General Wade quickly became dismissive and hurried back to his seat cutting off the conversation.

Redirect, your honor. Donelson stood immediately deciding to walk through the door that had just been opened. *I'm rather curious regarding just that, Mr. Pitts. The bullet striking the President in the head did immediately disintegrate into as you said dozens of fragments." Is that correct?*

Yes.

It is my understanding that there were numerous fragments in his head, correct?

Yes.

There were fragments taken from the seats, in the floor board. I've even seen in the FBI report that the windshield had been cracked by a fragment, and that one had hit the metal railing of the window guard separating the front seat from the back, is that correct?

Well, I've heard such but I'm not that certain of those as facts, sir.

But you do agree that the bullet hitting the President acted differently than the other bullet that you now say could not have struck both the President and Governor Connally? Is that a correct summation of your belief?

It is. It did act differently. It immediately struck extremely hard bone causing it to basically release a great deal of energy that blew the bullet apart.

Given that you do not believe the same bullet struck first Kennedy and then Connally, how many shots do you believe were fired?

It is not my job to speculate on such but to examine the evidence that I'm given.

But surely you must have some idea of how many shots, the evidence of which, you examined. Would it be correct to say that there were only three shots?

I'm not certain that the statement represents a fair assessment of the evidence based on my examination.

Would you then believe it a fair assessment to say that more than three shots were fired?

Perhaps that would be a fair assessment.

Just one more question, Mr. Pitts. In examining all the evidence that you have examined in this case, is there anything that you have examined that would make you believe beyond a reasonable doubt and within a moral certainty, that Lee Harvey Oswald fired that rifle at President Kennedy's motorcade? Can you say that with a factual degree of certainty?

Mr. Pitts paused, looked at Oswald, then up at the judge and then over to the jury. *I cannot.*

Thank you sir.

You may step down, Mr. Pitts. Next witness, Mr. Cavendish.

The Defense calls Dr. Charles Carrico.

Dr. Carrico, would you state your name for the record?

Dr. Charles J. Carrico.

And what is your occupation?

I am a surgeon in practice at Parkland Hospital here in Dallas.

And on the afternoon of November 22, 1963, at approximately 12:32, did you receive information that the President of the United States was on his way to the Emergency Room?

I did.

And how is it that you came to be in the Emergency Room?

I was consulting with a patient who was in the ER that we believed would need surgery when the call came in from the Dallas Police.

And did you have any indication of the seriousness of the situation before the President arrived?

We were told to expect serious injuries to someone in the President's party.

When the President was brought to you and you initially examined him, did you fear for his survival?

The President presented with very serious wounds. The wound to his head was sizeable. There was a 5 cm by 17 cm defect of the posterior skull, the occipital region. There was an absence of the calvarium or skull in this area.

And placing that in perspective to inches, Dr. Carrico, how large would that be?

That would be approximately 2 inches by 6 ½ inches.

That is a considerable amount of skull to be missing. And where would you locate that defect as you have called it?

It is a fairly sizeable wound and it was on the right side of his head in the parietal/occipital area. There were fragments of both cerebellum and cerebrum in the wound.

When the President was wheeled into the emergency room, were you the first doctor to attend to him?

Yes.

How old were you when you attended the President?

28

And what was your status at the hospital?

I was a second year surgical resident.

On viewing the head wound, were you able to deduce from which direction the bullet had struck the President?

I was unable to deduce for sure the entrance. Nothing seemed very clear. Although there was so much of the right side of his skull displaced and missing, it would be very difficult to determine under the circumstances with which we worked.

No further questions.

Cross examine, General Wade?

The state has no questions of this witness, your honor. Wade hardly looked up from his notes as he passed on questioning the witness. While there had been some passes from both sides during the long drawn out questioning, with more than 50 witnesses having testified, but this pass was significant because of what the witness had said. General Wade was not willing to question it.

Next witness Mr. Cavendish.

The defense calls Commander James Humes.

A murmur shattered the otherwise quiet room as the Commander dressed in his Navy uniform entered the courtroom. General Wade looked up from his legal pad when he heard the name and glanced over at Cavendish the unmasked look of surprise on his face. Tom thought he noticed General Wade start to rise from his chair to make an objection, but thinking better of it relaxed back into his seat. Tom turned to Judge Brown and noted the small smile evidencing itself on the face of the court's presiding officer. Tom supposed that even the crafty legal mind found it a bit of a kick that he had pulled this off.

State your name please, for the record, sir.

I'm Commander James Humes, United States Navy.

And Commander Humes, where do you work.

I work at the Bethesda Naval Hospital in Maryland not far from Washington, DC.

And in what capacity do you work there?

I work in the pathology department.

In such a capacity do you perform autopsies??

Certainly.

Isn't it true that you are indeed appearing at this trial of your own accord and against the advice of your superiors?

Let's just leave it that I am here of my own accord.

I want to ask you Commander about the night in question of November 22, 1963. Did you and your colleagues on that night perform an autopsy on the body of John Fitzgerald Kennedy?

We did.

Can you describe to me the scenario at the beginning of the autopsy?

The President's body was presented to us in a normal military shipping casket. ...

I beg your pardon, Dr. Humes. Are you saying that when you first received the President's body it was not in the same coffin in which it departed Dallas?

Well, sir, I'm not sure what it was in when it departed Dallas, but it was in a military shipping coffin when we received it.

OK, continue.

We opened the coffin and removed the body from the body bag.

Excuse me, again, Commander. I'm sorry to interrupt. You are saying the body was now in a military coffin and that the body in the coffin was in a body bag?

Yes, sir. The body was in a body bag.

And at what time did you begin the autopsy?

We began the autopsy at approximately 2000 hours.

That would be 8:00 PM Eastern time, correct?

Yes sir. That is correct.

Can you attest to the chain of custody of his body from the time the ambulance arrived at Bethesda Naval Hospital until you took possession of the body for the autopsy?

I cannot, no sir.

According to your observation at the autopsy would you describe the wounds to President Kennedy?

We found two entrance wounds to the President and two exit wounds. The first wound was one to the back even with the third thoracic vertebrae at about the right coracoid process. I tried to probe this wound but was unable to do so much beyond the length of my pinkie. I believe this bullet possibly was forced out the throat causing that wound. The wound appeared to some of the doctors at Parkland as an entrance wound. The second wound was in the occipital region of the back of the head. The force of the explosion blew out much of the parietal section of the skull and impacted some of the temporal lobe and the frontal lobe. A good portion of brain tissue was displaced.

In your professional opinion what conclusion did you reach in regards to the origin of the shots; do you believe they came from the front or the back?

In regards to these two shots, it is my opinion that they came from behind the President.

Is there any way based on the autopsy that one could tell who fired the shots?

Dr. Humes chuckled a bit at the question. *No sir, if I could, we would have quite a business, now wouldn't we?*

In the FBI report, the agency reports that the first shot hit the President in the back. It further reports that the second shot hit the Governor in the back, but there is then a correction to that stating that based on forensics the first shot may have hit both the President and Governor Connally. And then the third hit the President in the head. Based on your examination of the President's body and what you know about forensics and *ballistics, is it your belief that a single bullet hit the President and then traveled through the Governor causing his five injuries?*

No sir. I do not accept that as possible. I do not know of any of the three doctors who performed the autopsy who accept that as a conclusion.

So, let me see if I understand. How many shots do you believe were fired?

That is outside the realm of my ability to say. I was not present at the assassination. I can only tell you how many shots hit President Kennedy.

I see. And how many do you believe hit the President?

It is my professional opinion based on the autopsy that two shots hit the President.

But it is also your opinion, isn't it Doctor, that none of those shots also hit Governor Connally, and is that correct?

That is my professional opinion.

Thank you sir. Your...oh, I did want to ask you one further question.

Yes.

Why do you think your commanding officers did not want you to testify?

Sir, you would have to ask them.

Nothing further.

Cross, General Wade.

No questions.

Call your next witness Mr. Cavendish.

The defense calls Earlene Roberts.

When the older lady with salt and pepper hair was comfortably seated Tom Cavendish leisurely approached the witness stand.

Good day, Mrs. Roberts.

It's Miss Roberts.

OK, I want to ask you about the date in question November 22, 1963. Do you remember that day?

Of course I do, that was the day that President Kennedy was killed.

And where were you working at the time?

I was working for the Johnson's as a housekeeper at 1026 North Beckley.

And was Lee Harvey Oswald a boarder there?

I didn't know him by that name. He registered as O H Lee.

But you came to find out later that he indeed is Lee Harvey Oswald the defendant in this case. Isn't that correct?

Yes, that be him right over there. She pointed to the defendant.

And on the day in question, did you see Mr. Oswald?

Yes, he came in right around 1:00 that afternoon walking in a hurry. I said to him "You in a hurry aren't you?"

What did he say?

Nothing. I was trying to get the picture working on the television set. A friend had called me and told me about the President being shot. I thought she was pulling my leg. She said, "Turn on your television set." I turned it on and I could hear 'em talking but couldn't see a thang.

What did Mr. Oswald do?

He went to his room.

How long was he in there?

About 3-4 minutes.

And then he left?

Yes.

Did anything else happen that you think is important about that?

Well, yes sir. They was a police car that stopped just as he went to his room. It honked twice and I looked out the window. I use to work for a police officer and sometimes he will stop by and tell me something that his wife wanted me to know. I thought maybe it were him, but when I looked out the window I didn't recognize the car number. It weren't the same. Then they drove on off.

Did you see Mr. Oswald again after he left the house?

Oh, yes just a few seconds after he left the house, he was walking out the door zipping up a jacket, he didn't say nothing, so I looked outside to see where he was going and he was standing across the street waiting at the bus stop.

What time would you say that would be that you saw him at the bus stop?

It would have been a few minutes after one. Couldn't have been much more than around five after though.

Did you see him again after that?

The next time I saw Mr. Lee was on the television. Lord, I couldn't believe it.

Thank you, Miss Roberts. Your witness, General.

Miss Roberts, what type of jacket was it that Mr. Oswald had on?

It was one of those zipper jackets?

I'm going to show you a jacket marked exhibit 45. Is this the jacket that the defendant was wearing when he left the boarding house?

Does it have a zipper?

It does.

It looks like the one he had on but it seems to me that his might have been darker than that.

Thank you ma'am, I have no further questions.

Next witness.

Cavendish continued to call witnesses all afternoon. He called Mr. Truly to ask about Oswald's work history and habits. And while he was on the stand, Cavendish asked him about the gun Oswald told him Truly had been showing off just a couple of days before the assassination.

I don't recall bringing any kind of rifle to the office, sir; I just don't, Truly insisted.

Do you own a rifle? Cavendish asked.

Yes, I own several.

Can you tell me the make of any that you own?

I don't understand what any of this has to do with anything. I didn't bring a rifle to the depository.

Your honor?

The witness will answer the question.

I have an old Remington rifle, a Winchester, a Mauser and a couple of antique Muskets.

And you are positive that you did not bring a rifle to the depository and show it to workers there including Mr. Oswald?

To the best of my memory, sir, I did not.

The parade continued. Cavendish called an employee from a record store on Jefferson Street who attested to the agitated state he witnessed from Officer Tippit just moments before the officer was killed. He testified that Tippit had come into his store about 12:45 and used a phone on the counter. He couldn't tell who he was speaking with or about what they were talking. But he could testify that the officer seemed very upset.

He called Ruth Paine to the stand to ask if she had seen Oswald leave with anything on the morning of November 22 when he left from her house to go ride with Buell Frazier. Frazier had testified for the prosecution that Oswald was carrying a package of some sort that he said was curtain rods. In their meetings, Oswald had denied that he was carrying anything other than his lunch. On cross, Cavendish had shown Frazier the bag police said they had found on the 6th floor and asked if that was the bag Oswald had been carrying.

No sir, it wasn't that big. It was like a sack you get in a grocery store.

When he asked Mrs. Paine, she said the only thing she remembered seeing Oswald carry was his lunch. Cavendish confirmed this by calling to the stand several of the people with whom Oswald worked at the depository. Not a single person recalled Oswald carrying a package into the depository that day or any other day except his lunch.

S. M. Holland and Richard Dodd, both railroad workers who had been on the triple underpass during the assassination were called. Both reported seeing persons behind the fence and smoke coming from there during the shooting. They both believed that at least one shot had come from there. Holland was absolutely adamant that the third shot came from behind the picket fence. He had been interviewed by the FBI although Dodd was nowhere mentioned. Lee Bowers, who was working in the train tower during the assassination reported seeing two guys behind the picket fence before the assassination and others driving through that seemed totally out of place.

Cavendish decided to end with another power elite who would leave the hearings with an impression the jury was not likely to forget.

The defense calls as its final witness the honorable Senator Ralph Yarborough.

Senator Ralph Yarborough.

The distinguished politician walked to the front of the courtroom head held high, took the stand, where the oath was administered and was seated.

Senator Yarborough, I am going to dispense with the pageantry usually afforded to those taking this stand. Everyone present knows who you are and that you are a Senator from the State of Texas and have had a very distinguished career in this state. So let me begin by asking you in regards to November 22, 1963. Did you participate in the motorcade for President Kennedy on that date that went through downtown Dallas?

I did.

And in which car were you riding?

I was riding in the car immediately behind the Presidential Security detail.

And who else was in the car with you?

I was accompanied by Lady Bird Johnson and Vice President Johnson. We were in the back seat. I was seated on the left side. Officer Jacks was driving and Agent Youngblood, who was head of the Vice President's Secret Service detail, was in the passenger seat.

Can you tell us what happened that day as the cars made the turn left on Elm from Houston Streets?

We were just turning the curve slowly and had just straightened up when I recalled hearing a report.

You identified it as a gun shot?

Yes, almost immediately. I spent time in the military in World War II and I'm familiar with guns.

What was going on in the President's car?

Because of the position of the Secret Service agents I could see nothing in the President's car until we came up the other side of the underpass. I could see Clint Hill, the Secret Service agent spread eagle over the back of the car pounding on the back of the seat with an anguished look on his face. I knew from that the President had been hit.

Do you have an opinion based on your experience as to the origin of the shots?

When the first shot fired, I saw a couple of the Secret Service agents turn to the right and look to our right. I felt the shots had come from behind us.

All of the shots?

Yes, all three of the shots came from behind us.

You reported to the FBI that there was a strong smell of gunpowder, in fact, if I may quote your affidavit you said,"it clung to the car all the way to Parkland Hospital." Do you recall saying that?

Yes.

Was there a wind that day, Senator Yarborough?

Oh yes, a very smart one.

Did you hear anyone else say anything about the smell?

I think I heard a couple of people perhaps say the same thing.

Do you recall from which direction the wind was coming?

Yes, it was basically in our face?

That being so, then sir, and if the shots came from behind you, how would you be able to smell gunpowder?

I'm not sure how to answer that?

I don't think it needs an answer, Senator, I think it speaks for itself. Nothing further. General, your witness.

Senator, do you recall seeing people in windows?

Oh yes, there were dozens of people in windows all along the route.

Did you notice any difference in their disposition than those who were on the streets?

Distinctly. The people I saw in the windows all looked somber, like they were not too pleased that President Kennedy was here.

Did you see anyone in the Depository window as you passed?

No sir, I don't recall having looked up there.

And sir, again, how many shots did you hear?

There were three shots. They were very distinct. The first seemed separated by several seconds and the second and third were separated by perhaps 1 and ½ seconds.

Thank you sir. I have nothing further.

Next witness Mr. Cavendish.

Rising to face Judge Brown, Tom Cavendish clearly stated, *having called thirty three witnesses, the defense rests.*

A small buzz started once more in what had been a very hushed audience. The gavel brought the courtroom back to order.

We are going to break for lunch and when we come back the closing arguments will commence. General Wade will you be prepared to deliver your close when we return?

Yes, your honor.

Mr. Cavendish, will your team be prepared to follow the prosecution.

Absolutely, sir.

We will recess for lunch and will be back in session at 1:30 this afternoon.

All rise.

Donelson looked at Cavendish. They both looked at Oswald as the guard came to take him to the holding cell.

Well, this is it, isn't it, Mr. Cavendish. The trial is nearly over. They are going to send me to the electric chair, aren't they?

Now Lee, I don't know. I believe I've done the best I could do. The closing arguments may be critical in persuading the jury. Go get some lunch and some rest and I'll see you in a bit.

The guard led Lee away. When the door to the hallway had closed Cavendish turned to Donelson and said, *what are our chances?*

I've been watching the jurors out of the corner of my eye. Your arguments, our arguments, have resonated with them. But one has to wonder how much sympathy for the slain President will rule the roost. Will they want to be known as the jury who let a man go who may have killed a President?

Good question. I wouldn't.

Chapter 22- The Prosecution Closes

Gentlemen of the jury, I am speaking to you as the lead prosecutor of this case. But I am also a citizen of this community, a community that is hurting and aching for justice to be done. Dallas is not an evil place overtaken with hatred and violence. When President Kennedy came here on November 22, I do not believe there was the intent on the part of most of our citizenry to do him harm. But harm did come, and now justice must prevail. I believe that we have substantially proven our case. But this case is greater than all of us. Are there unanswered questions and things that don't seem to fit too well? Yes. But this isn't just about Dallas trying to get answers for ourselves. While it occurred in our jurisdiction, these crimes are about our country. On November 22, 1963, our country suffered a terrible loss. Only four times in our country's history has a President been assassinated. In each of those prior cases, a lone gunman took aim and killed our leader. This case has great similarities to those. President Kennedy was larger than life for many of our younger people. He was gallant, charismatic, charming, handsome, distinguished, educated, and eloquent. He challenged us to personal greatness—pushed our nation forward to the future in a new and exciting way. Men of his talents are rare and irreplaceable. At 12:30 on that horrible Friday, Lee Harvey Oswald, in an act that few of us can comprehend or figure out, fired three shots from the sixth floor window of the Texas School Book Depository and ended Camelot. You must, gentleman, insure that he pays for the injustice he has served to our nation and our community.

We have presented in this case evidence showing that Lee Oswald, the former defector, was seen carrying something suspiciously the size of the rifle he used to gun down the President to work that morning wrapped in a paper bag. Buell Frazier and his mother testified of seeing him with such a package that morning. At the exact moment of the assassination, not one person in the TSBD could testify as to the whereabouts of Oswald and all the defense has been able to show is a very grainy picture purporting to be Oswald on the stoop of the front door.

Look at the solid evidence, gentlemen. The rifle found on the sixth floor, not in an office somewhere in the depository, but on the sixth floor where numerous witnesses testified in this trial the shots originated, belonged to Lee Harvey Oswald. Oh I know he says he didn't own a rifle. But the mail order company from which it was ordered sent it to a PO Box which he rented. Ruth Paine testified that he indeed did own a rifle. The police reported not finding the rifle where it was usually kept in the garage on that fateful day. It had Mr. Oswald's prints on the rifle. Kind of strange for someone who says they didn't own one.

Mr. Oswald's prints were found in the sniper's nest. Witnesses testified seeing him in the window. And one young man actually saw this man pull the trigger on that rifle. And let us not forget that the same rifle, the same man, seriously injured our beloved Governor Connally and his behavior also led to the wounding of a citizen who was standing near the ambush. Most of the witnesses, and there were over 100 present in Dealey Plaza, testified in their affidavits of hearing three shots coming from the direction of the School Book Depository.

And how did Mr. Oswald act after the President of the United States has been gunned down right outside the building where he has only worked for barely a month? He leaves at the first opportunity. He tries to take a bus, but to no avail. Then he hails a cab and goes to his boarding house where he gets a loaded pistol and leaves again going only who knows where. And in the moment of chance, Officer J. D. Tippit happens on him at 10th Avenue as Oswald is walking across Patton Street. They have words. I don't know what was said, but it caused Officer Tippit to get out of the car, draw his gun, but before he was able to use it, Oswald pumped four shots into his body killing him almost instantly. And there are no less than half a dozen witnesses who saw this tragic event and identified Oswald as the assailant.

So on to the Texas Theater Mr. Oswald goes, leaving behind death and destruction on every hand. He enters the movie theater without buying a ticket raising the suspicion of workers who report the incident to the police. But mind you, the police are already combing the area for the suspected gunman of Office Tippit, and with a very good description, find him inside watching a movie. Watching a movie, gentleman! This man who has already gunned down the President of the United States, the Governor of Texas and a law enforcement officer of Dallas, is now sitting watching a movie. And when Officer McDonald approached him, once more Oswald grabs his gun and attempts to shoot his way out of his predicament. But the officers would overpower him and bring him in. And, of course, the lawyers for Mr. Oswald have mounted no defense at all in regards to the charges having to do with that assault. Those charges stand and you are obliged to find him guilty on those charges regardless of what you decide on the others.

The defense team has attempted to make the Dallas Police Department look like a bumbling bunch of Keystone Cops. Instead of proving the evidence wrong, they have tried to get you to believe it was mishandled, misidentified, perhaps even planted. They have tried to convince you that a large scale conspiracy assassinated our President. Listening to all the rumors and innuendoes that have made the rounds, I'm surprised someone hasn't come along and blamed our current President and accused LBJ of pulling the trigger even though he was in a car just two back from the limousine the President was in. There was here a loud snicker from someone in the audience causing General Wade to pause and turn toward the audience. When silence was observed, he continued.

We have laid down the facts, my friends, as clearly and as concisely as we have been able to do. Nothing that the defense has presented has in any way denigrated the evidence in this case. It is crystal clear that Lee Harvey Oswald had motivation and opportunity. He is clearly a communist sympathizer who hated John Kennedy for his hardline stand against Russia, a country to which this man defected just a few short years ago. There is the obvious—the obvious that for some reason the defense wants to turn into the sinister. They question the veracity of a picture taken in the backyard of the Oswald's home by his wife. In this picture, as you have seen, Oswald is holding the rifle in question, that rifle that killed our President and wounded our Governor, he added pointing to the rifle on the exhibit table. And what is their claim—that the picture has been doctored. They raise questions they claim have no apparent answers. I would suggest most of the questions they raise are imaginary. They seek to raise a smoke screen so that you will ignore the evidence. Were there three shots? Without a doubt. Almost every witness that we have called in regards to this matter has affirmed that there were three shots. What was the motive? I believe it was to merely stop Jack Kennedy because Lee Oswald hated him for what he did to his beloved Russia and for what he had done to Fidel Castro and Cuba.

I know you have heard the testimony that there may have been questions about the injuries to Kennedy and Connally. The fact of where they were hit is not quite as important as understanding from where and by whom. President Kennedy is dead! He is dead because that man, sitting right there, decided that he could act as God and take his life from him. Officer Tippit is dead! He is dead because that man, sitting right there, decided he would take the life of the officer instead of face justice. He took the coward's way out. Lee Harvey Oswald is no more than a low life, un-American communist who deserves based on the evidence, to be found guilty of all these charges and sentenced to death! Camelot is dead, but justice is not!

Gentlemen, you sat patiently and listened carefully to witnesses explain the evidence we have against this man. He had many aliases; he was living a crazed life. He was activist one moment in New Orleans passing out pamphlets supporting Castro in Cuba, and just a quiet husband and father in suburban Dallas working in a factory. Just last summer he ventures to Mexico trying to get into Cuba, then comes back to Dallas where at the suggestion of Ruth Paine settles back down again to a job at the Book Depository but moves out of the Paine house into a boarding house and comes home only on the weekends even though a co-worker lives near the Paine home. He wished for the spotlight. He wanted to be important. He received a dishonorable discharge from the military. He denounced his citizenship and went to Russia! How he even got back into this country is anyone's guess.

The defense has denied Mr. Oswald's culpability in the assassination of the President and the wounding of Governor Connally by dismissively saying that no reliable witness can place him on the 6th floor at the time of the shooting. But we have presented witnesses that saw him in the window. They identified him. The defense wishes to have you believe that someone else went to the Paine garage and took Lee Oswald's rifle out of the blanket he kept it wrapped in, put the blanket back in place so that it appeared undisturbed, snuck it into the depository without anyone seeing it, snuck a shooter into the depository without anyone seeing them, and fired the gun, hid the gun and got out of the building without anyone seeing them, and I'm telling you that the defense explanation is backed up with what evidence? I could conjecture that an elephant robbed a bank, but until I present evidence of such, it is merely the accumulated thoughts of the imagination. What proof do they have? Let them show us their evidence that their version of events fit. If they do and it does, then I'd be the first to say acquit this defendant. But our evidence does fit. His rifle, his pistol, his bullets, his finger prints, and his identification as witnessed by no less than half a dozen people during this trial and others whose testimony you will find in the affidavits.

Some have suggested that we have shortchanged the prosecution in that we did not call every person who witnessed all these terrible crimes that took place. But there are many reasons why we have not called some of the witnesses. We have not called Mrs. Kennedy or Mrs. Connally because we did not believe it was necessary for them to have to relive their pain of that moment. You have their statements. We have not called the Secret Service agents, Hill, Kellerman, and all the others who were around the President that day. You have their statements. We have not called the some 100 people who witnessed the assassination in Dealey Plaza both sitting in their cars over on Commerce and Main Streets or standing on the sidewalks and grass along the final paces of the motorcade route. You have many of their statements.

What does that leave us with? It leaves us with a mound of evidence pointing directly at Lee Harvey Oswald. Lee Harvey Oswald is charged with pre-meditated murder of John Fitzgerald Kennedy, President of the United States. You must find him guilty. The state believes we have shown that he alone is responsible for this heinous act. Lee Harvey Oswald is charged with attempting to murder Governor John Connally. The state believes that in his attempt to kill President Kennedy that Oswald also brought great bodily harm and suffering to Governor John Connally. He is charged with criminal mischief in the wounding of James Tague an innocent bystander in Dealey Plaza. The state believes that only Mr. Oswald is to be held responsible for this action. Lee Harvey Oswald is charged with the murder of Officer J. D. Tippit. While it was not pre-meditated, it was under extenuating circumstances as he attempted to flee from the committing of multiple felonies. The state believes that it has proven beyond a reasonable doubt that Oswald solely is to blame for this officer's death. Justice demands he be found guilty.

And what about the crimes that took place in the Texas Theater? Lee Harvey Oswald is charged with assault of a police office, attempted murder, assault with a deadly weapon, resisting arrest, illegal possession of a firearm, as well as trespassing and a few other minor charges. The state has shown that Lee Oswald is guilty of these charges and the defense has not answered. On these charges you must render a verdict of guilty as charged.

Gentlemen, you have much work to do. Take your time and carefully examine all the statements that have been made. And the state believes that when you have done so, you will find

Lee Harvey Oswald guilty as charged and will sentence him appropriately. It is your duty. Thank you.

Chapter 23- The Defense Closes

Gentlemen of the Jury, good afternoon.

Good afternoon, some replied.

From the beginning of this trial the prosecution has attempted to portray Lee Harvey Oswald as a lone nut. Even today, General Wade has brought to our memory the three prior assassinations of Presidents and attempted to get you to believe that all those were performed by lone assassins, and that therefore, this assassination of President Kennedy is no different than those having taken place prior. But on several points he has obviously forgotten his history. While all three of the prior assassinations were the work of a lone gunman, in the Lincoln assassination a large conspiracy of Confederate sympathizers was uncovered. Four persons were hanged for the assassination of Lincoln and the attack on Secretary of State Seward. Others were sent to prison. A Congressional inquiry actually probed whether Secretary of War Stanton might have been complicit.

In all three of these, the person who actually pulled the trigger leading to the President's death, quickly and arrogantly confessed their guilt. Booth was killed before he could be brought to trial. Guiteau, the assassin of President Garfield was convicted and hanged. Czolgosz, the assassin of President McKinley was almost beaten to death before his trial, but was found guilty and executed. In all three cases, none of the killers denied having done so. And now this prosecutor points to Lee Harvey Oswald as a disturbed young man seeking fame, yet, he denies the charges. Were he seeking fame, it would have been far easier for him to confess and be condemned to death as were the others. But in this, he has not followed their pattern. And there is an important reason why Lee Harvey Oswald has not confessed to any of these crimes, including those at the Texas Theater. It is because he is not guilty.

Gentleman of the jury, I would have you consider carefully all the testimony you have received in this trial. First let me state what this trial is not about. This trial is not about my client's political beliefs. He has stated over and over to the press that he liked President Kennedy and that he had no problem with the President. This trial is not about the time that my client spent in Russia or about his Russian wife, or anything having to do with his father or his past.   This is solely and singularly about the events that happened on November 22, 1963.   The prosecution has even hurled allegations at Lee Oswald for the attempted shooting of General Walker, a crime for which my client has not been charged. Yet General Wade has inferred in his rhetoric that if Oswald would try to shoot General Walker, then he must be guilty of shooting President Kennedy. There is no logic in that conclusion seeing how the two persons are diametrically polar opposites politically.

What evidence does the prosecution insist on in condemning my client? They say Oswald's rifle was in the depository. But interestingly officers in their sworn affidavits swore that the gun found in the depository was a Mauser. Now they want to dismiss this as a mistake made when just glancing at the gun. They handled the rifle. They gave it to Fritz who discharged a live round from the chamber. They signed off on statements giving it seems now false testimony about what they had found. There were no fingerprints on the rifle. This rifle, he said pointing to the rifle on the evidence table. The rifle they claim belonged to my client which he has denied owning. Only a palm print was found on it and that underneath the barrel in a position that could have only been made when the rifle was disassembled. What would have been of interest would have been a comparison of the palm print supposedly lifted from one of the boxes to compare with that of the barrel of the rifle. One thing I can guarantee about that, there is far less surface on the barrel than on the box. Might it be that a full palm print would not have matched Oswald after all?

They found three spent cartridge casings they have matched to the rifle. Would you not expect that they matched the rifle? They had to, didn't they? Were they not to match we would readily know that a conspiracy is at play. And even though they do supposedly match, it does not tell us at all who pulled the trigger. But it is at this point that a problem occurs with the chain of custody of the evidence.

According to an eyewitness, Mr. Alyea has testified in his affidavit that Fritz picked up those casings so that he could take a picture of them, film them, and then placed them in his pocket before Lieutenant Day had an opportunity to photograph them as they were found. Secondly, Mr. Alyea has further testified that the official photograph released by the Dallas Police Department does not match what he initially saw as far as location on the floor or proximity to each other. Third, while both the gun and the casings might seem to implicate my client, neither of those findings (if indeed it was a Carcano found in the depository, and the evidence indicates that it was a Mauser) neither of those findings, the rifle or the casings prove that my client, Lee Harvey Oswald pulled the trigger.

You know there is another problem with the prosecution case that they have seemingly ignored. If you noticed carefully, at least three of their witnesses, the two men in the window just below where the shots were said to have come from, and Mr. Brennan who supposedly saw Lee Oswald in the window, heard only two shots from the window. Think about it, gentlemen, three casings, but the people who were closest to the supposed origin of the gunfire, these two men who were less than 12 feet from the shooter, said they only heard two shots from that location.

And of course, we are to believe Mr. Brennan's testimony of having seen Oswald in the window when he says he was standing 15 feet back from the window, and I challenge anyone to see through that row of boxes that sat only 2.5 feet from the window. Can Mr. Brennan see through boxes? Hardly. A hearty chuckle from an audience member caused Judge Brown's eyebrows to rise at the outside corners. He reached for the gavel, but quiet returned.

And what are we to do with the host of witnesses who heard or saw a shot or shots fired from the Grassy Knoll from behind the Picket Fence? Officer Hargis, on a motorcycle on the left rear bumper of the President's car, splattered with the

President's blood immediately dismounts his bike, leans it over on Elm Street and runs up the pavilion to the fence, gun drawn where he encounters police officers already there, when we know there were no officers stationed back there. Jean Hill, one of the two ladies standing about as close to John Kennedy as anyone in the motorcade said she saw a flash come from the picket fence and was sure it was a gun being fired. And let's not forget her frightening testimony of being led away by unknown men from behind the picket fence claiming to be Secret Service or FBI. And what do we make of this stakeout in front of her home that continues to this day. What possible motive would the FBI have in placing a car in front of her house?

What about the testimony of Lee Bowers, and the railroad workers who were on the Triple Underpass. These workers were so convinced that someone had fired from behind the fence that they went over there immediately and found numerous footprints and cigarette butts on the ground and mud on a car bumper as though someone had stood on the bumper. Lee Bowers was able to describe the men even though he was some distance from them. And let us not forget to include the sworn testimony of Chief Curry and Agent Sorrels who initially reported believing the shots had come from the railyard area. Gentleman, don't forget where they were. The car they were in would have been almost parallel to where these other witnesses reported hearing the shot.

In fact, of the some 100 witnesses whose affidavits you have from the Dallas Police Department, 70 of them reported either hearing or in some way knowing that a shot had come from behind the picket fence.

Now we are not trying to say that no shots came from the depository. We are merely allowing the evidence to speak to us. No evidence of Oswald having fired a rifle according to the paraffin test, no smell of gunpowder on the sixth floor. Not one person who was on the sixth floor of the depository reported the smell of gunpowder, but many witnesses in the motorcade and on the ground reported smelling a strong odor of gunpowder. Look at the wind direction. It was coming at their face as Senator Yarborough stated. If a gun had been fired in the depository, wouldn't there have been a strong smell of gunpowder? The Dallas Police, yet again failed to follow the simple protocol of evidence collection.

The prosecution made the finding of Oswald's fingerprints in the place where he worked paramount to sealing the case. If I went to your workplace, would I find your fingerprints anywhere? Probably everywhere, right? Doesn't mean you committed a crime. But yet, the police do not find it alarming that there is a single fingerprint they found that cannot be identified as one belonging to a worker in the building. May I suggest that fingerprint could well be that of the real assassin?

General Wade misspeaks when he says that the young man who testified had identified Lee Harvey Oswald as the shooter in the window. Remember what he said, "I didn't see anyone except their hands and the bald spot."

In fact, and this is a fact, there is not one witness that saw Lee Harvey Oswald in that window firing the gun. There are witnesses who saw a gun in that window. This young boy saw hands and a bald spot. I don't believe that Mr. Brennan saw anything but boxes. Of the hundreds of people, not one person saw Lee Oswald in the window. Even one of the journalists in the procession saw a gun in the window but didn't see the shooter. The best they have is a bald spot. And isn't it interesting that they have a witness, the young boy, who has stated that a construction worker saw a man with a bald spot run out the back of the depository right after the shooting? Who was that man? I don't know. General Wade doesn't know. The police obviously don't know. But I do know one thing. It was not Lee Harvey Oswald because at that exact moment he was enjoying a soft drink on the second floor as attested to by both Officer Baker and Mr. Truly.

The prosecution believes it sinister that Lee Oswald would leave the scene given all that was going on. General Wade asked what was he doing? Why was he fleeing? And I would like to know that as well. But let's consider a couple of things. Lee didn't just flee with the sound of the last shot, did he, as one might expect from a person who has just committed a serious felony. He is on the second floor finishing up his lunch and a drink that he is enjoying. In all seriousness, do you really believe that someone who has just killed the President of the United States is going to go downstairs and buy a pop from a machine and stand there calmly and drink it before fleeing?

When Lee Oswald sees that things are becoming chaotic and that the building he is in has become the center of attention, I believe that Lee realized he was being set up to take the fall for this crime. I don't know how much Lee Harvey Oswald knows about what was supposed to happen. He hasn't talked with the police and he hasn't told me much. I do believe that he was involved in the conspiracy. He isn't charged with that, however, so I'm not here today to defend him against that charge. And I am not at liberty to disclose what he has told me. But he isn't reacting as a man who has committed a crime. He does, however, soon begin to react as a man who knows he is being set up for one.

Mr. Oswald walks out of the building through the front door! Does that sound like the actions of someone who is running from a crime? Before leaving the premises he points a newsman toward the pay phone in the hallway. Then he looks about for a bus as he walks outside. He walks down Elm a few blocks and gets on a bus. But soon the bus is stuck in traffic. Lee seems in a hurry. He's near the bus station. He could have hopped a bus and been gone. Perhaps he is supposed to meet someone. I don't know, he hasn't told us. His actions seem to indicate such. Going to a theater after all that has happened seems totally insane. So he hails a cab to take him to Beckley but the cab lets him out 2 blocks from his boardinghouse. Why? Was he fearful someone might be waiting for him at the boarding house? Someone he suspects is supposed to silence him. He gets a jacket and presumably his pistol and leaves walking not straight down Beckley toward Jefferson, toward the theater. If he was going to the theater even if it was to meet someone, why would he go away from the theater? He is walking crossing over Patton, walking in a direction that isn't consistent with going to the theater. I think I know where he was going. I think he was going to a person's home known to the court but who shall remain nameless until after this trial. If one draws a line between the two points of this person's home and the boarding house, they are nearly on a straight line.

It would be ridiculous for me to stand up here and tell you that there aren't some witnesses to the Officer Tippit shooting who have identified Oswald as the shooter. However, as I believe you have seen, there is a great deal of disagreement among the witnesses as to the facts of the matter. Even some of the reported actions of Officer Tippit are questionable. Why did he go into the record store seemingly agitated and use the phone? Who was he calling? Why didn't he contact dispatch when he saw a man whom he evidently believed matched the description of the APB that had been given? What did he say to the young man he called over to the car. You heard Helen Markham's testimony. "They seemed friendly," she said. Why did a couple of the witnesses testify that there were two shooters? The stories seem all over the place. It is indeed a tragedy what happened to this officer. But there are great questions concerning the ballistics reports. Those shell casings don't match the make of the bullets one for one. It is impossible that you have different makes of bullets in Tippit than the brands of shell casings. The prosecution has not attempted to explain this. You just can't get past that. Also, gentlemen of the jury, keep in mind that in at least the case of three of the witnesses who have positively identified Lee Harvey Oswald as the shooter of officer Tippit, these witnesses have reported the firing of only three shots, not the four that we know for a fact were fired. This goes directly to their credibility as witnesses.

And now to the actions in the Texas Theater--how would you feel? I'm not sure why Oswald was there. He told me that he just decided to go see a movie, but I'm not buying that. But to be sitting there and suddenly see all these police officers coming at you is scary. He didn't know what they were going to do to him. Fight or flight. He couldn't escape, so he fought.

And he fought hard, and the police officers hit him as well, didn't they? This man was scared for his life. I believe he knew he was marked for death as the patsy. And what did he tell reporters and the police as soon as he was in custody? "I am a patsy."

I wish we had more answers. And there is ample evidence that we do not have access to in this trial. We have been given a great amount of testimony, statements, videos and photographs. We have poured through a plethora of this material and much of it has been entered into evidence. But there are things we do not have access to. We have been refused access to the government's records on Lee Harvey Oswald, and that, in and of itself, raises questions as to why someone who is just "a lone nut" as Hoover has labeled him, ...well frankly, what is there about Lee Oswald that the government doesn't want us knowing? Cavendish looked over at Lee when he said this and noticed the scowl on his face for the first time in the trial. *I have it on good authority that the records involving Lee Harvey Oswald number into the tens of thousands of pages. Seriously? My father was in WWI and I can assure you his military record doesn't have near as many pages.*

One of the leading witnesses of the assassination was a man named Abraham Zapruder who videoed the entire route of the motorcade from the beginning of Elm Street to the triple underpass. So it is a very good window into the assassination. While newsmen like Dan Rather have seen the video, and it has been seen by the Secret Service and the FBI, it has not however been made available to us for this trial. We have subpoenaed it. Even Judge Brown has signed an order for it to be released. It has been ignored. The film was sold to Time Life. They have closed the door to our requests saying that they do not wish to release it for public viewing. And we have had a defendant who has been less that forthcoming with us on his life. The government has declined to tell us much about some of the events that we think brought us to this state. And the reality is that it could be there is something on the Zapruder video that would vindicate my client. The jury will never know because it isn't being allowed to be seen by them.

I'm not here to argue that Lee Harvey Oswald is an ideal citizen. I'm not here to deny that Lee Harvey Oswald isn't guilty of something. But what I am here to tell you is that the government has not proven within a reasonable doubt and to a moral certainty that Lee Harvey Oswald killed John Kennedy and the other things herein charged. The burden of proof was theirs. I believe that anyone who seriously looks at the evidence in this trial will have serious doubts about the facts as presented by the State. And that is why you gentlemen must come back with a verdict of not guilty. I thank you for your service. I thank you for thinking prayerfully about your decision.

Chapter 24- The Verdict

The judge gave his final instructions early the next morning warning the jury that they were to be driven in deriving a decision based on the facts. He told them the affidavits and testimony transcripts were at their disposal and were to be used in their discussions and deliberations. *This is not to boil down to just a vote on each count, but a true deliberation of the evidence. The country demands that you render a verdict based on evidence and not on feelings, or any other factor.* Most jurors nodded agreement as the instructions were delivered.

Cavendish and Donelson met briefly with Oswald in the conference room before he was taken back to the county jail. Within just a few moments of leaving the courthouse and returning to their office a few blocks away, a call from the court clerk sent them scurrying back.

There is no way they have reached a decision this quickly, Sylvester said as the two lawyers quickly walked back to the courthouse. They reached the front door of the courthouse about the same time as General Wade.

General, you have any idea what's going on?

Yeah, I think so. It has to do with that Zapruder film, I suspect.

When they came into the courtroom a projector and screen had been set up in the courtroom. The clerk had cleared the courtroom and officers stood guard at the door. The windows had been covered so as to allow no one to see into the room.

The judge is in chambers and wants to see you stat.

The three lawyers walked into the chambers where they found a gentleman they did not know standing in front of Judge Brown's very cluttered desk.

Gentleman, we have an interesting scenario. This is Frank Pullman from the FBI. He has in his possession one of the copies of the Zapruder film made the night of the assassination. He is answering the order for it to be delivered to my chambers

245

and has only now arrived with it. *As you are aware, the jury has begun deliberations. While it is not totally unusual to call them back to the courtroom to look at evidence or to answer questions, this one is a bit different.*

How would bringing them back in to see the film be different, your honor? Cavendish asked. *The film was mentioned during the trial. I for one believe it would be the right thing to do.*

I would agree, added Sylvester.

Your honor, I actually tend to agree with the defense on this. If you have the video and don't show it to them when you could have, then there is grounds to appeal whatever verdict is rendered.

I have passed a note to the jury foreman to let them know that the video just arrived, that I am calling counsel into chambers and asking them to tell me what their pleasure would be. Judge Brown seemed exhausted. The trial had gone on for some two months. It seemed as though there would be no end to it and just as it was being reached, now this.

Gentlemen, I also much tell you something else in strictest confidence.

What is it, Judge Brown? Are you OK?

No, I'm not, General. This trial has worn me down. But last night I received a call at my home, a threatening call.

NO! Sylvester interjected.

The person on the other end said that if I didn't make sure that Oswald died, I would die with him. This morning our dog was laying on our front porch. He had his throat slashed.

You told the police, I trust? General Wade responded.

Yes, they are at my home now trying to find clues.

The clerk knocked on the door and then opened it. *The jury has responded to your note.* The clerk handed a piece of paper to the judge. He opened it and read it. He glanced up at us before standing.

They want to see the film.

The lawyers assembled in the courtroom, brought in the jury and carefully explained to them that in his opinion, it would be a distraction to bring in any but the press pool representatives. No camera would be allowed to take pictures or anything of that nature. The jurors, he explained, were being allowed to see the film because of its frequent mention in the courtroom and that even though it was only now being delivered to the court, it was, in the opinion of both he, the prosecution and the defense, appropriate to be shown to them now. He told them that it would only last a few seconds and that it would be shown to them five times. He told them that the prosecution nor the defense would be allowed to say anything regarding what is shown on the video. He said it was to be permitted the same value of evidence as anything else they had seen such as the pictures, the Nix video, and the testimony of the other witnesses.

The room darkened and the video began. The tension in the room was palpable. The jurors seemed to be confused that there was no sound. He let them know that there was no sound recording only images. When the frame came when the President's head exploded and he violently moved back toward his left and then fell toward Mrs. Kennedy there was a gasp among the jurors. One man began to weep. The court reporter was muffling sobs. Even the judge turned away for a moment and wiped a tear from his eye. Sylvester sat stunned. They both looked at Oswald who had a weird expression on his face. It was almost a knowing, satisfied look. Cavendish shivered and stood up. He walked back behind the railing into the second row of benches. At this moment he didn't want to be near Oswald. His stomach was churning.

After the final viewing of the video, the jury was dismissed back to chambers where they continued deliberations.

******

It's been five days and no word, Sylvester said as they ate with some others from the law office at a restaurant nearby. They had left word with the court as to where they could be found. Judge Brown and his family had been taken to a safe house under heavy guard and Oswald had been placed under maximum security in total isolation. He was allowed no visitors except a priest, and his food was carefully checked for poisons.

Not far down the block in another section of the jail sat Jack Ruby the man who knew much but wasn't talking. *They have got to find him guilty and execute him,* Ruby was thinking, *else we will have to find a way to shut him up permanently. I'm sure they will come after me as well. With me out of the way, no one will ever find out what happened. And they ain't smart enough to figure it out on their own.*

Two more days went by. A runner for the court came into their law offices on a Thursday afternoon and said the judge wanted them back at court. The jury submitted a question or two and another request. They wanted to see all the videos again.

Three more days went by and come Monday morning, all the parties were brought to the courtroom. The jury had reached a verdict.

The crowds moved into the hard benches, as many as could possibly crowd into the area until the officers closed the doors and stationed a guard at the door. There were numerous armed guards inside the courtroom as well. Two standing on either side of Oswald's seat and four stationed to the front of the courtroom. Oswald was led into the courtroom shackled hands attached by chains to the foot shackles. These were removed and he was allowed to sit beside us at the table relatively free to move around in his seat. But with two large guards standing right behind him, there wasn't much room to move.

Several people from General Wade's office were at his table this morning awaiting the reading of one of the most anticipated verdicts of the century.

Judge Brown entered just as the jury was being seated.

I understand the jury has reached a verdict, is this correct Mr. Foreman?

A thin man at the first chair position stood. He was well dressed in suit and tie. He looked nervous. None of the jurors were making eye contact with anyone except the judge.

We have your honor.

The foreman will hand the verdict to the bailiff.

The judge looked at the papers he had been handed. He showed no sign of tipping his hand as to the verdicts. He handed the papers back to the bailiff to hand to the clerk.

The clerk will read and record the verdict of the jury. The defendant will rise. I will also remind the audience that this is a courtroom and I will expect decorum to be maintained.

On the first count, the murder of John F. Kennedy, President of the United States, we the jury find the defendant Lee Harvey Oswald, not guilty.

A roar of protest went through the courtroom. People were on their feet shouting at the jury. The judge was banging his gavel as loudly as he could.

You will sit down and be silent or I will not only clear this courtroom, I will arrest every person in here. Now sit down!

Order was soon restored but not until Sheriff Deputies removed a couple of guys in the back who started fighting.

Continue, please with the reading of the verdict.

On the second count of attempted murder of John Connally, Governor of Texas, we the jury find the defendant Lee Harvey Oswald, not guilty.

Again a sense of denial pierced the silence of the courtroom, but the murmuring settled quickly.

On the third count of murder of J. D. Tippit, Police Officer of the city of Dallas we the jury find the defendant Lee Harvey Oswald, guilty as charged.

What?! Oswald shouted. *I didn't kill him.*

Mr. Cavendish, control your client immediately!

I placed my hand on his arm and Sylvester told him in no uncertain terms to be quiet.

On the fourth count of assault of James Tague, we the jury find the defendant Lee Harvey Oswald not guilty.

On the fifth count of assaulting a police officer, namely Officer McDonald, we the jury find the defendant Lee Harvey Oswald guilty as charged.

On the sixth count of attempted murder of a police officer we the jury find the defendant Lee Harvey Oswald guilty as charged.

On the seventh count of resisting arrest we the jury find the defendant Lee Harvey Oswald, guilty as charged.

Thank you Mr. Clerk. The jury has heard the reading of the verdict in the seven counts of the indictment. Is this the verdict of the jury, so say you one so say you all.

It is, the foreman responded.

In the matter of recommendation of punishment on the capital offense, does the jury have a recommendation?

We do your honor. It is the recommendation of the jury on the offense of murder of Officer Tippit that Lee Harvey Oswald receive the death penalty. On the other counts for which Lee Harvey Oswald was found guilty, it is the opinion of the jury that he should receive the maximum sentence allowed by law.

So say you all?

We do, they all responded.

Do I need to poll the jury, gentlemen?

We are satisfied, Cavendish was quick to respond. Lee looked at him with a serious anger that was threatening.

The deputy will take the defendant into custody. I thank the jury for your faithful execution of your duty. You are dismissed with the court's thanks. The jury rose and immediately walked through the door taking them to the back where a dozen armed guards waited to escort them from the building to a safe location. They would board their bus and be driven there by another armed deputy.

I will take into consideration any further motions. Seeing none I will set sentencing for August 16th. 2:00 pm. If either side has motions to be made before that time you may file them. This court stands adjourned.

We did the best we could do, Lee, Cavendish said to Lee as the officers were once more shackling his feet and hands. This time there would be no more returning to the courtroom to hear testimony. It was over.

Thank you, sir for what you did. But it wasn't enough. I didn't kill that officer. You know that, don't you? Why didn't you get me off?

I couldn't get past some of the evidence, Lee. I believe you are lucky that you fared well on the assassination charges. Frankly, I expected worse. We must have done something right.

What happens now?

In a couple of months the judge will probably sentence you to death. If I'm guessing correctly, all your appeals will be turned down quickly and by Christmas, you'll be dead.

The officer led Oswald away. Cavendish and Donelson exchanged glances but neither said anything on the walk back to the office. Tom needed a shower. Sylvester just wanted to go somewhere and throw up. The trial of the century was over. And with probably few exceptions, no one felt like celebrating.

Afterward

What has been written is a work of historical fiction. While it is based on a premise that the reader knows did not happen, the *what if it had* concept took hold of me reasonably hard and would not let go until I had written this book. I am aware that the premise is nothing new. There has even been a movie starring Loren Green made some years back. And while our knowledge of the events of that fateful day in 1963 are vastly greater today than they were in the aftermath of their occurrence, the revelations that time has brought only seem to lead us further into questioning.

It was during college in approximately 1978 when I first began to be enthralled with all the questions. With each new revelation my intensity grew stronger. Every frame of the Zapruder film is forever etched in my mind. Yet I'm convinced it holds few real clues as to the identity of the shooters. Yes, I do believe there were multiple shooters but I do not believe that Lee Harvey Oswald was one of them. I am fully convinced that he was every bit the patsy he claimed to be. When I and my daughter journeyed to Dallas for the fiftieth anniversary, and even as I was surrounded by interested questioners in the Subway across from the Depository, on that cold November day, I was cognizant that just a few hundred feet from where I was sitting, Jack Kennedy lost his life. We must never lose sight of the horrendous tragedy that took place that day, nor of the injustice that was done with first the murder of Lee Harvey Oswald brought about by the inept security measures of the Dallas Police Department and the unprofessional investigation conducted by that agency along with the federal agencies. The nation was done wrong when the Secret Service stole the President's body and flew off to Washington. Much of the questionable aftermath could have been avoided, I'm convinced, had a proper inquiry been developed beginning with the autopsy being performed by the Texas coroner.

Conspiracy can be seen by those who wish to see it. The reality is that the more we know the less we learn. I believe those who plotted the assassination of John Fitzgerald Kennedy wanted it that way, yet there are so many documents (thousands of pages dealing with Oswald alone) that are yet to be released. And now we have reached a point where few people truly care. They look at it as history of half a century ago with no apparent repercussions for anyone still living. But the implications of such a callous handling of history are unacceptable. One opens almost any history book and it pronounces Lee Harvey Oswald as the lone assassin of the President. Yet, he never had a trial and he denied his involvement in the shooting to his death. If for no other reason truth and justice demand that we know. It is as Chief Curry was videoed as saying (you can see it on You Tube), they did not have enough evidence to convict Oswald of killing the President.

There are many areas I have not attempted to cover in this work. What I wanted to do was recreate the situation of those days after the assassination and what would have transpired based on the knowledge they had without all our modern technology, digitization, and without all the files (some of which have since been destroyed such as Hosty's file on Oswald and the Secret Service file on the killing of the President and perhaps the Hoover file on Kennedy). What did they know and what would they have presented in court? Did they have enough for conviction? It was also needful to bring to light what is apparent to many students of history, the Dallas Police, the FBI, and the Secret Service did a remarkably sloppy job. Protocols were violated; laws were even violated. I'm convinced that Oswald's Constitutional rights were violated. Would he have received a fair trial? No more than did Jack Ruby.

A puzzle contains many pieces with far too many colors. Only when the whole picture is pieced together does the visual come to life and make sense. For four decades I've worked to try to make sense of the pieces. Having been encouraged to write something about my research, I found this avenue a fitting way to relay my views. I can only pray that the events that brought such a tragic end to the life of John Kennedy and changed our nation in such a profound way will never again in my lifetime be reenacted on the canvas of human history.

I have endeavored to stay as true to the written record as is possible. I have read the affidavits of dozens of witnesses as well as the book written by Chief Curry. I've looked at autopsy pictures and every video known to exist regarding the assassination. I've walked the Grassy Knoll on a number of occasions. I've been in the depository. I've been on the triple underpass and stood behind the picket fence. But perhaps no visit was more painful to me than when just last summer I stood at the grave of John Fitzgerald Kennedy and said in my silent prayer, *Jack, I sure wish I knew what happened.*

Much of the words in the testimony that you have read are from the affidavits or Warren Commission Testimony. In regards to hard evidence, I've made nothing up. In regards to dialogue, it is the work of fiction. While some names do reflect the people involved in the case, the main character lawyers Cavendish and Donelson are completely a work of fiction. What I have attempted to add are the questions any right thinking lawyer would have thought to ask had Oswald gone to trial. It is my intention that these questions will cause people to pause and realize the truth has not been told by history. It must not be disregarded.

The pictures that have accompanied this work of fiction come directly from either the Warren Report, the Dallas Police Department or from researchers whose work has been credited.

Pictures

A view of Dealey Plaza from the Triple Underpass (K.Pruitt)

The Warren Report alleges that Oswald shot three times from this sixth floor window (K.Pruitt)

The Texas Theater on Jefferson Street where Oswald was captured (R.Pruitt)

The grassy knoll and picket fence as it looks today. It would have been near the larger tree where witnesses believed a shot had been fired (K. Pruitt)

The Sniper's Nest

From this area young Euins would have watched as the President's car went by. He hid behind this concrete wall when shots were fired. Across the street is the County Jail. Just to the left of here along the wall was where Brennan claimed he saw Oswald in the window of the Depository. (K.P)

The graves of President and Mrs. Kennedy at Arlington National Cemetery in Virginia (K. P.)

Oswald's Grave

(R. Pruitt)

Authors in the Sixth Floor Museum, November 22, 2013

Suggested Reading

It may be that the reader will want to further pursue information relative to the assassination of President John F. Kennedy. Among the multitude of hundreds of books that have been written regarding the events of November 22, 1963, these are the ones I have found the most credible and the most helpful. There are others, but I mention these particularly.

Fetzer, James H. (2000). **Murder in Dealey Plaza: What We Know Now that We Didn't Know Then about the Death of JFK.** Chicago: Catfeet Press.
Lifton, David S. (1980). **Best Evidence: Disguise and Deception in the Assassination of John F. Kennedy.** New York: MacMillan.
Thomas, Josiah. (1967, 1976). **Six Seconds in Dallas: Irrefutable Evidence that Oswald Could Not Have Killed JFK Alone.** New York: Berkley Publishing.

History also owes a debt of thanks to the outstanding work of early writers such as Mark Lane, Chief Curry, Edward Epstein, William Manchester, Sylvia Meagher, and Robert Groden. There have been very few who have become renowned for their support of the Warren Commission Report. Time has continued to reveal to us more information with the newer releases of documents, digital technology and scientific studies that have now proven the x-rays were staged, we have little reason to believe the original findings are truthful.

Notes

Made in the USA
Lexington, KY
12 June 2018